# Adelina

## Yvonne Rogers

The Book Guild Ltd

First published in Great Britain in 2017 by
The Book Guild Ltd
9 Priory Business Park
Wistow Road, Kibworth
Leicestershire, LE8 0RX
Freephone: 0800 999 2982
www.bookguild.co.uk
Email: info@bookguild.co.uk
Twitter: @bookguild

Cover photograph of Adelina Patti © Victoria and Albert Museum, London.

Typeset in Aldine401 BT

Printed and bound in Great Britain by CPI Group (UK) Ltd, Croydon, CR0 4YY

ISBN 978 1911320 791


British Library Cataloguing in Publication Data.
A catalogue record for this book is available from the British Library.

*For my daughters, Arianna and Sarah Jane*

# Introduction

"Did I ever tell you your great-grandmother was Madame Patti?"

My mother dropped the words casually while she was pouring out my second cup of tea. I was home on holiday from Italy and we had been catching up on family news about aunts, uncles and cousins, the way we always did after we hadn't seen one another for a few months, but nothing she had said so far had prepared me for any surprises.

"Madame Patti?" I shook my head, perplexed. The conversation was taking a strange turn. I stole a glimpse at my mother but she looked her normal, cheerful self as she added a slice of lemon and passed me the sugar.

Madame Patti? The name sounded vaguely familiar but I couldn't place it. I had always understood my granny was an orphan. Why this sudden information? "Well, no, I don't remember you ever mentioning it. Who was she, exactly? And you mean she was my great-grandmother? Your grandmother?" By now she had caught my full attention.

Evidently, my mother, now in her seventies, wished to share some family secret. She hesitated for a moment and looked away, unsure whether to continue the conversation or let the matter drop, but then put her cup down and gave me the most incredible piece of information.

"Madame Patti was one of the most famous opera singers of her time. A great lady. Italian. With a castle in South Wales. But I'm sorry, I don't know much more than that. Perhaps you'd like to do some research when you go back to Florence."

"But…" It didn't make sense. "Why is this the first I hear of it?"

My mother shook her head and sighed. "Everyone in the family wanted to keep it a secret... those who believed the story, that is. My sister, your Auntie Dolly, told me about it a few years ago. I thought you might be interested. You can believe it or not, that's up to you."

And do you believe it?" I asked, intrigued.

"Sometimes I do, when I think of my mother. She was, well, very Italian in many ways. But on the other hand it does seem rather far-fetched, and perhaps it's just one of your Auntie's flights of fantasy."

Fantasy or not, once I was back in Italy as soon as I had a free afternoon I decided to join the British Institute Library in Florence and with the help of a friendly librarian and my husband up a tall ladder, found several dusty old volumes on the top shelf of the music section that were about to change my life.

What I discovered astounded me. Adelina Patti had been the unrivalled star of nineteenth century opera, possibly the first real star. Her name had been a household legend across the whole of Europe, from Moscow to Madrid, as well as from north to south America where people slept in the streets just to catch a glimpse of her.

One thing led to another. Devoured by curiosity, I was always on the look-out for more information, bought and borrowed old volumes, read century-old newspapers and magazines, and in time did a thorough research in Italy, London and South Wales until I had discovered the entire life and work of this extraordinary lady, and her even more extraordinary career.

Whether my mother's story has any truth in it will never be known. Officially, of course, Adelina Patti had no children and I never came across any hint of scandal relating to the fact.

My grandmother grew up in Victorian London. She never mentioned her mother, probably protecting herself and her unfortunate status as an illegitimate child by silence. She never had a birth certificate (her birth was not officially registered). My mother thought she was born in the year 1870, 71 or 72. She was christened Laura Geraldine Adela and I remember her telling me how proud she was to be a true Londoner born within the sound of Bow Bells.

So very little is known about Geraldine, as she was called, in the early years of her life apart from the fact that she was fostered out at birth to two 'Aunts', court dressmakers serving the rich and titled ladies of London. She was given the surname Lloyd and had the typical Victorian education for girls covering the three "Rs" and not much more. She remembered her Saturday mornings picking up pins and threads of cotton from the carpet under the Aunts' workroom table but this boring task was counterbalanced by the excitement of visits to opulent West End houses with her aunts when they fitted gowns.

For many years, my grandmother preferred to avoid the subject of her childhood but sometimes she reminisced to my mother, the youngest of her nine children, about monthly invitations to "luncheon" at Manchester House (now Hertford House, Manchester Square). She described the dining room with its rich upholstery and oil paintings, the furniture, and her mysterious host, "a kind old gentleman". Towards the end of her life she gave way to sudden nostalgia and asked her sons to take her to London for the day, with special emphasis on a visit to Hertford House, Manchester Square. Going from room to room in the mansion that houses the Wallace Collection, she recognised paintings and the dining room where she had eaten as a child. "I used to come here once a month when I was small," she told them. "I sat at this table and had luncheon with an old gentleman. Look what he showed me." And to their astonishment she pressed a panel on the wall to reveal a secret passage.

In the 1870s, when Geraldine was a child, Hertford House was no longer the property of the Dukes of Manchester but was occupied by Sir Richard Wallace and his French wife, and had already been altered and amplified by the architect Thomas Ambler to house their collection of paintings and antiques. So it was very similar to the way we see it today. Richard Wallace does not appear to come into my grandmother's story directly. But he would have had occasion to meet Adelina Patti in Paris where they frequented the same circles. In the late 1860's she was friendly with the Empress Eugénie and the Emperor Napoleon III and the Marquess of Hertford, Richard's father, was an habitué at the French court.

So why would Sir Richard Wallace take the trouble to entertain a rather plain little orphan girl who was being brought up by dressmakers? There were several interesting possibilities. He could have been checking on her progress for Adelina as a friend. Or he could have lent his home to the Duke of Manchester (rumoured as being the father) for the purpose of meeting his illegitimate child. Alternatively the "kind old gentleman" could have been Adelina's friend and solicitor George Lewis, acting on neutral territory for his illustrious client. A sceptical cousin suggested he could even have been the butler! The possibilities are endless. If my grandmother knew the identity of her host, she kept the secret well.

The other story in my family concerns the Duke of Manchester. It was sometimes whispered that he was Geraldine's father. Obviously there is no evidence to support this. The idea appeared to me to be very farfetched until one day, researching into Adelina Patti's young days, I discovered to my amazement that they were in fact very good friends. William Drogo, 7th Duke of Manchester, known to his friends as Kim, had been Adelina's witness at her wedding and had proposed the first toast to the newlyweds.

Was he enamoured with Adelina? Or were they just good friends? She was already a star feted by international society, slim, dark-eyed, vivacious, attractive and famous. He was twenty years her senior, a racy member of the Prince of Wales' set and she would have been flattered by his attentions. It was also general knowledge that shortly after her marriage to Henri, Marquis de Caux, she realised she had made a terrible mistake.

I am certainly not trying to prove anything, these are mostly suppositions based on family secrets. Obviously my grandmother's real story will never be known and if there were ever any records these have long since disappeared. But there were many similarities between my grandmother and Adelina Patti. They were both tiny, and with an energy and verve far beyond the average. Like Adelina, my grandmother took a size one in shoes. And like Adelina (baptised Adela Juana Maria) she had that unusual second name, Adela. My grandmother loved singing and two of her daughters took after her (one having her voice trained for the stage). Up until the time of her marriage when she was about eighteen, my grandmother received a regular allowance from an unknown source, paid by a firm of London solicitors whose name is lost in the past. From the day of her marriage, the allowance was stopped.

When Geraldine was a teenager, the "aunts" emigrated to Australia. Because she insisted on staying in England and was fond of children, they (or whoever decided for them) agreed to place her in a highly recommended family in Buckinghamshire as a nursery assistant. When she was eighteen or so she fell in love and married Francis Thorn, the eldest son of a well-to-do local family and their first son was born just a few months later. A scandal! The Thorn family considered her below their status and had opposed the match, so it was not surprising that when poor Francis died of heart disease at only thirty-six, they severed all connections with her. Geraldine, a young widow with seven children, was forced to sell their home to survive. But not too long afterwards she remarried, had two more children (the last being my mother) and lived quietly and serenely in a small cottage in Somerset until her death in 1946.

I was only a child but I still have a clear picture of her in my mind, a sprightly little old lady who sometimes came down by train to visit us in Dorset. She sang me ballads and the Music Hall songs of her youth, and filled the house with her incessant, lively chatter. I was always sorry when her brief visits were over, and looking back it isn't difficult to believe that she really was Adelina's daughter. She did not have much money but was always careful with her appearance, slim and neatly dressed. "Remember that you can always judge a lady by her accessories," she told me. "You can wear a sack but if you have good shoes, bag and gloves, you'll save appearances." Poor or not, she was a true lady.

Like Adelina, she loved animals and filled her home with cats. She played the only instrument that would fit into her tiny crowded cottage: a spinet. For years I played at dressing up with a fringed silk shawl and a pair of size one black satin shoes with Louis heels, finely embroidered with coloured glass beads, that she had worn when she was young.

After studying the life of Adelina Patti I have asked myself several times why my grandmother, a woman of spirit and character, never tried to make any claims because she lived through difficult times and money was often short. The lady who could have been her mother was one of the richest and most famous women in the world, living in splendid luxury in her castle in South Wales, cosseted by at least forty servants and with an enormous collection of jewels. It must have been a question of pride. After all, it is not pleasant to be abandoned at birth. She was never heard to mention her mother.

I do however have my own little scrap of evidence. I have a letter from my aunt who wrote that when she was a child she was singing one day with her sister when Francis Thorn's sister came into the room. "It's not surprising that you both have such good voices," she told them. "After all, your mother's mother was Adelina Patti!"

# 1

Pushing back strands of hair that were sticking to her forehead with the heat, she fanned herself with a sheet of music. She would never have believed it could be so hot in London, even in summer. Alone, the silence became oppressive, broken only by the steady ticking of the clock on the mantel. Perhaps she had been optimistic to insist on staying in town and giving most of the servants and Louisa the rest of the day off.

Earlier she had tried sitting out in the shade of the apple trees but there was no air to stir the leaves and soon she had felt a prickling in the small of her back where the muslin dress stuck to her skin she had come indoors and sponged her body with cool water and changed into a silk *peignoir*. She was alone and had no need to dress up today.

Another Covent Garden season was over. The last notes of '*Home, Sweet Home'* always a favourite encore, had died away. The usual bouquets had rained on stage and at last the applause had subsided when, bowing and blowing kisses, bending to fill her arms with flowers, she had made it clear that this was really the last encore and backed gracefully into the wings. Leaving the theatre that last evening she was left with a sense of something achieved, of gratified pleasure, but also of anticlimax. Today she felt none of that elation she had always enjoyed at the end of a London season but was restless and vaguely ill-at-ease, as though she had been the centre of attention at a party and suddenly all the guests had turned and left. It was the year 1869 and Adelina Patti was twenty-six years old.

This room, her *salon*, was still crammed with her favourite treasures, although a row of packing cases with wisps of straw escaping from the top were a sad reminder of her imminent departure. Seeing them lined up there along the wall like passengers waiting on a railway station, the thought that she must soon leave Pierrepoint House forever only made her all the more nervous. In the coming days she must personally supervise the packing of her special things.

Idly her fingers brushed the glass on a photo in its ornate silver frame. Tsar Alexander II of Russia and the Tsarina, stiffly in pose, stared back, so unlike the friendly couple she knew. They had given her the signed photograph last December during her Russian tour and she smiled, remembering how he had asked her to call him *Papa* and how the Tsarina had brewed her tea backstage in a samovar, "To keep up her strength". They were both very dear to her.

She picked up a celluloid souvenir gondola from Venice and then put it back next to her favourite china dog, chipped at the base, not surprisingly after all his travels with her since she was a child, from New York to Mexico and Cuba.

One of her papier-mâché bonbons boxes, empty but cherished for its pretty colours, had fallen to the floor and she placed it back on the oval table next to a French tobacco box and the signed portrait that Alexandra, Princess of Wales, had pressed into her hands during her last visit to Marlborough House. And then, as always, her eyes strayed to the family portraits, Papa Salvatore, Mamma Caterina, her sisters, Amalia and Carlotta, and her brothers, Ettore and Carlo, lined up along the mantel on a heavily fringed drape. Most of all she missed Papa, who had always been there, encouraging her before and after every performance, sharing her triumphs, consoling her when she was troubled.

In an effort to keep her *salon* cool the blinds had been lowered and the room had taken on that shaded, mysterious air of a Mediterranean villa when the shutters are closed against the outside world. She loved Pierrepoint House, privately renamed Rossini Villa, in Atkins Road, Clapham – her own quiet corner of London. The old-world villa in its pleasant garden had become the perfect retreat from the bright lights of public life. She had spent happy summers here with Papa and Maurice[1], learning to ride, watching the cricketers during her walks on

1    Maurice Strakosch, her tutor and manager since her childhood

the Common, even coming to grips with her first English novels. From here they had set out on the drive to Covent Garden on the evenings when she was singing. Six years of happy memories.

She sighed. All that was about to change. She was a married woman, a Marquise, as her husband never failed to remind her, and although at first she thought having a title would be enough to compensate for Henri's shortcomings, it was of little comfort now. He had decided they must give up the villa and return to live in Paris. It would be a final break with the past and she was more than a little sorry. She could almost hear Papa saying, "I told you so".

Picking up a Venetian vase, a wedding present, she turned it over in her hands, admiring its glint of greens and blues, the colours of the lagoon. Did she really have to go? Was it possible that she had broken free of the confines of life with Papa and Maurice only to find herself trapped in an even more restricting set of rules and commands? Of course, Henri was polite enough, he was a gentleman, but he expected his word to be final.

Henri had chosen this moment for a brief trip to Paris, officially to make arrangements for their new accommodation and to take care of his private affairs although she had pleaded and argued that these matters could well have been dealt with by others. This was the first time they had been separated since their marriage and she had felt put aside when he kissed her briefly and left for Victoria Station with his manservant and a trunkful of clothes. Although lately she had to admit that his presence had begun to irritate her, on the other hand she felt he should not have left her alone at this particular time. But then, he understood little of the emotional strain of an opera singer's life on and off the stage.

She shuffled through the music sheets spread across the top of the piano. This 1869 season had been particularly demanding. Covent Garden the opera house, had formed a coalition with Her Majesty's Theatre, which had recently been destroyed by fire. So the two opera companies had joined forces and Adelina, as usual, had been very much in demand; in fact it had been one of the most crowded seasons of her life. She had sung with Mario, her old Italian friend who was still a popular tenor and a handsome partner although he was getting on a little in years, the Swedish prima donna Christine Nilsson, the dramatic soprano Therese Tietjens and the French baritone Faure. Their greatest success had been *Don Giovanni* and they had given several repeat performances with her Zerlina and Mario's Don Giovanni always bringing the house down. And then there had been *The Barber of Seville, Dinorah, Don Pasquale, La Figlia del Reggimento, La Gazza Ladra, Rigoletto* and *La Sonnambula*. A dizzying one-season repertoire.

The 'Royal Italian Opera' columns of *The Times*, which Henri insisted on reading aloud at the breakfast table, had been lavish with praise, and it had given her intense pleasure to hear herself described as "one of the most accomplished actresses that ever trod the lyric boards". This was what she had been longing to achieve for some time now, to bring the level of her acting as near as possible to that of her voice. She could hardly believe what they wrote of her Amina, "the whole performance exhibited the genius of Madame Patti in the happiest light and may justly be recorded as a legitimate triumph".

Endless applause, success, praise, flowers, gifts –it was all very gratifying but the constant switch of roles did take its toll. Like the rest of the company, she was a little tired when the curtains swished across the stage after their last performance and they had taken their last bows. How strange, how disquieting it was now to find herself, for the first time in her life, utterly alone, if one didn't count a couple of servants somewhere in the back of the house.

Suddenly she came to a decision. Self-commiseration and brooding would get her nowhere. This unaccustomed solitude did have a positive side after all: she could relax and do whatever she pleased. Adelina Patti, Queen of the Opera, already a star at the top of a brilliant career that was to span a lifetime, stopped prowling around the room, kicked off her slippers and lay down on the most comfortable couch. She may as well make the most of her freedom: moments like this were rare enough. She adjusted a pile of cushions under head, others beneath her feet. Helping herself to a peach from the bowl of fruit at her side she bit into its soft pink ripeness, careless of the juice running down her chin, wiped away with her sleeve. It did not matter. Henri was not here to reproach her for her behaviour, "unsuitable for a Marquise" and her public was not here to see. Now that she had bitten down to the stone the peach tasted bitter and she tossed it aside.

The room was stuffy, filled overpoweringly with the scent of flowers, making her drowsy. There were flowers in every corner and on every available surface, bouquets in vases and complicated arrangements in baskets standing on the floor. She had them brought home from the theatre but some were already beginning to droop in the heat. And mixed with their scent was the fresh, pungent smell of new wood and straw that came from the packing cases. There was still so much to be done…

For a moment the thought crossed her mind that she should sing a few scales. A lifetime of self-discipline deplored her laziness. The piano beckoned invitingly. But she was so tired, her limbs heavy, and gradually her eyelids dropped and she slipped into an uneasy sleep.

# 2

Born in Madrid on the tenth of February 1843[2], under the sign of Aquarius, Adelina was a romantic idealist but with a concrete practical sense, especially where money was concerned. She had those qualities of fascination, independence and geniality that are associated with Aquarians on the one hand, and a sometimes childlike naivety on the other; a contradictory character, but with a total dedication to music.

She was nearly born on stage. Her mother, the Italian soprano Caterina Barili, already the mother of seven children and once again nine months pregnant, had nevertheless insisted on keeping her annual engagement with the Italian Opera in Madrid. Her voice was in excellent form so why should she disappoint her Spanish public?

Caterina was singing one of her favourite parts, Norma, when on the evening of February 9th, just before the curtain went up on the last act, the birth pains started and she collapsed on stage. She was rushed back to her hotel but as things turned out Adelina was not born until the following day.

The life of Caterina Patti Barili, born Caterina Chiesa, was almost as good as a story for the opera. She had been discovered by her first husband (a music teacher and composer, son of a well-known soprano) when, singing, she was drawing water from a fountain in Rome. Signor Barili, entranced by her beauty and her voice, married her and trained her for the opera. Their marriage had been a happy one until he died,

---

2   Some sources specify that this was actually the 19th February

leaving her a widow with three sons and a daughter and very little else. Luckily by this time she was able to fend for herself, being a favourite with the San Carlo Opera in Naples and popular in other Italian cities. Donizetti even created the part of the heroine in *The Siege of Calais* for her. She was therefore launched in a successful career when she met Salvatore Patti (a tenor with the same operatic company) a Sicilian from Catania. His darkly handsome good looks "swept Caterina off her feet", they were married soon after and had four children in quick succession.

Strangely, after the birth of Adelina, Caterina's voice was never to be the same. Although she continued to sing for several years, the strain of that *Norma* had been fateful and later she was heard to complain, "Adelina has taken everything from me, even my voice!"

Meanwhile, back in Madrid, on April 8<sup>th</sup> 1843 in the parish church of St Luis, the baby was christened Adela Juana Maria. Not long afterwards the Patti family returned to Italy.

Adelina, as she was called, grew into a lively, healthy child with a voice that was already making itself heard, although none of the family could have guessed at its potential. When she was two, Salvatore Patti accepted the management of the old Palmo`s Opera House in New York and the family moved to America. Unfortunately this venture turned out to be a failure and he took on the management of the larger Astor Place Opera House, the family settling into an apartment on the Bowery. Adelina's first memories were of when she was three and was taken to the theatre in the evenings to hear her mother sing. At a hour when other children of her age were tucked up warmly in bed, she sat on the edge of her seat between her brothers and sisters, spellbound by what was happening on stage, immersed in the music and the magic of the opera, drinking in the atmosphere, the colours, costumes and lights, never missing a note. Later, back in her bedroom, she would be unable to sleep for excitement and would dress up in one of her father's old red-lined cloaks and her mother's hat and feathers and go through the whole opera as she remembered it, singing each part in turn. She was even the audience, applauding at the end of each act and throwing bouquets, which she made up from twisted paper. In this way the seeds of her musical education were sown, and they would soon shoot up in such a fertile ground that few singers have been lucky enough to find because there was music everywhere at home. Her older sisters, Amalia and Carlotta, who had been left behind in boarding school in Milan but soon joined the rest of the family, were both talented sopranos and dutifully practised their scales and trills. The other step-brothers and step-sisters were also musical, and scales and arias echoed from room to room. Little Adelina listened and learnt. Now she saw them all again vividly in her dream: Ettore, who had given her her first singing lessons; Clotilde, who had already sung in public for years; Nicolo and Antonio, who were both good basses; temperamental Mamma and dear Papa, her kind, reassuring rock.

She was back in the large, shabby, rented apartment at 170 East Tenth Street which Mamma did her best to brighten up with flowering plants and their personal bits and pieces brought from Italy, the family all seated around the table for supper with Papa ladling out bowls of steaming minestrone. They lived a life of highs and lows. Papa lost his job as theatre manager and it was up to the children to keep the family fortunes afloat with their singing. Sometimes there was less meat and more macaroni on the table, sometimes objects disappeared when they were taken to the pawnbrokers, but nobody complained except Mamma. They were living from day to day.

The most carefree was of course the youngest, Adelina, who, oblivious to problems and encouraged by her mother, sang all day long. She repeated arias she had heard and the popular ballads, copying her sisters, singing as she played with her dolls or concentrated on her colouring book, and by the time she was six she already knew several opera parts by heart. She remembered well the first time she surprised all the family with her performance when she was six or seven. Amused, they stood her on the table so that they could all see her and, to their amazement, she attacked what is perhaps the most difficult and most beautiful aria of all, *Casta Diva*, which even many accomplished sopranos are afraid to tackle. Their initial amusement soon turned to silence as the first slow notes of the aria from Bellini's *Norma* came across the room in an effortless childish treble. After their stunned reaction they had all become emotional and her parents brushed away a few tears. Papa had later confided, "That was the moment we realised we had given birth to a genius!"

Adelina had come to the rescue and saved the family from poverty by turning professional at the age of seven when Salvatore Patti, by now convinced that his baby daughter was a potential goldmine, arranged for her to give her first concert. Ever since she had first performed for the family, her brother Ettore had been giving her lessons and they had taken her to hear famous singers such as Jenny Lind, Madame Grisi, Bosio, Sontag and Alboni, so that when her contemporaries were still chanting nursery rhymes, she already knew the arias from *La Sonnambula* and *La Traviata* by heart.

Her first public performance was for a charity concert in a certain Tripler's Hall in New York. Once again she had been stood on a table so that the audience could see her, a tiny dark-haired child with large, intelligent eyes, sure of herself and with no trace of stage fright. Clutching her favourite doll she sang the rondo 'Ah, Non Giunge' from *La Sonnambula* and 'The Echo Song' made popular by Jenny Lind. The audience was taken completely by surprise. How could such a tiny figure produce such notes? Some may have thought there was a trick somewhere. A first incredulous silence gradually turned to warm applause and for the very first time she realised how intoxicating it could be to sing in front of a real audience, to carry them along with the power of her voice, to hold them in her hands. All that applause was for her. The sensation was sheer excitement.

They called her a child prodigy, a star. There was more coaching from Ettore and piano lessons from her sister Carlotta and soon she was judged ready for the big step, and had set off on her first professional tour with Papa, never to look back. To seven-year-old Adelina it was all rather like a game. She never thought of being exploited so early in life because after all she was doing what she enjoyed most, singing. She adored singing and it took precedence over her dolls and the trunks full of pretty new dresses and suits with matching pantalettes, the velvets, taffetas and silks. It was no hardship to take up her career so young because not only was there the excitement of performing on stage but there was the fun of travelling with Papa.

Shortly after they were joined by Maurice Strakosch, her brother-in-law who had married Amalia when she was only fourteen, and who was to act as tutor, manager and accompanist and stay with her until she married.

During the next six years Adelina gave more than three hundred concerts, travelling all over the States and as far south as Mexico and Cuba. She had her share of adventures: earthquakes that shook the theatres, a scorpion in her bed, strange hotels, but she took it all in her stride. She quickly picked up the languages of the countries they visited and only had to listen to an opera two or three times to know it almost by heart. Papa was convinced she was a genius. Above all, she was earning large sums of money. Family treasures came back home from the pawnbrokers and the Pattis were once again living in comfort. They were all proud and pleased with her and now, when she went home, she was given lessons by the opera singer Madame Paravelli who also taught her to read and write.

She had no need of voice training in the normal way since it came quite naturally to her. Madame Paravelli and Ettore were wise enough not to interfere with her natural talent, but limited themselves to teaching her correct breathing, to sustain tone and to exercise her scales. She was still small for her age, but her voice was judged very surprising for its volume and purity. She discovered that the 'shakes' Amalia spent hours trying to perfect cost her no effort at all, and the same applied to all the other embellishments in vogue at the time. She was eight when, after Amalia finished singing at a family concert, she approached her with a smile that was not without a touch of malice.

"Do you think you've just done something great?" she asked. "Now you will hear me!" And she promptly demonstrated the way it should have been done.

Every homecoming was the occasion for a *festa in famiglia*. Mamma went out of her way to be nice and baked a chocolate cake, Adelina's favourite. When she was home she was the spoiled and pampered baby. There would be a new doll waiting for her and new dresses for her tours, trips to the theatre and rides in the park. It was an unusual childhood, caught up as she was in the net of increasing fame and importance. She had few friends, being so often on the move, and those children she did have occasion to play with soon had to be left behind with tearful partings and promises that they would never forget her. And home at 170 East Tenth Street, in what was then a residential area but was later to become the ill-famed Bowery, not all the mothers were happy to have their daughters play with Adelina. Not only was she Italian but she was from a family of opera singers! She was also headstrong, bossy and a little reckless and fond of dangerous games like balancing on fences or following the band down Broadway.

Fortunately, neither as a child nor as a young woman, was she ever aware that it was considered a disadvantage to be Italian. On the contrary, she came to realise that she was in many ways privileged, different from the other children she met who always lived at home and went to school. But although she was doing what she loved most, there were inevitably times when she felt lonely in strange hotel rooms and, bored, she even counted the raindrops running down the windowpanes for something to do.

By now word had spread that there was a new child prodigy and soon her name was becoming known all over America. People flocked to the theatres, curious to see and hear her. Although a photograph taken in a studio shows a solemn faced child with hair parted in the centre and drawn tightly back into plaits and dark, inscrutable eyes in an oval face, she was really just the opposite, quick to smile, vivacious and communicative. Adjectives used to describe her varied from self-willed and quick-tempered to affectionate and amiable. Her repertoire included the arias she had learnt at home and popular ballads like 'Comin' thro' the Rye', 'The Last Rose of Summer' and 'Home, Sweet Home', destined to be favourite encores for the rest of her life.

With no formal schooling, she was quick to pick up reading and writing at home and languages and geography on her travels. Bilingual in English and Italian, by the time her tour ended she also knew Spanish and French. Like most little girls Adelina had a passion for dolls. Maurice Strakosch recalls in his autobiographical *Souvenirs* how once in Cincinnati she asked him to bring her doll to the theatre and he promised to do so but then completely forgot. The moment came for Adelina to go on stage but she flatly refused to do so unless Maurice brought it to her. He rushed out of the theatre although it was already packed and the audience growing impatient, by some miracle found the right doll and hurried back with it. As soon as she had her favourite doll in her arms, Adelina dried her tears and bounced on stage 'singing as beautifully as ever' as though the incident had never taken place.

Apart from these occasional *capricci* she was fundamentally a good and obedient child especially where music was involved. She only had to hear that something was bad for her voice and she avoided it completely. She once refused a dish at dinner to which she had been invited by girls of her age, saying "No thanks, I dare not taste it if there is any pepper in it, Papa would be terribly angry!"

She was, in fact, a little in awe of her Sicilian father, whose word was final, although she loved and respected him. Salvatore took great care of her. He prepared her for her public appearances, laying out the dress she would be wearing on stage and the boots, gloves, jewellery and ornaments for her hair. It was Salvatore who plaited her hair, tied on her bonnet and fastened her cloak, not forgetting a scarf to protect her throat. Since everybody else spoiled her it was fortunate that he knew how to be severe and the strict self discipline he taught her as a child was to remain with her for the rest of her life. By now newspapers raved about her enthusiastically in the over-flowery language of the day, describing her voice as 'Exquisite', 'Wonderful' and 'Amazing', and the well-known conductor Luigi Arditi confessed to '… weeping genuine tears of emotion' the first time he heard her sing, and writes of '…the extraordinary vocal power and beauty of which little Adelina was, at that tender age, possessed'.

At last her long tour in North and South America came to an end. It had been rewarding financially as well as spiritually. Adelina's share in the profits was a clear twenty thousand dollars, a considerable fortune for the times, and Salvatore wisely invested it in a summer residence for the family in the countryside not far from New York. By the time her thirteenth birthday came around, she had the secret conviction that she would become the world's greatest soprano; it came as a very unpleasant surprise when Maurice Strakosch (with the full approval of her family) told her that her voice should now take a rest so as not to force it during the delicate period of adolescence. Her concerts came to a halt. Adelina was angry, frustrated and impatient. She considered herself the victim of a plot. She had been poised to take flight on a brilliant career only to have her wings clipped and heaven only knew for how long. To make matters worse, her mother insisted that she used this interlude to learn such boring occupations as sewing and embroidery, arguing that, "the voice is soon lost and the operatic stage is a most uncertain means of livelihood". There was no choice but to obey but as Adelina stitched half-heartedly, her mind was not on the needle and thread but wandered away to the day she would become a prima donna. When the despised sewing basket was brought out every morning, one look at Mamma's set expression was enough to silence any protests, so she resignedly put on her thimble, selected a length of coloured silk and sat humming to herself *sotto voce* – any real singing being strictly forbidden – while she jabbed the needle into the cloth. And when even Caterina could see that her daughter was sick to death of 'petit point' she was allowed to set it aside and take out her colouring book and paints.

★★★

A year went by. Her voice, rested and refreshed, was now a pure soprano which easily reached the top F and to her delight her parents were persuaded to let her take off on a tour of the southern States and the West Indies with the pianist Gottschalk. Maurice was away at the time, otherwise he would never have given his consent, but fortunately her voice did not suffer in any way from the trip.

This was to be the last of her childhood concert *tournées*. At fifteen, Adelina still had the slight figure of a child but she already possessed the determination of a woman, and back home again on 22nd Street she settled down to studying in earnest, particularly those roles which were to make her world famous: Lucia in *Lucia di Lammermoor*, Rosina in *The Barber of Seville* and Amina in *La Sonnambula*. Seeing her firm intention to launch herself as soon as possible on a full operatic career, her family, alarmed, now did their best to stop her. Caterina argued that at fifteen Adelina was far too young, she must wait a little longer and meanwhile learn the art of dressmaking. So once again, Adelina resigned herself to the inevitable. How could she make them understand that what to others might seem like very hard work, to her was pure enjoyment and cost her very little effort?

Life did have some lighter moments though and it was pleasant enough to be living with the family once again, especially now that things were easier and they were living comfortably.

Christmas and the New Year were celebrated in style, going to a few smart parties with her sisters. She was surprised and delighted when, at last, Maurice took her side and decided that she was now ready to be launched on a career. After much pleading with his senior partner at the New York Academy of Music (which had replaced the old Astor Place Opera House in 1854 and where he was now co-director) it was at last agreed that she should have an audition. A lot of people thought her too young and inexperienced to jump straight into a leading role but the audition was a success. The orchestra conductor Muzio fell in love with her voice after hearing just one song and she was engaged right away for the part of Lucia in Donizetti's *Lucia di Lammermoor* at the fee of one hundred dollars for each performance. Her cachet had been higher as a concert singer but that was beside the point. At this stage of her life she did not care about money but only about her dream coming true, and she lived through the following days and weeks in a state of mounting excitement. Not only was she about to make her debut in opera but it was to be in a starring role. Caught up in a whirl of lessons with Signor Muzio, fittings for her three costumes and running through the part time and again with Maurice, Lucia filled her days and nights; she *was* Lucia.

She lived in a state of excitement and hardly slept. Then came the day of the full dress rehearsal with the tenor Brignoli in the part of Edgardo and the theatre half full of invited guests and it all fell into place and went wonderfully well.

The memory of the opening night was to stay with her forever. It was the 24th November 1859 and she was sixteen years old. In spite of having been excellently coached in the part by Signor Muzio and sailing perfectly through the dress rehearsal, before the curtain went up she was in a turmoil of fright and apprehension. What if it was a terrible *fiasco*? She peeped through the wings and saw the theatre was crowded. There were the regular opera-goers and also a public who had come out of curiosity to see how the child prodigy would survive the test. For the very first time she had a moment of sheer stage fright. But then the lights were dimmed, the curtain went up, the familiar music took hold of her and she was once again in control. She became Lucia and, to quote the *Musical Courier*, "She took the house by storm". The enthusiasm of the public on that first night in New York was an enthralling experience to a young girl of sixteen making her first appearance in an opera and it surely went to her head far more than the champagne they toasted her with after the performance. Adelina had become an overnight sensation. For the rest of that season she sang to packed houses. All the seats were sold out at the Academy of Music. And, incredibly, during that same season, after *Lucia* she sang in no less than fourteen different operas. She had already studied a few of them but the majority were completely new to her. A formidable memory made it possible for her to learn a part in a few days and this, with her natural talent and her capacity for sheer hard work, were the three factors that would carry her to the very top. After this New York triumph, Adelina left on a successful tour of the Eastern States of America, Cuba and then New Orleans.

Recently another idea had been buzzing around in the head of Maurice Strakosch – he decided they would sail to England. He reasoned that London audiences, more sophisticated and critical than any they had faced up until now, would be a true test for Adelina and the right time was now, while she was seventeen, fresh and unspoilt. He was fairly sure her youth and her talent would have the desired effect, and wasting no further time he had contacted the well-known London impresario Colonel Mapleson, sending him a selection of Adelina's press cuttings.

Maurice Strakosch had been an astute manager and a good tutor and much of her success was due to him. They got along well, she made fun of his strong German accent and they were good friends. He could certainly rely on the right training. After studying as a pianist he had some success in Austria and Germany and then had the idea of becoming a tenor. He was lucky enough to study with the great Italian soprano Giuditta Pasta (for who Bellini had originally written *La Sonnambula* and *Norma*), who had by then retired to her villa on Lake Como; in this way Pasta's teachings, including the 'ornamentations' and 'cadenzas' fashionable at the time, had indirectly reached Adelina. After studying with Pasta for three years Maurice abandoned the idea of singing and went back to the more congenial profession of concert pianist, moving to America where he married Adelina's older sister Amalia. It didn't take him long, however, to discover that his little sister-in-law was the one with the most talent in the family, and he took on the job as her tutor and accompanied her on all her tours. He also got along well with Salvatore Patti and the three made a successful trio. The thought did cross Adelina's mind in later years that poor Amalia must have felt quite abandoned during her husband's long absences, but as far as we know she never complained. By tacit understanding all the Pattis and Barilis took second place to little Lina. She was the star of the family, the money-spinner who kept them all in comfort, and her wellbeing and success were of prime importance. So Amalia stood quietly aside as towards the end of March 1861 her husband and her father prepared to accompany Adelina across the Atlantic to try her fortune in London.

# 3

Her first glimpse of England was the Liverpool waterfront when their boat docked on a foggy April morning in 1861. One look at the oily black sea slapping noisily against the wharf and she returned to the comfort of her cabin until the moment came to go ashore. She was a good traveller and had enjoyed the novelty of the journey, full of happy anticipation, but even her enthusiasm was a little dampened by the sight of the dismal, sooty dockyard. She was glad when they were safely tucked into a first class carriage on the train to Euston, and as they travelled southwards, her spirits lifted. The green English countryside, neat gardens in front of every house when they passed towns and villages, fields of well-fed cows and sheep, patches of wild flowers under hedgerows (a sign that here too spring had arrived in spite of the cloudy sky), all gave her the curious sensation that instead of arriving in an unknown country, she had come home.

Papa and Maurice were not interested in the view speeding by through the carriage windows, but were busy discussing future arrangements, papers strewn over the seat between them. She knew that Maurice had been corresponding with the agent of Mr Edward Tyrrel Smith, manager of Her Majesty's Theatre, so she understood the gist of their conversation. Apparently this agent, a certain Colonel Mapleson, had arranged for contracts to be signed by both parties, one in London and the other in New York, and these had been exchanged through the post. If a trial run should prove satisfactory, Adelina would then be engaged for the season at Her Majesty's Theatre at a fee of £40 per week.

Details of her contracts did not worry her too much. She cared little, at eighteen, for such matters, confident that Papa and Maurice had only her best interests at heart and would take care of all the details. Instead she whiled away the time daydreaming of the London stage.

An unpleasant surprise awaited them, however, on their arrival. They were staying at the Arundel Hotel in Norfolk Street and Adelina had gone straight up to her room to refresh herself and take a rest while Maurice brought himself up to date with the situation. In less than half an hour he discovered the dismaying truth. During their voyage to England Mr Smith had found himself in grave financial difficulties and had been obliged to sell out to Mr Gye, the manager of Covent Garden. Consequently there was to be no season for Adelina at Her Majesty's Theatre and the contracts signed with Mr Smith were worthless. Neither was there any hope of compensation.

Maurice summoned the agent Colonel Mapleson to their hotel and aware by this time that something had gone wrong, Adelina joined them and was put in the picture. The others were nearly in a state of panic but Adelina's self confidence and *sang froid* came their aid. Outwardly unperturbed, she calmly suggested to Mapleson, "Why do you not try the speculation yourself? I am sure I would draw in the money."

Colonel Mapleson eyed this small, composed little woman seated on the hotel sofa. What could he lose by having a private audition right there? He asked her to sing, to have an idea of the quality of her voice, and without a moment's hesitation she broke into 'Home, Sweet Home'. Mapleson was very impressed. Later in his memoirs, he wrote, "I saw that I had secured a diamond of the first water".

He started looking for a suitable theatre right away. He dashed across to France to talk to the man who could hire him the Lyceum, and was successful. But by the time he returned to London he discovered that Maurice had spoken to Mr Gye at Covent Garden. Not only had Gye engaged Adelina for the season but he had signed a contract with her for a period of five years. Gye was an astute man and he had immediately recognised the extraordinary potential of this little Italian American, drawing up a contract that swung entirely in his favour.

The first three performances at Covent Garden were to be given free, as a trial run. If they turned out to be successful she was to be paid

£150 a month for the first year, £200 for the second, £250 for the third, £300 for the fourth and £400 a month for the fifth year, appearing twice weekly during the Italian Opera Season. Since their finances were beginning to run low, Maurice had agreed to the terms and had accepted £50 as an advance fee. Adelina listened only half attentively as Maurice went into the details. She was too excited at the prospect of singing at Covent Garden and another and even more important first night, this time in front of a London audience. Above all, she was delighted that her first appearance was to be as Amina in *La Sonnambula*.

There was little advance publicity about her London debut. No newspaper 'puffs' as they were called, appeared. Taking an all-round view Mr Gye had kept rather quiet about his new young find from America, thinking it best not to give her too much of a build up in case she turned out to be a dreadful flop; however things went he had protected himself. If her trial nights were not the success he hoped for, the contract was automatically cancelled. But privately he was sure he had a find.

There were few rehearsals and these were only partial so that not many of the other singers realised the force of the cyclone that was soon to hit the London operatic scene. One of the few mentions in the press was an editorial in the weekly *Musical World*, which commented on May 11th, "the interest becomes deeper when the debutante is so highly recommended, and expectation is elevated in proportion. Shall we hear and see a Malibran, a Persiani, a Lind, a Bosio...? In the meantime we wish every success to the youthful and much praised cantatrice, and trust that the result of Tuesday's performance may realize the most sanguine anticipations of her friends on the other side of the Atlantic." So someone had obviously followed her career and knew her potential.

She was excited about her forthcoming adventure but kept her feelings to herself, attending rehearsals, fitting costumes, practising her *solfeggi* daily and keeping to the simple routine of light meals and brisk walks as usual. There was the city of London to be explored. She took drives in the Park among the well dressed crowds, went window shopping in Bond Street and Oxford Street looking forward to the day when she too would have money to spend. She also visited Madame Tussauds like every other tourist.

Her ear quickly became accustomed to the strange Cockney accent of cab drivers and street hawkers, and soon she began to drop the Americanisms from her speech to adopt the more clipped English tones.

She loved the city with its smoke-grimed buildings and churches and the contrasting green of parks and gardens. She felt at home here among the busy crowds which reminded her of New York. There was also the fascinating fruit and vegetable market around Covent Garden Theatre where she had to pick her way between stalls packed tight with cabbages and carrots, lettuces and fruit on her way to morning rehearsals, careful not to slip on the mess of litter trodden underfoot in the cobblestones made slippery by Spring showers. The pungent smells, the noise, the shouting and bustle, this was to her the very heart of the city. Now she was eighteen, Adelina was an attractive young woman. Eduard Hanslick describes her in his *Music Criticisms* as "half timid and half wild". Her figure was still slim and almost childish, her movements agile. She had a mass of dark hair and she liked to change the style often, according to her mood, some days piling it high with ringlets falling in the nape of her neck, sometimes drawing it back into a chignon, sometimes plaiting it into a simple rope. Her most striking feature was her eyes: large, expressive and "dark as velvet".

Her looks were to play an important part in her success. Once when she mentioned to her father that she wished she had been an inch or two taller he had smilingly replied, "Italians say that the best wine comes in small casks." Encouraged, she did not let the matter worry her, and soon realised that her small frame was an advantage when she appeared in her favourite roles. Such a freshly youthful Zerlina, Lucia or Rosina was loved by the audience and she was so light on her feet that, as one critic put it, "She almost danced on stage".

The great day arrived, Tuesday May 14th. This time there was none of the stage fright that had attacked her eighteen months before at her New York opening. She had been warned that London audiences were critical, more jaded than their American counterparts. London opera-goers still had memories of her great predecessors to measure her by, people like Pasta, Malibran, Jenny Lind, Alboni, and Grisi. But Adelina had great confidence in her powers and refused to be intimidated.

As she attacked the first notes, for a moment she did feel a passing twinge of nervous fear but it vanished as quickly as it had come, and she passed happily into her aria *"Come per me sereno"* already at her best. By the end of the first act she had won the audience over completely. Once again she was submerged by wild applause. At the end of her performance bouquets were thrown onto the stage from all directions. Again and again she came to the front to acknowledge the standing ovation, the prolonged cheers and applause, first led by Tiberini, her Elviro, and then alone, gathering up as many of the bouquets as she could hold, smiling and waving her thanks, happy and more than a little overcome. Another triumph.

From then on it was easy. Audiences were spellbound, enchanted by the purity and beauty of her voice, her youth and grace. She had amazed them all, regular subscribers, the curious, the experts, the critics and the press.

It had been almost impossible to sleep that night and she lay awake for hours, going over the evening again and again in her mind. She had reached the success she had dreamed of and worked for all her life and the sacrifices she had made, even the two years' enforced rest were now all worthwhile.

Word spread quickly all over town. People coming out of the theatre raved about her to their friends, journalists wrote long, enthusiastic articles for the next day's papers and the box office was inundated with requests for tickets for her next performance. She was an overnight sensation and her long reign at Covent Garden had begun. Late the following morning Maurice came into her room and found her sitting up in bed sipping her breakfast chocolate, a bouquet of spring flowers in her lap. The hotel room was like a flower shop because she had insisted on bringing back as many bouquets as they could cram into the coach. Warm May sunshine filtered through the curtains. Her hair tumbled across the pillows and she looked like a child freshly woken from sleep.

Maurice smiled. He was obviously very pleased. "Lina, Lina, just listen to this." He spread *The Times* across her bed and read aloud, "A new Amina does not usually excite much curiosity among frequenters of the opera... There have been since the days of Malibran so many Aminas and nineteen out of twenty of them commonplace. Even the announcement of a new singer… is nowadays received with something like indifference…"

He paused, smiling at her puzzled expression before going on to the part that concerned her directly where she was described as, "A very young lady who made her first appearance last night as the heroine of *La Sonnambula* and who, we may add at once, created such a sensation as has not been paralleled for years".

The article went on to say that, although she had received little or no advance publicity and few of those present had any real idea of what to expect, "The debutante was at first calmly, then more warmly, then enthusiastically judged. And she who, to Europe at any rate was yesterday without a name, before tomorrow will be a 'town talk'." Maurice passed over a few lines that dealt with some technical shortcomings, described as inevitable in one so young but which he knew to be easily corrected. Useless to worry her with those, he would take care of ironing out any imperfections in good time. Quickly he went on to read, "There is an abiding charm in every vocal accent, an earnestness in every look and an intelligence in every movement and gesture that undeniably proclaim an artist 'native and to the manner born'. And let it be understood that these qualities of charm, of earnestness and of intelligence are not merely the prepossessing attributes of extreme youth, allied to personal comeliness, but the evident offspring of thought, of talent, we may almost add of genius, but assuredly of natural endowments, both mental and physical, far beyond the average".

Maurice paused for breath. There was more, much more praise of her voice, described as, "A high soprano, equal, fresh and telling in every note. "

All this time Adelina had been sitting motionless. She looked calm enough but her eyes were bright with tears. She did not need newspaper writers to tell her what she had always known but nevertheless it was moving to hear such praise after her very first performance in England. She thought for a moment of all the people who were at that very moment reading the 'Royal Italian Opera' columns of *The Times* all over the country. It would also be read abroad. The numbers were almost frightening.

As Maurice carefully folded the paper she caught hold of his hand. "*Merci, mon cher Maurice, je suis très contente,*" she whispered, speaking in

French as she often did in moments of great emotion. Now she forgave all the times he had made her lose patience and remembered that this success she owed, above all, to him.

Another eight days went by before she repeated her exploit, again in the part of Amina. Mr Gye realised that to keep the public waiting awhile was all good publicity. On the strength of her success Maurice had tried to change the terms of her contract. Mr Gye refused to do so but was induced to pay her an extra £100 for every additional performance on top of her monthly fee, which seemed to them fair enough.

From now on she was known as "Mademoiselle Patti" and the "Miss" was dropped forever.

When she arrived at the stage door in Flower Street she was amazed and a little frightened by the crowd that surged forward to catch a glimpse of her stepping out of her carriage. It took the force of extra policemen from Bow Street to hold them back. The theatre was already packed, the audience expectant, and she did not let them down. After the *Sonnambula*, three triumphant performances as Lucia di Lammermoor and five more repeats of *La Sonnambula*, Adelina made her Covent Garden debut in *La Traviata*. She was the youngest Violetta ever to appear on that stage and the critic of the weekly *Musical World* who had by now become her greatest fan, turned journalistic somersaults in his article: "Previous performances have not prepared us for the striking display of histrionic genius with which Mlle Patti delighted the public on Thursday night. Her last scene was truthful and beautiful. She drew 'the trembling tear of speechless praise' from many an eye, and no eulogy we might offer could exceed this spontaneous tribute to the histrionic powers of the young artist. If Mlle Patti played this scene so admirably, it may be readily supposed that where brilliant fluency of vocalisation was required she shone with almost incomparable lustre."

*La Traviata* was repeated and then it was the turn of *Don Giovanni*, which opened on 6th July with the great Madame Grisi as Donna Anna and Adelina as Zerlina. Don Giovanni was interpreted by the famous French baritone Faure and Masetto, Zerlina's husband, by the equally well-known Ronconi. Altogether, it was a memorable production. Madame Grisi had reached the end of her operatic career and this was her farewell performance. Many looked on Adelina as her natural successor.

Afterwards, when Maurice read aloud snippets from *The Times*, she was flattered to hear that, "We are inclined to think that only those who are old enough to have seen Malibran in the part can remember anything to match it".

And then, "She never for an instant loses sight of the character she is sustaining... Mlle Patti's Zerlina was a genuine artistic triumph and made an unmistakable impression on the most crowded house of the season." Praise also came from *Musical World*, which reported, "The performance of *Don Giovanni* derived a special interest from the appearance of Mlle Adelina Patti in the character of Zerlina, the happiest of her efforts and the greatest of her triumphs. Mlle Patti is gifted by nature with the requisites for succeeding in this captivating part." That June she had also had the honour of being summoned to take part in the State Concert at Buckingham Palace in front of Queen Victoria and Prince Albert who had attended several of her performances. Church music was called for and it was decided she would sing 'Jerusalem', Mendelssohn's 'Hear Ye Israel' and Hummel's 'Alma Virgo'. The Queen was never to forget the impression Adelina's voice made on her, and was to remind her of the occasion several years later.

The magical season went on and on. Londoners could not get enough of her and refused to let her go. After her sensational Zerlina she was a graceful Lady Enrichetta in *Martha* and then Rosina in *The Barber of Seville*, appearing both times with the well-loved tenor Mario. Press and public were at her feet. So by popular demand they repeated *Don Giovanni* for two consecutive nights and the curtain finally came down on the exhausted company on August 2nd. It had been a long and triumphant season for Adelina, and, tired but satisfied, she left London for a well-earned holiday by the sea.

Meanwhile Maurice and Salvatore Patti were sifting through the many proposals they had received following her London season. They decided to accept an invitation to the three-yearly Birmingham Musical Festival which was to be held that autumn, asking for a fee of five hundred guineas for four concerts. It was a high figure but Michael Costa, the conductor, insisted on her being engaged in spite of the committee's hesitation, and this insistence was to pay off because the crowds flocked to the theatre in Birmingham to see and hear her.

Then followed autumn tours in Britain and Ireland, with especially delirious crowds of admirers in Dublin.

In December she appeared in Berlin at the Royal Opera House. The German public turned out to be less enthusiastic than the British. However she did have one illustrious admirer in King Wilhelm, the future Kaiser, who attended all her performances and always came backstage to her dressing room to offer his congratulations, kissing her hand in a devoted gesture that she found quite charming, even if a little comical.

Then followed Brussels, Amsterdam and The Hague where she received a first approach from the management of the prestigious Theatre Italien in Paris, but the sum of £50 a night requested by Maurice proved to be too high. For the time being Paris must wait.

For some months now she had enjoyed the company of a companion engaged by Papa, a young Englishwoman, Miss Alice, and she was glad to have some female presence at last and a new friend to confide in.

They all celebrated her nineteenth birthday on the Continent and then towards the end of February, returned to London. It was good to be back and she felt even more strongly than before that she had come home.

# 4

A journalist once asked Adelina, "Madame Patti, what is the secret of your eternal youth?" Her reply was enthusiastic, "I loved the very joy of living and I revelled in the beauty of everything around me!" This was never nearer to the truth than in the spring of 1862. Happy to be back in London, she was looking forward to the coming season at Covent Garden and there was nothing to upset the serenity of their lives.

The Covent Garden season officially opened in April but her first appearance was scheduled for May 5th in a grand gala opening in *La Sonnambula*, by now her hallmark. It was the first "Patti Night" of the year and a journalist wrote, "The theatre was packed from floor to ceiling". Again a success with overwhelming applause and curtain calls, even more enthusiastic than in the past.

1862 was the year of the Great Exhibition and London was crowded with visitors, many of them more than happy to round off their trip to the city with a night at Covent Garden Opera House where Adelina had twice-weekly appearances, thirty-four in all. They presented the same programme as the previous year, adding the operas *Dinorah* and *Don Pasquale*. Music critics continued to praise her singing and acting. One wrote, "Beyond a slight increase of volume, no particular change was noted in her voice", but added, "there was a great improvement in her acting, no doubt due to the experience gained during the past year". Once again, Zerlina was judged to be her best role, the *Daily Telegraph* critic going as far as to write, "We doubt if any impersonation so exquisitely fresh, spontaneous and natural as Mlle Patti's Zerlina has ever been witnessed on the operatic stage". She was variously described in the press as "bright and faultless", "brilliant" and "full of freshness and originality". It was all more than enough to go to any young singer's head, but she pretended to show little interest in what they wrote. The season was a huge financial success and closed on August 15th with her benefit night, when she sang a selection of arias and closed with her favourite 'Home, Sweet Home'.

Arrangements had been made and contracts signed for the winter season in Paris but she was secretly a little concerned about such a long stay in the French capital. She now considered London her home and she had heard the French public were very critical. Maurice, however, was adamant. To set the seal on her fame it was essential that she win the approval of the French. As a lure he reminded her that in Paris she would have the opportunity to refurbish her wardrobe with gowns from famous fashion houses since she now had no lack of money for personal shopping. As a matter of fact up until now she had hardly ever handled money. Her father had always taken care of her financial affairs, investing her earnings carefully and already laying the foundations of the great fortune she would accumulate during her lifetime. The prospect of new dresses was certainly inviting and in the end she began to look forward to the trip. So they arrived in Paris the following November and once again she made her debut in *La Sonnambula* in the now very familiar part of Amina that Papa called her *porta fortuna* or lucky charm.

As she had expected, Parisian audiences were cool at first, but soon fell under her spell. It wasn't long before she had become the darling of society, led by the Emperor Napoleon III and the Empress Eugénie, who went six times to hear her at the Theatre Italien. They also gave her what was to be the first of many precious gifts, a diamond and emerald bracelet. Delighted and flattered she turned her wrist left and right, the gems flashing brightly under the lights. From that moment her passion for jewels was aroused to such an extent that she was to end up with a collection, mostly gifts from the crowned heads of Europe, that could be rivalled by few. The Theatre Italien paid her only £60 a night, although seats in the stalls sold for unheard-of sums. But her popularity grew by leaps and bounds in France and crowds that filled the streets around the theatre often had to be kept back roughly by the police. Her arrival in Paris, on the contrary, had not been over-popular with the local press. Several journalists were openly against her, going as far as to say she neither knew how to stand or how to walk on stage and that she was far too self-conscious. Some of her more jealous colleagues also criticised her "weak voice" or called her ugly! Now, overnight, after her first performance she had become *un rossignol*. Among her more celebrated admirers, apart from the emperor and empress, were the composers Berlioz, Gounod and Auber.

Coming back to her private life, the following January while they were still in Paris, her companion, Miss Alice, had to leave suddenly and Adelina found herself alone with no one to listen to her rather childish chatter. She was upset, missing female company and the hours discussing clothes and jewels, the shopping trips and the drives in the *Bois*.

Some weeks previously she had met the niece of an old friend of Maurice, a pretty German girl only two years older than herself, the blonde and blue-eyed Louisa Lauw. Adelina, struck by her friendliness and pleasant manner, immediately had the idea of sending for her and asking her to take her companion's place. Here we have a hint of Adelina's still childlike character in her relations to other people. Louisa writes in her memoirs, *Fourteen Years with Adelina Patti*, "When I arrived at Patti's, she received me in a morning negligée. She wore a charming Turkish costume, with her hair falling over her shoulders. Her pretty little face was disfigured by weeping. As soon as she saw me, she threw herself into my arms and sobbed bitterly. I was fortunately able to distract her attention from sorrow by some amusing anecdotes and a little innocent gossip. Although not much older than herself, I looked upon her as a spoilt child, to be flattered and comforted with stories. She soon laughed heartily and took me into her room to show me her treasures. Nobody could guess of what they consisted. Of an old picture book in which Adelina tried her skill with her paintbrush, some fashion papers, besides a few ornaments. She so completely recovered her cheerfulness that she sang some duets with me. But when I offered to wish her goodbye, her countenance darkened. 'No!' she exclaimed, 'I cannot let you go, you must remain with me as my friend and sister!'" How much of this little scene was genuine and how much was due to Adelina's acting talents we can only guess at. But the outcome was that Louisa was too flattered to refuse the offer and from the 6th January

1863 became the official companion to Adelina, and was to stay with her for the next fourteen years.

Perhaps the most important of Adelina's admirers at this time was the composer Giacomo Rossini. Born in Pesaro on the Italian Adriatic coast in 1792, up until the advent of Verdi, Rossini was considered the greatest living composer and consequently occupied a position of prestige and popularity in Paris where he was living. After his early successes, *The Barber of Seville, La Gazza Ladra, La Cenerentola, La Donna del Lago, Semiramide, William Tell, Othello* and other popular operas, he had passed a long period of inactivity. Twenty-five years went by. It was as though he had used up all his mental and physical resources in his youth.

In 1843 he married his French mistress Olympe Pélissier. The Rossinis returned to Paris in 1855 after a period in Italy and here the composer seemed to take on a new lease of life. His health and good humour returned and he began composing again, opening one of the most brilliant salons of the city. Artists and public figures were regular visitors at his *Samedi Soirs* and Adelina was no exception. Their early meeting had been a near disaster. She had sung him the *cavatina* from *The Barber of Seville*, 'Una Voce Poco Fa' with her usual charm but embellished with so many of her own "ornamentations" and additions that the maestro exclaimed, *"Brava, bravissima!* But tell me, whose music is this? It's completely new to me!" But soon even the elderly Rossini fell for Adelina and he wrote new pieces for her, calling her affectionately his "Pattina" (the suffix "ina" indicating "little"" in Italian).

Rossini enjoyed good food and wine and also a good joke. His friend Baron Rothschild on one occasion sent him some prized grapes from his vineyards and received this note, "Thank you. Your grapes are excellent, but I am not too fond of wine in pills." The Baron got the message and sent him a keg of his famous wine by return.

Just two days after her arrival in the Patti household, Louisa was delighted to be invited to dinner by the Rossinis, together with Adelina, Maurice and Salvatore Patti. It was a great occasion for the girls to dress up and they looked forward to an evening of good music and good food. The maestro sat between them at the dinner table, Adelina on his right and Louisa, 'La Biondina' (little blonde) on his left. On the other side Adelina found Auber the French composer who "made himself very agreeable to her". Another friend, almost always present as Rossini's guest, was James Rothschild who managed his financial affairs. Louisa tells us that Auber touched no food for he ate only once a day but that Rossini, on the contrary, was a confirmed gourmand who preferred the Italian style of cooking and did ample justice to macaroni. Adelina's friendship with the Rossinis was to continue until the composer's death in 1868 at his villa in Passy. Her sorrow was genuine: he had been almost like a second father to her. Nevertheless, she brought herself to sing a duet at his funeral, *Quid est Homo* from his Stabat Mater, with the contralto Alboni. But all this was in the unknown future when the party broke up, fairly early because Adelina had to rest, the following evening being her benefit night.

Her last days in Paris passed serenely and her next stop was to be Vienna. At the cost of being monotonous, it has to be recorded that her performances in Vienna were also a triumph and she was unprepared for the overwhelming reception she received at the Karl Theatre on February 28th 1863. There was a continuous, frenetic applause such as she had never heard before. The Austrians had taken her immediately to their hearts and there was one curtain call after another, encore after encore until she was afraid they would never let her go. Her cachet, too, was improving. She was now being paid £80 a performance by the impresario Merelli who had also arranged her tours in Holland and Germany the previous year. During her stay in Vienna the Karl Theatre made an unprecedented profit of £4,000. Patti fever was running high all over Europe.

A curious incident took place during her stay in Vienna, which was her first real experience of the reverse side of popularity. One Sunday at the beginning of April she sang at morning Mass in the church of St Augustine. There had been a crush inside the church as more and more people pushed their way in, anxious for a free glimpse of the diva. They appeared to forget where they were and broke into a spontaneous applause after Adelina had sung. Afterwards as she left the church protected by the arm of Maurice, there was a nasty moment when the crowd pressed forward, almost crushing her. In the confusion, pushed and pulled, her dress was torn, her hat pulled off, her hair dishevelled and the gloves she was carrying lost. She was badly frightened and shaken, nothing like this had ever happened before. Luckily she was saved by Maurice pushing her into a nearby doorway which happened to be the entrance to the home of the Turkish Ambassador to Vienna, Count Zichy. Upstairs the Countess bustled about comforting her and in due course the mob dispersed and she was able to drive home. But it took more than an unpleasant episode to spoil Adelina's stay in Vienna.

One day she met the famous music critic Eduard Hanslick, a meeting arranged by Maurice. She was well aware of his importance in the musical world and felt a little apprehensive, but to her surprise he turned out to be very pleasant and not at all frightening. He even confessed that he had not been particularly anxious to meet her either as she had been described as "unfriendly". A mutual liking sprang up between them and she was soon treating him on familiar terms like an old friend, a naively charming way she had with many of the important people she met. Eduard Hanslick became a daily visitor at the house where she was lodging. He found her natural and not at all the diva, and describes her in his *Music Criticisms*: "I can still see her before me, a small, pale, slender figure in a red wool Garibaldi blouse, seated in an armchair at the window, caressing her dog, Cora". He goes on to write, "I was soon on good footing with both, with the dog because I coaxed and with Adelina because I didn't. With her father, her brother-in-law and her faithful companion Louisa she had rented a small private apartment where she lived simply and quietly during this first year in Vienna. She had no fondness for parties, visits or flirtations and this coincided with the tastes of Strakosch, who took good care of her. Apart from myself, there were few visitors".

Hanslick says he often arrived at mealtimes and she would insist on his joining them, and he noted that she attacked her macaroni with gusto, her taste in food, too, tending towards the simple and genuine. After lunch she would insist on Dr Hanslick playing Viennese waltzes at the piano and then, having Maurice replace him at the keyboard, would twirl him around the room in waltz after waltz until he flopped, breathless, into a chair. He has nothing but admiration for Adelina's talent, saying she charmed him in operas he would normally have gone out of his way to avoid, but at the same time he deplores the fact that "a book was always the rarest item in her apartment". He tried to interest her in literature, giving her a copy of Charles Dickens' *Great Expectations* but was taken aback by her reaction. Returning the book she said that she had started it but did not intend to continue reading it – "It's nothing but lies, which nobody will make me believe. That an old woman wouldn't give up her bridal dress and her old wedding cake, it can't be true and isn't possible. I am no longer a child to whom one can give such things to read". At this time, Hanslick reports that Adelina was "good humoured and violent, inclined to sudden, quickly passing fits of temper, directed usually against Strakosch who tried to appease her. She had not yet learned to restrain herself, to be amiable with people for whom she did not care, an art which she later learned to perfection".

While she was living so quietly at home, Adelina was a great success professionally in Vienna. She conquered everyone, not only the man in the street but the Emperor Franz Josef of Austria who did not miss one of her twelve performances in the capital and always visited her backstage to compliment her afterwards. At the end of her visit he presented her with a royal order set in diamonds. Richer not only in terms of money and gifts (the management of the Karl Theatre gave her a solid gold laurel wreath) but in human relationships, and with the affection of the Austrians warming her heart (Josef Strauss himself had played the piano for her at a farewell party in Vienna), she travelled back to Paris. Rossini arranged a gala evening in her honour and now it was his turn to accompany her at the piano as she sang a duet from *The Barber of Seville*.

Their stay in Paris was brief this time, little more than a stopover on their way to Madrid, and on the morning of their departure Rossini called to present her with the parting gift of a Parmesan cheese knowing that, like him, she had a passion for sprinkling it over her pasta. In Madrid she was booked to sing at the Opera. During the journey, first by train to Bayonne and then by carriage over the Pyrenees, she again thanked her lucky stars that she was a good traveller. The steeply winding mountain roads did not worry her and she enjoyed the changing scenery and the stops at roadside inns for a meal and to stretch their legs. In good spirits but tired by the time they reached Madrid, she looked forward to a few days' rest. The Spanish were proud of the fact that she had been born in Madrid and were anxious to hear their "little countrywoman". Seats for her performances were quickly sold out. What better opera for her debut than her lucky *Sonnambula*? Her many curtain calls resounded to loud cheers and Queen Isabella, who had been present in the royal box, called Adelina to her side and invited her and Salvatore Patti to the palace a few days later. The queen was charming and friendly, putting them immediately at their ease, and insisted on hearing all the details of Adelina's fortuitous birth, her family history and the story of her rise to such fame. She listened attentively and congratulating her on her "brilliant successes" said, "Your account has interested me greatly, for now I can justly call you my dear countrywoman of whom I am proud."

A few days later, after Adelina's benefit, she sent her a magnificent pair of diamond and sapphire earrings. The benefit itself was a real gala night and after she had sung the stage was literally submerged by flowers, laurel wreaths and bouquets. Then two hundred canaries with coloured ribbons at their necks were released and flew around the theatre and on the stage. Adelina was touched by this pretty, original compliment and managed to catch two of the birds gently in her hands. From Madrid, where she had spent her twentieth birthday, she travelled back to London via Paris.

This time, following a friend's advice, they did not stay in a hotel but rented part of a house at 22 Clapham High Street. She immediately loved this quiet suburb of London which could only be reached by horse-drawn vehicle, and decided that she would like to settle here for the opera season every year, possibly in a larger house with a garden. With Louisa she enjoyed daily walks in the park and across the common. It was spring and the first shy flowers pushed their way through the grass, trees were sprouting green and for the first time she saw close to the reawakening of the English countryside. She took riding lessons, kept to a regular routine, practised scales in the mornings after breakfast, ate simply and went to bed early on the nights when she had no engagements. It was the serene, healthy life that was good for the voice. To save her the unnecessary stress of attending rehearsals for parts which she could probably have sung backwards, Maurice hit on the idea of standing in for her. Orchestra directors, particularly Mr Costa, were obviously annoyed by this but thought it best to turn a blind eye. A diva like Patti must be forgiven. She had no need for rehearsals? The silly mistakes of her fellow artistes made her impatient? Then naturally she need not attend. Maurice knew every move she must make, the length of each note she would sing, and after rehearsals gave her a report if there was anything particular she ought to know. So she enjoyed a pleasant interlude until her first appearance in May, once again in *La Sonnambula* This season she added several new roles to her Covent Garden repertoire. Adina in *Elisir d'Amore*, Marie in *La Figlia del Reggimento*, Ninetta in *La Gazza Ladra* and Leonora in *Il Trovatore*. She also reproposed Rosina in *The Barber of Seville* as well as singing in *Don Giovanni, Don Pasquale* and *Martha*. How any singer could switch her attention to all these parts without the benefit of regular rehearsals is almost unbelievable but Adelina took it in her stride, looking on it as a busy but very satisfying season. Of course the press had another field day and filled their columns with praise, finding her voice had grown in richness and volume and that she was singing with "wonderful brilliancy". The *Morning Star* critic was quite carried away, describing her Norina as "An incomparable combination of sparkling radiance and perfect grace", adding that, "…the simple truth is that Mlle Patti is not merely a singer who can act, she is heart and soul an actress".

Until now her life and career had spiralled dizzyingly upwards. She was cosseted, protected, admired, loved, the darling of European opera houses, utterly untouched by any breath of scandal. Her home life was serene, she could have asked for nothing better than for things to continue this way. So it was doubly worrying for Salvatore and Maurice when she became caught up in an unpleasant episode which they feared might bring her bad publicity although she was not too concerned and tended to laugh the matter off. What happened was that a certain young Baron deVille had become infatuated with her and continually pressed her with proposals of marriage. Salvatore had done his best to discourage him and as a result found himself and Maurice involved in a lawsuit. Under the name of James Macdonald, Adelina's "next friend", Baron deVille alleged that she had virtually been kept as a prisoner and treated with cruelty, her income pocketed by her father, and that she was not allowed out of the house or to receive letters or visits from friends.

As a result, Adelina was forced to go to the Court of Chancery and swear to an affidavit that stated: "There is not one word of truth in any of the allegations against my said brother-in-law or against my said father in any of the affidavits filed in this cause. I wholly deny that I am or ever was treated with cruelty by them, or that my liberty is or ever was controlled, or that I am or ever was controlled, or that I am or ever was kept short of money, or that my jewellery or any part of it has been appropriated by them. It is, however, true that the defendant, my father, takes care of the bulk of my earnings as an operatic singer for me, and I say I have the most entire confidence in and the greatest love for my dear father and also for the defendant the said Maurice Strakosch, both of whom have always treated me with the most affectionate kindness".

This was pure gold for the papers and scandal magazines. *The Penny Illustrated News* of June 13th published an article headed "The Patti Romance ". It was llustrated with an engraving showing her as Rosina and telling the whole story tongue-in-cheek, ostensibly taking her part and concluding with the words, "The nine days' wonder has collapsed and henceforward we hope the tattlers will leave Miss Adelina Patti in the undisturbed enjoyment of that domestic happiness which, everybody will be pleased to learn, sweetens her life and solaces the cares and toils of her professional career".

That summer Adelina was reunited with her sister Carlotta. Soon after their departure for Europe, Carlotta had begun a series of concert tours (possibly basking in the glories of her celebrated sister) that made her famous in America. She was described as having a fine, flexible voice that was never to reach the smoothness or texture of Adelina's but with which she had nevertheless had a certain success. Now, with Maurice intervening on her behalf, Carlotta had been engaged for a number of concerts at Covent Garden on nights when Adelina was not singing. She was prevented from trying her luck in opera because of a limp she had had since childhood, one leg being shorter than the other.

Then in the autumn she was signed on for a series of Promenade Concerts at Covent Garden, so for all this time the sisters were together and able to enjoy one another's company and catch up on one another's news. Adelina hoped her mother would also come to stay with them in London but Caterina Barili, for reasons known only to herself but which might have had something to do with jealousy, preferred to return to her native Rome where she was to live for the rest of her life. The busy life of an opera singer involved a lot of travel and in August Adelina set off with her entourage for a tour in Germany, France and Spain. Their first stop was at the Stadt Theatre in Frankfurt where she sang in *The Barber of Seville* in honour of the Emperor Franz Josef of Austria. For this night alone she was paid the unprecedented sum of £400. Her fees for subsequent performances were also generously high, a fact that led to a lot of criticism in the Continental press.

In Germany she sang the part of Marguerite from Gounod's *Faust* for the first time, then followed a trip to England for the Birmingham Music Festival, after which they returned to the Continent. Now something was to happen that would change her life.

In Paris she was introduced to the Marquis de Caux, Equerry to the Emperor Napoleon III, little guessing what an important part this meeting was to have on her future. She saw him as just one of the many fashionable gentlemen with perfect manners who vied for her attentions. She was quite unimpressed, not yet interested in suitors, smart society parties or invitations to the grand Parisien houses.

Her only great love was her music and she enjoyed visiting the theatre where, she said, she could "learn from others' mistakes". Engagements then took them to Spain once again but there was trouble brewing in the country, unrest which would eventually lead to the overthrow of the monarchy, and the atmosphere was tense. She had another meeting with Queen Isabella who was full of admiration and presented her with a large cameo brooch surrounded by forty pearls. But the menacing sound of gunfire in the streets and the air of hostility in the theatre when the Queen appeared, kept them in such a state of anxiety that they were relieved when the time came to leave Madrid.

Their stays in London now took on a fresh appeal. Through a friend they found just the home they had been looking for, "Pierrepoint House", an old world villa in Atkins Road, Clapham Park. This was Adelina's London home from now on until the year following her marriage. Once they had settled in she began to receive eminent visitors, the tenor Mario with Madame Grisi, the composer Belfe, even Mr Davidson , *The Times* music critic who had consumed so much ink writing about her since she had first arrived in England. For the first time she discovered the pleasure of entertaining friends in her own home, an art she was to perfect in later years. Her biggest success that season was when she stepped into the part of Margherita, as she was called in the Italian version of *Faust* when the soprano Pauline Lucca, upset by criticism in the press, deserted the performance.

Maurice as usual, read Adelina the best part of her press including that in the *Weekly Despatch*, "… she has thrown its beholders into a delirium surpassing all they have yet experienced… the performance is so wonderful that it is difficult to describe it without partaking of their excess". She had a series of photographs taken by Francis Slinger of Westbourne Grove on the set of *Faust* showing her in her favourite pensive mood, but remarked that she looked no more than sixteen (although she was now twenty one), with her dark hair hidden by a long blonde wig. When yet another season came to its successful conclusion she decided to take a holiday at Boulogne sur Mer where she enjoyed some sea bathing and recouped all her usual energy before setting off on tour, Homburg, Frankfurt and a Paris season before a series of concerts in Amsterdam.

On the surface it appeared a brilliant, enviable life. She had no worries and success was always assured. But something was still missing to make it complete and she was soon to discover what it might have been.

# 5

Romance edged its way into Adelina's life somewhere between the hors d'oeuvres and the dessert at a dinner party given by Italian friends in London. Adelina in her early twenties was still very much an adolescent at heart.

She had flirted and sung of love many times on stage but had never become involved in entanglements with the opposite sex, regarding her many suitors as mere background. But this time things were different. He was an attractive young merchant from Milan, an engaging conversationalist with warm brown eyes and a quick smile, flattering and full of Italian charm. It did not take him long to push all thoughts of music from her head.

Louisa, not feeling well, recounts that she had not gone to the party, so she was woken up by a highly excited Adelina on her return home. She was forced to listen to Adelina while she described every detail of the evening and her conversation with "Signor M." (whose name she never specifies). When Louisa was introduced to him a few days later she found him "handsome and of very engaging manners". For Adelina the days and weeks that followed spiralled into a crescendo of happiness. Their meetings, though chaste, were frequent and *appassionati*. Signor M. visited them with Salvatore's approval and before long they were engaged.

When Salvatore was formally requested his daughter's hand in marriage he gave his consent but with reservations. He insisted they wait a few years. Although he liked the young Italian he preferred that he made a position for himself before marrying his daughter. Also, Adelina must consolidate her musical career and put aside more money before she should think of taking such an important step. It was frustrating to the young couple but Salvatore was inflexible, so they limited themselves to twice-weekly meetings in the drawing room of Pierrepoint House, Louisa tactfully leaving them alone as they sat hand in hand in the window seat, or strolled out into the garden.

It was a love affair based largely on looks and sighs, with the occasional thrill of a chaste kiss. They did not often discuss their future together, the years separating them from marriage seeming to stretch ahead endlessly. She would obey and wait as dear Papa desired, but her lover was growing steadily more impatient.

Romance or no, the season had to go on. This year Mr Gye added Donizetti's *Linda di Chamounix* to her usual repertoire. This opera had brought her success in Paris so she must now present it for the very first time at Covent Garden. Obviously the critics were unanimous in their praise. Her passion for music came back stronger than before and she threw herself into her parts with enthusiasm, scarcely noticing at first but then becoming more and more aware of the fact that her young Italian fiancé was beside himself with jealousy. Jealous of her stage lovers, jealous of her public when they shouted their approval and showered her with flowers, jealous of anyone who as much as looked her way or came near her, jealous to such an extent that life was becoming difficult. Secretly Adelina was flattered. To the inexperienced, naïve girl of twenty-two, this meant that he must love her very much.

It came to a point that her fiancé could control himself no longer. His passionate Italian nature caused the pot of jealousy to boil over and he gave Salvatore an ultimatum. He must give his consent to let Adelina marry him immediately. He could wait no longer. Wisely, Salvatore, concerned at the change that had come over the young man who was so obviously unwilling to share Adelina with her public, began to have serious doubts about the engagement. What would become of his daughter's career if she married someone so possessively jealous that he could not even bear to see her stage Romeo embrace his Juliet? So he refused to give in. If this young Italian wanted his daughter it must be on his own terms and when he was ready to give his consent. There followed a violent argument between the two which ended in Signor

M. storming out of the house and banging the door with a finality that made the old bricks tremble. He never returned.

Louisa tells us that Adelina "was beside herself with grief and wept bitterly when she heard of the sudden ending of her love idyll. Her woman's pride was deeply wounded at the idea that the man she had honoured with her affection could thus leave her. She began to doubt the sincerity of his love and she never again mentioned his name".

Sadly disillusioned, she could also have kicked herself for being such a fool, to have fallen for the first handsome Italian face and irresistible charm that crossed her path, to have exposed her feelings to Papa, Maurice and above all Louisa. Although her friend was sympathetic and did her best to be comforting, she probably thought her quite childish. From now on Adelina decided she must be more cautious in her approach to men. The best thing to do was to put all thoughts of romance behind her and start afresh. She turned again to music. That at least would never let her down.

Meanwhile, there had been several important engagements in her diary. In May she had made her second appearance at a Buckingham Palace State Concert, singing a selection from *A Midsummer Night's Dream*. But perhaps the most emotionally intense moments had been when she had sung several times at the Handel Festival, held every three years at the Crystal Palace, to the accompaniment of an orchestra of five hundred instruments and choirs of three thousand voices. Her own voice had rung out clear as a bell over and above that immense sea of sound as she sang 'I Know that my Redeemer Liveth'. This season was also to see the inauguration of the morning Patti Concerts at St James's Hall. These were to become a popular feature on the London musical scene. With Pauline Lucca, her old friend Mario, the tenor Brignoli (Edgardo in her New York debut as Lucia) and the baritone Graziani, accompanied only by a piano, she sang many of her favourite songs, almost always ending with her own personal rendering of 'Home, Sweet Home'.

Her immense popularity was catching. Possibly, it was considered *chic* to be a Patti fan. After all, musicians, conductors and above all journalists worldwide raved about the wonders of her voice. The name Patti drew in the crowds everywhere she went. The magazine *Orchestra* wrote, "The remarkable popularity of Mlle Patti and the charm about her, apart from those powers which make her singing so specially attractive, were quite enough to secure a large audience".

They were now living in considerable prosperity and in September she hired a lady's maid who was to become her close friend and confidante and stay with her for thirty-five years. Her name was Karolyn Baumeister, but Adelina fondly called her Karo. Karo followed Adelina on all her European and American travels and acted as a good buffer between her and the dangers of the outside world. "I can tell Madame's real friends from the flatterers," she said. She was expert at keeping away those people she did not trust. And it was Karo who suggested which *mise* she should wear, who arranged her gowns and jewels for every occasion including her theatre costumes, and who took care of all the intimate details of her daily life.

As the year 1865 drew to a close, Adelina became increasingly nervous about her planned visit to Italy where she was to appear for the first time. Her natural curiosity about her parents' homeland was edged with worry about singing in front of audiences who knew most of what there was to know about *bel canto*. Their party set off from Paris, taking the Moncenisio route over the Alps to Turin, where they stopped briefly before travelling south by train to Florence. In this beautiful old city Adelina was booked to sing for ten nights. They arrived in Florence in early November under sheets of pouring rain. Nevertheless she was charmed by the medieval city on the banks of the river Arno, surrounded by gentle hills and the green Tuscan countryside with villas nestling between cypress trees and olive groves. Beneath the persistent rain, the water of the Arno, heavy with mud washed down from the valleys, had turned the same yellow ochre colour as the buildings that lined its banks, but in spite of the weather she could not resist driving around the city to admire the Duomo, the Palazzo Vecchio and the churches and piazzas. She was booked to appear at the Teatro Pagliano (now the Teatro Verdi). The moment she stepped on stage she heard an unexpected surge of applause and all her nervousness vanished. Italians had been waiting a long time to hear the diva and her Amina was greeted by an enthusiasm unusual for Florentines. Altogether she considered her first appearance in Italy a success.

On the reverse side (and Adelina was probably never to know it) not all the critics had been impressed. On 19th December 1865, a few days after her departure, the local paper *La Nazione* in a long front-page musical review, criticised her performances as being all alike, whether she was singing the part of Rosina, Lucia or Amina, and "lacking in sentiment and taste". The music critic Biaggi wrote that, "The clay and the shape are there but there is no spark, no breath of life". He admitted to all her technical merits and the extraordinary beauty and extension of her voice, but had the impression of, it being, yes, a beautifully polished and executed presentation, but lacking in feeling. He was perplexed by her choice of encores: 'The Echo Song' and a Strakosch waltz, following so closely after the magic of Rossini, Bellini and Donizetti (and these were those same encores that had sent her American and English audiences into a frenzy).

But although the more discerning ear of the Florentine music critic had detected a lack of feeling in her singing, technically perfect but without that essential ingredient of *passione*, this was not so with the bulk of the public, who were quite satisfied. Mario, who in private life was the Marchese di Candia, and his companion Madame Grisi, were present at her first performance in Florence and threw her a bouquet from their box to the delight of the audience. The couple were popular locally, possessing the splendid Villa Salviati just outside the city, which they had made even more prestigious with valuable paintings and sculptures. It was here that Adelina was invited the next day for a dinner in her honour.

Florentines had to wait several days for her second performance. This was not a publicity trick to keep them warm, but simply because she was suffering from a badly inflamed throat due to the damp weather. No local specialist could be found to cure her (one doctor called in pronounced solemnly that she would lose her voice altogether if she did not give up singing immediately!) so it was left to Maurice to do so, using the contents of his portable medicine chest. The cure worked and she was soon back in form.

By coincidence her stay in Florence combined with a state visit by the king and queen of Portugal, guests of King Vittorio Emanuele of Italy and his family, and on Thursday 23rd November they all descended on the Teatro Pagliano to hear her sing Amina in *La Sonnambula*. The local newspaper reported, "On Thursday evening Signora Patti, after having sung with that magisterial art that has made her famous, in one of the intervals between acts was invited to the royal box where their royal highnesses the kings and queens of Italy and Portugal were seated. The celebrated artiste, moved and grateful for the very high honour, accepted the invitation and was received by these august personages with affability and flattering praise. The public that crowded the theatre were extremely pleased by the spontaneity with which the queen joyfully greeted the artiste, demonstrating that true merit was worthy, in her eyes, of the very highest honours".

Adelina had added more crowned heads to her long list of admirers. The bearded and bewhiskered King Vittorio Emanuele was so taken with her that he returned with the King of Portugal on 28th November for *The Barber of Seville* and then again on the 15th December made a special trip to Florence from Turin for *Lucia di Lammermoor*, her last performance in that city.

The diva received a warm welcome in all four of the Italian cities she visited, going on to Turin, Bologna and Rome. An eyewitness reports that the Italians "shouted and applauded and wept like children with sheer delight, following her carriage in thousands from the stage door to the hotel where they serenaded her till they were tired".

The party spent Christmas in Turin where the king came to hear her sing again and where she was "repeatedly toasted in the local Barolo and champagne!"

Despite this heady star treatment at only twenty-two, Adelina somehow managed to remain unaffected and relatively unspoilt. Italy had been the tonic that she needed to smother the last symptoms of her unhappy first love and back in Paris after a stop in Marseilles she was again visited by the Marquis de Caux.

The past few months had been full of emotions, excitement and social engagements. She felt the need to relax and was happy when, shortly after her birthday, they crossed the Channel on their way to London and settled back into the tranquil routine of life at Pierrepoint House.

★★★

Mr Gye had prepared a varied programme for the 1866 season at Covent Garden. Added to all the old favourites she was to star as Annetta in

*Crispino e la Comare* for which she wore a delightful costume with a low-necked velvet bodice and pleated skirt with an over-bustle that showed a good three inches of leg above her ankles. She was also to sing Caterina's part in *L'Etoile du Nord* and this was to become a regular fixture for several years. Her partner in *Lucia di Lammermoor* was the handsome French tenor of Greek origin Ernesto Nicolini. Neither Adelina nor the critics were very impressed by his performance and his contract was cancelled. Nicolini went back to France and would not reappear on the London stage for five years when he would be found "very much improved". Nothing at the time pointed to the devastating effect he would one day have on Adelina's life. The familiar carousel continued and in the autumn they returned to Paris. Mario lent them his elegant apartment on *Avenue de l'Imperatrice* which he seldom used, and this meant that they could entertain in style. Among their frequent visitors were the composer Auber, always one of Adelina's admirers, the illustrator Gustav Doré, the Swedish soprano Christine Nilsson, a close friend, and the Marquis de Caux with his two inseparable friends Viscount Daru and Baron St Armand. Whether she liked it or not Adelina was beginning to make an impression on Paris society and as well as her regular Sunday evenings at home she also threw several parties. Celebrities began to look forward to invitations.

In the spring of 1867 she was visited by her old friend from Vienna, the music critic Eduard Hanslick. He was surprised to find her becoming such a socialite. Gone was the little girl in the red blouse who had pulled him into a waltz in Vienna. In front of him now stood a gracefully attractive young woman of twenty-four, a charming and attentive hostess surrounded by a swarm of infatuated suitors who buzzed around her like wasps around a pear tree in summer. He noted that "she treated them with the same friendliness and impartiality, and without a thought of serious involvement."

At the end of the Paris season Adelina gave a grand ball in her salon. She invited all her friends and many acquaintances… members of the Diplomatic Corps, high society and representatives of the world of art. Louisa recounts in her memoirs that while Adelina was dancing with a handsome young Spaniard, the Marquis de Caux, who had arranged the cotillions, never took his eyes off her "from which I drew my own conclusions, destined later to be verified".

By contrast, at home in London, she did very little entertaining and only invited close friends to Pierrepoint House. Clapham Park was her private retreat and she wanted it to remain so. The Covent Garden season came and went to packed houses. An innovation was Gounod's *Romeo and Juliet* with Mario as her rather ageing Romeo. The rest of the programme more or less repeated that of the previous season.

After a performance in Hamburg the party took a short holiday in Baden, the then fashionable gambling resort that was a favourite with the Prince of Wales. Here they met up with Mario and his family, and, shortly after, the persistent Marquis de Caux arrived. Louisa writes, "I did not altogether believe the marquis when he assured us that he had come solely on account of the September races".

Since there was very little for Adelina to do in Baden but rest and take walks or drives in the surrounding countryside, she found herself looking forward to the marquis's daily visits. He was an accomplished raconteur and kept the girls amused with his stories. She found him quite attractive physically too, in a refined, aristocratic way. He was not tall but neither was she. He was elegant to the point of perfection both in dress and manner.

Little by little he managed to knock down a few bricks in the wall she had built around her feelings towards the opposite sex. They took a romantic walk arm in arm through the woods one evening after they had been to dinner at an old castle and the gossip Louisa, who was following behind, remembers that "Adelina pressed closer to the arm of her escort, declaring that she had never before spent such a delightful evening nor felt so happy".

Adelina was being irresistibly drawn towards this man twenty years older than she was. Now she looked forward to his daily visits and told him she dreaded the time when she would have to leave. He was constantly on her mind and Maurice, guessing what was going on, hastened their departure for Wiesbaden where she was to sing next. Like Salvatore Patti, Maurice was not at all impressed by the Marquis de Caux. After appearing in Mayence and Frankfurt Adelina was excited at the thought of returning to Paris. She could not see the Marquis for long because it was his turn to leave for Biarritz with the Empress Eugénie, but with Salvatore's permission she was allowed to correspond with him through Louisa. Adelina, fancying herself in love again, counted the days to his return.

When his party returned to Paris he resumed his daily visits and two months later they became engaged. According to Louisa, Adelina had almost done the proposing herself. When she asked him for the latest gossip one evening in her dressing room, he had jokingly replied that the latest news in town was their engagement. She had turned and looked him straight in the eyes, replying simply, "And why not? I hope you do not object?"

Startled, and for once taken off guard, she could swear he almost blushed. And then after a moment's hesitation he managed to stammer, "Oh no, certainly not. I should be the happiest of mortals if it were true!"

"It would make me happy too" she replied. He caught her outstretched hand between his and kissed it devotedly. Had he understood rightly? Was she joking? He could not believe his good fortune. He would probably never have dared to ask her to marry him, being aware of his shortcomings. Henri, Marquis de Caux, although a prominent member of the French aristocracy, had run through his fortune, spending lavishly on expensive women and high living. He had little money apart from his modest allowance as Equerry at Court. But to his joy the message in Adelina's eyes told him she was not making fun of him. She was in deadly earnest. Overcome, he hugged her tightly and then turned and rushed out of the room. After this unexpected reaction, Adelina was worried that perhaps he had not fully understood that she wished to marry him. So Louisa was entrusted with the delicate task of sounding him out the following evening when they were all dinner guests of the Ambassador Khalil Bey. Louisa reported that all was well. The marquis too was beside himself with happiness at the prospect of their marriage (as well he should be considering the fortune that he was about to come into).

Following the etiquette of the times, two days later he sent his friend Viscount Daru to request Adelina's hand formally, and Salvatore Patti gave his consent. At once the question arose, should she continue to sing after her marriage? The viscount was of the opinion that to continue a stage career would not be fitting for a marquise, but Salvatore argued that the money she had in the bank was not yet sufficient to keep her in the style to which she was accustomed for the rest of her life. Obviously, he was familiar with the financial shortcomings of the marquis. For the time being the matter remained open.

One of the most enthusiastic promoters of the match was the Empress Eugénie who was genuinely fond of Adelina. She and the emperor hardly ever missed one of her performances at the Theatre Italien and were always among the first to applaud the diva and throw her bouquets. Adelina was frequently received at court *en famille* and Eugenie probably saw the match as the ideal way to keep her protégée in Paris. She urged her to continue to sing for the next five years and then, after securing a sufficient fortune to keep her in comfort, to join her at court as a dame *d'honneur*. In this way they would avoid the problem of having to live on the marquis's income of £400 a year.

Once news of their engagement became known, events took a turn as melodramatic as any opera. Anonymous letters began to arrive. Papa received them by the dozen, the majority telling him how de Caux had frittered away his family fortune, how he had had countless scandalous 'affaires' and how he only wished to marry Adelina for her money. There was quite a lot of truth in this and Salvatore grew uneasy. Surely there was no smoke without fire? Like any protective father he only had his daughter's best interests at heart and, preoccupied, he decided to forbid the marriage.

He wrote the marquis a stiffly-worded letter asking him to drop all pretences towards Adelina and cease all visits to their house. Furious at this intervention on the part of Salvatore, Adelina rebelled. This time she was not going to let her feelings be trampled on or to let her father dictate all the rules of her life. She accused him and Maurice of keeping her in a gilded prison and warned them that any restrictions would only serve to strengthen her determination to marry Henri. She openly opposed her father for the first time in her life. This was followed by a period of hide and seek, with Henri following her all over Paris. She found him everywhere she went, whether she spent an evening with friends or took a box at the theatre. Maurice and Salvatore, always with her, were mystified by his continuous presence. How was it possible that he knew all their moves and planned excursions? Later she was amused when she discovered his trick… he had them followed everywhere at a distance by his coachman and as soon as he was informed of their whereabouts he rushed to the same place. The headstrong and romantic Adelina longed to be with him. All this subterfuge only served to increase her desire.

It was unbearable to be so near but unable to speak to him, to take his arm, to allow him to kiss her hand. All physical contact was forbidden. She continued to take it out on her father as soon as they were home and away from curious ears. Salvatore argued in vain, entreating her to forget the marquis and to consider other proposals if she was so set on marrying, but she refused to listen. She would shut herself in her room and cry herself to sleep, or as Louisa tells us, "Her only solace was in playing the guitar. She generally retired early to her room and she often remained awake till dawn playing the most fantastic strains. Despite my idolatrous friendship for Adelina, I frankly own that I would rather have gone to sleep, but when I knew that she liked me to listen to her performances I applauded enthusiastically until she dozed off from sheer weariness".

After almost a month of enforced separation she unexpectedly came face to face with Henri at the home of their mutual friend Baron Thal. For once Papa and Maurice were not with her. Adelina rushed into his arms and he had held her close to him, regardless of their hosts. She could do no more than repeat his name over and over again while he kissed the tears from her cheeks, they were together again and nothing else mattered. Kindly, Baron Thal offered them the use of his home whenever they wished to meet and they were also able to steal an hour together every afternoon when she drove with Louisa in the Bois de Boulogne. They got into the habit of picking Henri up in a prearranged meeting place and he climbed into their carriage and drove around with them for an hour, holding Adelina's hand while he amused them with his stories and stealing a kiss whenever he fancied Louisa was looking the other way. These meetings were all the more delightful because forbidden and in direct defiance of Papa. But of course this state of affairs could not go on forever. Adelina was coming up to her twenty fifth birthday, no longer a child, and she was desperate by now to be a married woman. She chose her moment with care, braving Salvatore one evening after dinner. He was sitting in his favourite chair by the fire nursing a glass of brandy, mellow after a good meal. She approached him almost timidly, sitting at his feet and resting her head on his lap as she had so often done as a child. "Papa" she said quietly, "I must talk to you".

There was no need to say any more. "It's the marquis isn't it, my dear?"

"Papa, I must marry him. My mind is quite made up. I swear that if I do not marry Henri I will never marry anyone else. And…" she added almost as an afterthought, "I am almost twenty-five." She did not add "and still a virgin" but that was implicit. Neither did she threaten to take Henri as her lover if their marriage was forbidden but from the calm finality of her tone Salvatore would have guessed at that possibility. It was a common enough situation in the theatre world, heaven only knew.

For a long moment he was silent, turning the brandy glass around and studying the golden liquid as though it were a crystal ball that could decide his answer. And then he sighed. "My little Lina, if it is what you most desire then I suppose I must give you my blessing. If your future happiness really depends on this marriage, if in spite of all the arguments I have used you are still set in your mind, then *va bene*, marry him and be happy."

Almost before he had finished speaking she sprang to her feet and embraced him, his white beard tickling her cheeks as she covered his face with kisses. Dear, dear Papa, she had always known he would give in to her in the end. Her joy was so infectious that he was forced to smile in spite of himself. But in his heart he was troubled and would never accept Henri as the ideal son in law. Seizing the moment, Adelina decided to waste no more time. They would be married in London at the end of the season. And with a swish of her skirts she rushed off to tell Louisa the good news.

Reflecting, Salvatore told himself it was partly his fault. By opposing her wishes he had only succeeded in fanning the smoking coals into flame. Could he blame her? Should he have continued to stand in her way and deny her this chance of happiness? He remembered those first blind moments of passion for Caterina and how he had not hesitated to marry her, a widow with four children. The years had not dimmed his memory. Nevertheless he was not happy with the situation and was convinced in his mind that his daughter's professed love for de Caux was nothing more than a passing infatuation. His Caterina had been a whirlwind stirring all the family into constant activity and he smiled, remembering her quick outbursts of fury when she was not above threatening the children with the object nearest to hand, usually the poker. Happily these storms had alternated with sunny spells when her *joie de vivre* and enthusiasm carried all the family along during those difficult early days in New York. There was a good dose of her mother in his youngest daughter, more protected and cared for than Caterina had ever been but nevertheless subject to sudden violent outbursts of temper. It had been impossible for the two of them to live under the same roof and when he had brought Adelina across to England, Caterina had returned to Rome. In her own words, "Two primadonnas in one family are one too many!"

The break had been inevitable. He had chosen to follow his daughter in her career and his wife had taken second place. Caterina was now living happily in Rome and received a generous monthly allowance from her daughter and followed her successes with interest and a considerable amount of pride. And now their little Lina was set on marrying that worn-out roué of a Frenchman. God knew he had done his best to prevent it. He was certain the fellow would run through her money in no time as soon as he could get his scented little hands on it. Not for the first time Salvatore wished Caterina were here by his side to give their daughter some good advice. Perhaps the girl had missed a mother's guidance all these years, in some ways she was still very much a child.

Finishing the brandy he eased himself out of his comfortable chair, his tall figure slightly stiff. With a bit of a shock he realised he suddenly felt old. He had lost the second battle he had ever had with his youngest daughter and in spite of her obvious happiness he was sad.

★★★

As though to thwart any danger of her father changing his mind, Adelina set about making preparations for her wedding right away. The first thing she did was to order a simple wedding gown in white satin trimmed with lace from her favourite *atelier*, the House of Worth, together with a summer trousseau.

Parisiens gave her a great send-off and after her last appearance, her benefit night, smothered her with flowers and bouquets. Amongst her farewell gifts were a pair of pearl and diamond earrings from the Empress Eugénie and a huge bunch of moss roses from Henri sent especially from Nice. Adelina returned to London with a light heart to prepare for the coming season, her last as Mlle Patti. Shortly after they were joined by Henri at Pierrepoint House and Salvatore made a great effort to be civil and gracious to his future son-in-law.

There was nothing new added to her Covent Garden programme that year and she passed blithely from one part to another, Rosina, Zerlina, Norina (in *Don Pasquale* which she had already interpreted three years previously), Lucia, Martha, Juliet, Amina and Marie (*La Figlia del Reggimento*). It was a packed programme, particularly for a young woman with her mind on preparations for her forthcoming marriage, but she was Adelina Patti and not to be confused with ordinary mortals. Henri returned to Paris for a brief stay so as to resign his position at court. Although at first he had been opposed to his wife continuing her career, he had been forced to give way. He did not want to risk losing her again. He would be following Adelina on her travels and must resign his position as Equerry. In Paris he was relieved to find that his mother, the Duchesse du Valmy, who had formerly objected to her son marrying "an actress" had at last given her long-awaited consent, thanks to her daughters, the Comtesse de Reculot and the Princess Ginetti. Another obstacle had been overcome.

Henri returned to London with the good news and preparations for the wedding went ahead. When it came to discussing the church ceremony Adelina realised that although she had been baptised and brought up as a Roman Catholic, her family had not had much time for churchgoing or observing the conventions and she had never been confirmed or received the first communion. As a result these ceremonies were now carried out in haste with Madame Grisi acting as godmother at her confirmation.

The 1868 opera season drew to its close and the date of the wedding was fixed for July 29th. The weekly magazine *Illustrated London News* startled its readers with the news, fortunately unfounded, "… The Royal Italian Opera closed on Thursday last with a performance for the benefit of Mlle Adelina Patti. On this occasion the captivating prima donna took her final leave of the stage, if it be true (as reported) that she is now Mme la Marquise de Caux". Many people were under the impression that once married she would give up her operatic career and she did not bother to enlighten them. She was well aware that Maurice had signed a contract for her to appear the following winter at the Imperial Opera House in St Petersburg for a period of three months, to be followed by a month in Moscow, another tour that would bring in a huge amount of money. And by now she was interested in the material side of her contracts and not just the enthusiasm of the public for her voice.

Give up singing? How absurd. Nothing could be further from her mind. For the time being she threw herself into her coming role as the Marquise de Caux. A titled lady! Sweet music indeed to her ears.

★★★

Like most brides she woke up early on her wedding day. Louisa, Karo and her new young maid fussed over her until she was dressed in her wedding gown and she stood in front of her long mirror to see the effect. "Madame looks like a princess!" Karo told her and Adelina, studying her reflection, was pleased, she even felt like a princess in the white satin dress from Worth, her hair beautifully arranged around a circlet of orange blossom. If her face was unusually pale it was covered by her veil and could not be seen. Inwardly she was shaking but she did her best to hide her emotion, there was no point in letting them see her nervousness. Her only regret was that so few of her family were here to share her happiness. Amalia had fully intended to come but had arrived in France too tired out by the journey from America to face crossing the English Channel. Mamma, for reasons known only to herself, had preferred to remain in Rome. Carlotta had an important engagement in France. The Barilis stayed in America. Only dear Papa and her brother in law Maurice were here to support her. Her moment had arrived at last. She was about to give her biggest and best-ever performance and she had not felt so nervous for years. Her father was waiting for her at the foot of the stairs, smiling reassuringly, and when she reached the bottom step he took her hand and tucked it into his arm. The bridesmaids clustered in the hall chattering excitedly and all dressed alike, and when she appeared they all burst into a spontaneous applause. They were Mario's daughter Rita di Candia, Maria Harris, Alexandrine

Zanzi and Louisa. The evening before Prince de la Tour had given a wonderful dinner party for Adelina and Henri at the French Embassy and perhaps she had drunk a little too much champagne because she was feeling a bit giddy, or was it the emotion?

The house had been transformed for the occasion, they had obviously been working overnight. Garlands of flowers hung from the banisters tied with white satin bows, and a profusion of flowers and potted palms decorated every room. Yesterday a large marquee had been set up in the garden to accommodate the more than sixty guests who had accumulated although she had insisted she wanted only a "small, quiet reception" and here too there were garlands and British, French, Italian and American flags.

Through the open door she saw that it was raining, a fine incessant downfall, and the servants were waiting with raised umbrellas to escort them to their coaches. When Salvatore saw her disappointed expression he quoted the old Italian saying, "*Sposa bagnata, sposa fortunata!*" A bride wet with rain is a lucky bride.. And lucky she was indeed and had been from the day she was born. She held on tightly to his arm as he led her down the carpeted pathway to their waiting carriage.

Word had spread that Clapham's most important citizen was on her way to be married and the road to the church was lined with waving spectators. She waved back, some of the tension leaving now that she was on her way. It was a brief ride from Atkins Road around the Common to the church, and for a moment the white spire of St Mary's reflected an unexpected ray of sunlight that pierced the grey sky, another lucky omen. It was a beautiful ceremony.

The following day 'The Times' wrote, "For a time at least one of the most engaging and accomplished vocalists and actresses known to this generation is lost to the stage, she may even be lost to it altogether. Mlle Adelina Patti was yesterday married to the Marquis de Caux, a French nobleman connected with the Imperial Court. Long before eleven o'clock the Roman Catholic Church of Clapham Common, belonging to the Redemptorist community, was crowded to excess and many well known faces were to be recognised there. Signor Mario, Madame Grisi, Mr Gye, Mr Costa, Mr Augustus Harris and Signor Tagliafico were among those present. When the ceremony had been performed by the officiating clergy, the Hon. and very Rev.Father Plunkett, assisted by the Rev. Fathers Burke and Cleary, the civil contract was signed in the vestry, the French Ambassador Prince de la Tour d'Auvergne and M. Mure acting as witnesses on the part of the bridegroom and the Duke of Manchester and Mr Costa on the part of the bride… Mass was performed at the conclusion of the ceremony, but oddly enough, and to the disappointment of many present, not a note of music or of song was heard throughout the entire service."

It had been Adelina's idea to have a simple ceremony with no out-of-tune choirboys to distract her during this the most important day of her life. The organ did strike up a few notes as she arrived on Salvatore's arm, and again as they left. She lifted the veil back off her face in the vestry and it was only then that her nervousness left her and the tight constriction in her chest that had almost stifled her breathing vanished as if by magic. Radiantly pretty, the colour back in her cheeks, she embraced Henri, Salvatore and the witnesses, Mr Costa who had directed her so many times at Covent Garden and her friend Kim, the Duke of Manchester. Louisa tells us that the congregation had "… listened in perfect silence to the words of the priest and followed intently the ceremony at the altar. When Father Plunkett put the customary questions to the bride and bridegroom, Adelina uttered such a loud 'Yes' as if she intended it to bind her to her beloved Henri even beyond the grave."

As Adelina left the church Louisa records that she was "radiant with happiness". Back at the house the couple were jostled left and right by the large crowd of guests and received their congratulations before they all proceeded to the marquee in the garden where a wedding breakfast had been prepared. And the Duke of Manchester proposed the first of many toasts to the happy couple. Afterwards, the weather having cleared up, they all posed for a group photograph in the garden by a certain Mr Southwell. Adelina then led her guests back indoors to look at the display of wedding presents including a costly gift from the Emperor Napoleon and the Empress, a sapphire and diamond bracelet from her mother in law the Duchesse de Valmy (prevented from being present by ill health) and another bracelet in diamonds and rubies from Louise, the Duchess of Manchester. Then there was a set of antique coral mounted in gold from her old friend Mario, her Romeo, Don Giovanni and Faust, who had whispered to Mr Sutherland Edwards during the reception that "The Marquis, much as he might be attached to his fascinating bride, had never made love to her as much as he, her constant lover, had done!". There were many other valuable gifts in silver and gold, paintings, sculptures and Venetian glass.

A few close friends stayed on after most of the other guests had left, to speed them on their honeymoon in Paris, throwing white satin shoes after their carriage. And then they were alone. Another phase of her life had begun and, like many new brides, she kept twisting the wedding ring around on her finger to reassure herself that it was really true.

# 6

Who exactly was Adelina's friend William Drogo, 7th Duke of Manchester, known to his friends as Kim?

Described as a rather wild young man he had been sent to Hanover, officially to study German but more likely as an attempt to calm his boiling spirits in the chilly Teutonic atmosphere. Instead, he had fallen in love with Louise, the fascinating daughter of his host, Count von Alten, and they were married in July 1852, just three years before he succeeded to the dukedom.

Louise set about conquering London society with her beauty, gaiety and wit. After presenting her husband with five children, two sons and three unfortunate daughters brought up with a rod of iron, she then turned all her attentions to her lover, Lord Hartington, known as 'Harty Tarty'. She flaunted the affair so blatantly in the face of all London that people wondered at Kim's apparent imperturbability. In fact, the last real sparks of affection for his wayward wife had long since been extinguished. His reaction to her behaviour was to ignore it and to trust that his friends and acquaintances would do the same.

An incurable gambler, he devoted himself to playing for higher and higher stakes and to lavish entertaining at Kimbolton Castle in Huntingdonshire, his family estate. He rode to hounds with such enthusiasm that he had "broken nearly every bone in his body". A leading member of the Marlborough Club, of which the Prince of Wales was founder and President, he had also dabbled a little in politics but without much success. Like many others in his set, his days and nights were devoted to killing hours of idle boredom, and his close friendship with Bertie, the Prince of Wales – frowned on by Queen Victoria who considered him and Louise bad influences on her son – was an easy way to any society lady's couch.

Although Adelina had met Louise in Hombourg, where to the impressionable young girl's delight they had spent some time together (she wrote her a letter of thanks from Paris after receiving a signed portrait from the duchess) it was the duke who was a frequent visitor to Pierrepoint House.

Since the day of her marriage, they had met on several occasions. He had attended most of her performances at Covent Garden and Adelina and Henri had been guests of honour at a house party at Kimbolton Castle in the spring. They had exchanged invitations to dinner, had met at Marlborough House, and he sometimes dropped in for tea.

It was therefore no great surprise to Adelina when, struggling out of her dreams of the past on that summer afternoon in 1869, she awoke to see her visitor pulling up a chair to sit near her. He couldn't help staring. This afternoon she was particularly attractive, like a child rumpled from sleep, her hair down in great silky black skeins with curls around her pretty face, so unlike the *svelte* prima donna he usually found.

Although nothing had been said in so many words, for some time now he had the impression that his young friend was already a little disillusioned with her French marquis. Some of the gilt was evidently beginning to wear off their marriage. After all, the fellow was middle aged, only a year or two younger than himself and although he had led a brilliant life at Court in Paris and was well connected, it was common knowledge that he was far from being rich. And word had reached his ears that there were frequent arguments in this house. His mind flashed back to her wedding when he had been her witness and had kissed her goodbye in this very room. He had to admit that he had felt a faint twinge of envy for de Caux, as he carried his prize away triumphantly on honeymoon. Louise had not been present, perhaps a little jealous of his friendship with the diva in spite of her professed affection, but she had sent a nice bracelet as a wedding gift. Although Louise was a star in her own right, considered the most beautiful, fascinating and ambitious of London society women, it would have been difficult competing with Adelina Patti on her wedding day and she knew it.

Kim Manchester, absorbed in his thoughts but keeping his eye on her, was aware that she was going through the motions dictated by etiquette, taking his hat, gloves and cane and placing them carefully on a chair, excusing her rumpled appearance as she smoothed the creases in her gown, something soft in an apricot colour with ribbons and lace trimming, pushing her unruly hair back off her face and ringing for tea, all in quick, flurried movements that betrayed her nervousness. Then she plumped up the cushions on the divan and sat down carefully rearranging her *peignoir*, crossing her hands in her lap.

This afternoon the house seemed strangely deserted. There were none of the usual servants around to do all these things. No butler had opened the door, no parlour maid appeared and there was no sign of that German fraulein who usually placed herself so squarely between them when he called.

Perhaps he shouldn't have come unannounced. They both felt ill at ease. Although they were living in an age when gentlemen of a certain rank were expected to take advantage of teatime visits to their married lady friends while husbands were conveniently out (a fashion set by the Prince of Wales who often left his hat and gloves on a chair), Adelina had never found herself in a similar situation. Certainly no thoughts of lovers had ever crossed her mind. Always heavily chaperoned, first by Papa and Maurice and then by Louisa, Henri and Karo, never in her life had she entertained a gentleman quite on her own.

After several awkward minutes the kitchen maid, hastily spruced up for the occasion, appeared and was sent off to prepare a tray of tea. Adelina played the part of hostess, covering her confusion with an endless flow of chatter, trying to forget that she was half undressed and above all trying to ignore the significance of his gaze. But the afternoon was warm; the atmosphere in her salon heavy with the scent of roses, magnolias, lilies and heaven knew what other flowers that consumed the air they breathed. And it seemed only natural then that her friend should sit next to her on the sofa, carefully place his cup and saucer on the table and put an arm around her shoulders, drawing her closer.

After a first startled reaction of surprise, she turned to look at him. Gently, he placed a finger beneath her chin to raise her face to his, and then, gently at first, he kissed her. Even when he pulled at the satin bow that tied her negligee and his hand slid down to caress her, she did not protest but suddenly everything else, her past, Henri, Papa, Louise, propriety and *bon ton* faded and vanished into the hot air of a summer afternoon.

★★★

Henri returned from Paris, all their cases and trunks were packed and the house took on the deserted air of a theatre after the audience had filed out. He was preoccupied with the turn events were taking in Europe, the Prussian threat to France. There had been much talk of imminent attacks, of crises and of alliances in scraps of conversation overheard at dinner but most of it had passed over Adelina's head. As long as she was not directly involved and her engagements were not affected she did not worry unduly. Of course she realised it was different for Henri. Those properties of his which were left were in France and so was his ageing mother the Duchesse de Valmy, that noble lady who Adelina had at first found so awesome, and who had so objected to her as a potential daughter-in-law. Later by using all her wiles, charm and *savoir faire*, Adelina had overcome her prejudices and had won the old lady over.

Not only did Henri have his mother to worry about, but there was also the question of the Empress Eugénie's promise to appoint Adelina as "Dame d'Honneur" at the French court if she decided to retire from the stage after the agreed period of five years. Privately, this was Henri's greatest hope. He did not know that his little wife had mixed feelings on the subject. However the problem was to resolve itself because events were soon destined to come to a head and the French Second Empire swept away forever.

In the year following their marriage they had lived for the most part in Paris, where they had enjoyed a sparkling social life and a brilliant round of parties and entertaining, and Adelina had been feted as the first real life marquise ever to star in opera. Now, the London season over, they were due to move back to France. Paris was Henri's home and she liked it well enough. Besides, her sisters Amalia and Carlotta had now settled down in Paris with their families and Papa. The empress had also written pressing them to return soon, the Theatre Italien not being the same without Adelina. Tomorrow they were leaving Atkins Road. She took a last long look at the half empty rooms, stripped bare of her personal belongings. It was the end of an important chapter in her life. These old walls had witnessed her happy London days and also her secrets.

Unwillingly, her thoughts slid back to Henri. Shortly after their marriage she had realised that he was possessively jealous, scarcely leaving her alone for a moment, unwilling to let her out of his sight. Sometimes she was afraid that if provoked his jealousy might even lead to violence. Naturally, the appearance he presented to the world suggested none of this. He had a pleasant manner and was always perfectly turned out and impeccable in a stiff shirtfront and carefully knotted tie, gold watch chain across his chest, a fresh flower in his buttonhole; well groomed, his beard was cut in the latest fashion to reveal part of his chin; his hair was smoothed back. Quite the dandy, he moved in all circles with the perfect self-assurance of the true aristocrat. She did not doubt that he loved her although at times she was aware that she irritated him, that he found her childish and naïve.

Their worlds were further apart than she had guessed, and as time went by she found they were quarrelling more and more often over sheer futilities. She only had herself to blame. Papa had warned her that she was making a mistake. Gradually, insinuating itself into a corner of her mind, was a wriggling doubt that perhaps Papa had been right after all. On the other hand she had to admit that Henri, in spite of his faults, had proved a devoted husband, showering her with a thousand little attentions. He was also looking after her interests well. Her bank account was flourishing under his management, in spite of Papa's forebodings. And the night Henri had returned from Paris his passion for her had known no limits. Sighing with a vague sense of loss and regret she closed the door of her salon and climbed the stairs to spend what was to be her last night in Pierrepoint House.

★★★

Their possessions were sent ahead to Paris but Adelina was booked to perform during the month of August and the beginning of September in Bad Homburg, and naturally Henri, Louisa and Karo accompanied her. It was an easy matter for her to conquer Bad Homburg audiences and in particular King William of Prussia, her fervent admirer, in whose honour they gave the *Trovatore*. Afterwards in her dressing room, as he bent to kiss her hand, she asked herself how it was possible that this charming person could be considered such a danger to France and the French, and so feared by Henri.

Bertie, the Prince of Wales, who was taking the waters at Baden Baden, also turned up specially for the performance and was, as usual, full of praise. He reminded her how "his favourite prima donna" had only recently been guest of honour at a dinner at Marlborough House, sitting on his right and captivating everyone present with her "sparkling wit". Adelina was flattered. But at the same time she was wary. After all, Bertie was a close friend of Kim Manchester. Men talked. Was it just her imagination or did she detect an interested gleam in the canny eye of the Prince of Wales that had not been there before?

But she had little time for introspection, which had never been one of her traits. Next on the programme was *La Figlia del Reggimento*, one of her favourite roles and she was looking forward to the first night when suddenly her happiness was shattered by unexpected bad news. Her dear Papa, Salvatore Patti, had died suddenly in Paris where he had been living since her marriage. Blinded by genuine grief she turned desperately to Henri for consolation. But of course, obligations to her public had to take first place over and above any private sorrow.

Later, the Queen of Prussia begged her to sing in Baden, and as usual her Lenora in *Il Trovatore* was met with rounds of applause and praise. At last, the season over, she could return to Paris and give way to her feelings. A veil of grief hung over her heavily, the city was strangely empty without Papa. All her life he had been her guide and her dearest friend, and she owed everything to him. Now he was gone. He had never approved of her marriage, her one defiant gesture that had wrenched her away from his protection. She prayed he had forgiven her before he died.

It was late October and the season for sadness. Henri had taken an apartment in the Hotel du Rhin in Place Vendome. Here they were visited by Amalia Patti and Maurice Strakosch, also both in deep mourning. Maurice had preferred to leave her after her marriage, although Henri had asked him several times to remain as Adelina's tutor and manager. He had, however, left on good terms and had secured her contracts for future appearances at the main European opera houses for a total value of 1,600,000 francs extending over a three-year period.

Maurice Strakosch was of the opinion that artistes of the theatre should never marry. In *Souvenirs d'un Impresario* he writes, "The joys of the domestic hearth are not always for artists, family life is rarely suited to those idols of the public whose existence is passed in an imaginary world, and who sometimes have neither the time nor the wish to appreciate the happiness to be derived from the peace and calm of a simple life". So, although Maurice had come to accept her marriage to Henri as a *fait accompli,* like Salvatore Patti he did not approve of her choice. This is why he decided to graciously bow out of her public life and had turned impresario, promoting the careers of other promising singers.

The period of mourning could not last long, Adelina was too popular to hide away and invitations poured in. They were frequently invited to the Tuileries as guests of the emperor and empress, and soon after her return to Paris she was besieged by journalists urging her to take part in a benefit concert in aid of a young actress, a certain Sarah Bernhardt who she had never heard of, but who had lost all her possessions in a fire. Wishing to do some good in memory of her father she accepted. Henri complained that she was lowering herself, this actress being quite unknown and Adelina a star. But in the end he gave his consent and the concert was held at the Odeon Theatre on 5th November.

Louisa Lauw writes in her memoirs, "After the concert, the latter (Sarah Bernhardt), clad in a black woollen gown, timidly approached the great singer and offered her a small bouquet, and being too shy to utter a word of thanks she kissed her hand. Who could have guessed that so insignificant a girl would develop into the famous Sarah Bernhardt of today and astonish the world by her acting and her quarrels?"

There followed a sparkling Paris season at the Theatre Italien with the diva throwing receptions for the crème of Paris society and even inviting the Crown Prince of the Netherlands as well as a gathering of French aristocrats living out their last days of splendour before the imminent fall. There is also a musical fact to remember. For the Crown Prince, for the first and only time, Adelina and her sisters

Amalia and Carlotta sang together a special trio from the opera *Il Matrimonio Segreto* and it is recorded that the Dutch prince was "quite entranced".

Then it was time to make preparations for her forthcoming tour in Russia, beginning in St Petersburg on November 15th. Her Russian tour the previous year had been an overwhelming success and she wanted to repeat it. She remembered well how the public had gone wild in St Petersburg. Tickets had sold out at lightning speed at the unprecedented price of a hundred roubles each and the Jockey Club had arranged for flowers to the value of six thousand roubles to be thrown to her on stage. That first night she had received no less than forty curtain calls and among her most enthusiastic admirers were the tsar and tsarina.

Russians, she discovered, were as generous with their gifts as they were with their affection. The public had presented her with a diamond brooch that had belonged to Catherine II. Tsar Alexander gave her diamond earrings and she had received many other equally costly gifts from the nobility.

On her Benefit night she had chosen to sing *Don Pasquale*. As she entered her hotel with theatre applause still ringing in her ears, to her amazement she had been greeted by a fanfare of trumpets and the sight of the entire staircase decorated with flowers and a chorus of young girls dressed in white scattering her path with blossoms. And then six Russian generals in full dress uniform had lifted her in a flower-decorated chair and had carried her up to her apartment where a crowd of friends and admirers were waiting. They all sat down to a gala supper and the party had broken up at four in the morning. It had been a glorious tour that she hoped to repeat.

The new gowns from her favourite couturier Worth were delivered, her trunks packed, and she set out again for St Petersburg with her entourage, well wrapped in furs against the rigours of a Russian winter.

It was another triumph. The wild scenes repeated themselves and she allowed herself to relax and be carried along happily on the tide of the Russians' enthusiasm. Her public presented her with another priceless gift: a large pearl brooch set in twenty-five diamonds. To add to her joy, Tsar Alexander officially appointed her Court Singer and invested her with the Order of St Andrew with his portrait set in brilliants on a gold medal. All this was carefully noted down by Louisa Lauw.

It was a lengthy tour and continued until February, winding up with an extra gala concert on March 3rd.

On March 16th she sang in Liege and here it was reported that her voice was more beautiful than ever, "possessing an added dimension". Here for the first time she sang 'Valentina' in French and the critics enthused she had "never been so great". Henri read out the conclusion of the music critic in the Paris 'Figaro', "*Le rossignol à pris le vol de l'aigle!*" (The nightingale has taken the flight of an eagle). From her triumphs in St Petersburg and Liege, she returned to Paris to sing *Linda de Chamounix* on March 29th and Rosina in *The Barber of Seville* two days later.

On April 2nd it was the turn of *La Traviata* and five days later *Rigoletto*. The composer Giuseppe Verdi, who made no secret of the fact that Adelina was his favourite singer, was present, and sent her his card one evening after a performance with the words, "To my only and real Gilda". And her friend, the French composer Auber, offered her a bouquet of Normandy roses with a card saying, "The diamonds you wear are beautiful but those you place in our ears are a thousand times better!"

★★★

The 1870 season at Covent Garden had already opened by the time they returned to London with the soprano Mathilde Sessi singing for the first time in front of an English audience and "meeting with a favourable reception". Adelina was to appear later when the season was well under way.

On May 14th the *Illustrated London News* reported that "…The return of Madame Adelina Patti and the reappearance of Signor Mario (the latter after an interval of two years) were the special events of the past week at the Royal Italian Opera. The Barber of Seville, on Saturday, brought back both these public favourites… "The reception of both was of the most enthusiastic kind, the first entry of each having been greeted with loud and long continued applause by an audience that occupied every seat of the house. The Rosina of Madame Patti again exercised that charm which the refined grace and brilliant vocalisation of the accomplished singer must have for cultivated ears and taste. In the cavatina 'Una Voce' in the lesson scene (introducing 'O luce di quest'anima'), the encore 'Home Sweet Home' and in every scene in which Rosina appears, the mingled geniality and brilliancy of Madame Patti's performance were such as belong to the highest order of stage singing".

Back home, and in better voice than ever, after a tour de force including leading roles in eight operas, she spent the summer in London. There were plenty of weekend invitations to country homes for the darling of society and her husband, and the time passed pleasantly; they were very much a part of the social scene. But then, as a result of the Franco-Prussian war and the difficulties of life in Paris, a group of French exiled family members began to arrive, starting with Henri's mother and followed by Carlotta and Amalia with Maurice Strakosch and their children.

In spite of the unhappy circumstances the sisters were glad to be together again until on September 7th they received a telegram announcing the death of their mother, Caterina, in Rome. Adelina had not seen her mother for several years, she had never been as close to her as she was to her father and they had had their moments of friction, but it had been Caterina who first encouraged her as a child in New York, set her imagination alight by allowing her to visit the theatre and urged her on to sing. Her death, together with increasingly alarming bulletins from France, cast a shadow over the Patti household.

That August had brought news of defeat after defeat of the French army at the hands of the Prussians. Even relations between French Henri and German Louisa grew strained. The French army was besieged at Metz with insufficient supplies, Alsace was lost and Napoleon III first withdrew his troops to Chalons and then marched north only to be caught in a trap. On September 2nd he was forced to surrender at Sedan with his army of 83,000 men.

The French Emperor was by now a sick man detained as a prisoner at Wilhelmshohe, and Henri feared for his life. Meanwhile the Empress Eugénie, helped by an American dentist in Paris, succeeded in escaping to England and took lodgings at the Marine Hotel in Hastings. Adelina and Henri paid her a visit and found her "as lovely and charming as always, quite philosophical about their plight but blaming herself for the misfortunates that had overtaken France".

Although the emperor had surrendered, the new French government was determined to hold out against the Prussian invaders. They were still grimly defending Metz and were confident of being able to defend Paris too. But as the German army advanced, telegraphic communications from Paris were cut off and the only way of sending messages out from the capital was by carrier pigeon or by hot air balloons!

In spite of the entire French nation rallying round and taking up arms against the invaders, Strasburg fell on September 27th and exactly one month later the army of 180,000 at Metz was forced to surrender. With Europe in a turmoil Adelina calmly planned ahead, determined to carry out her engagements. Mid-October found her in St Petersburg again, collecting even more successes, bouquets, gifts and jewels and then she went on to Moscow where she had three concerts booked.

Her outward calm was soon almost to be upset by an incident in her dressing room at the Grand Theatre before the curtain went up. Thanks to the self-control learnt as a child, particularly during her travels in South America when she had faced dangerous situations several times, she was now able to prevent disaster by keeping a cool head. A careless maid had left a spirit lamp burning at the foot of a cheval mirror and as Adelina stood in front of the glass adjusting the flowers in her hair the muslin dress caught fire and she was quickly enveloped in flames. Louisa and her maid rushed screaming to help, wrapping her in rugs and towels while all the time she stood quite still and without a trace of panic. But once the fuss was over and the flames put out, she quietly fainted for the first and only time in her life. Bits of charred muslin were later distributed as souvenirs to the theatre manager and her fellow artists! The rest of her time in Moscow was the usual success and Louisa notes that she was presented with a magnificent silver gilt tea service as a farewell gift.

But life was not so happy now home in London. With the excitement of the Russian trip over Henri grew more depressed as the days went by. Adelina did her best to cheer him up in the only way she could think of by organising receptions and musical evenings at home but she watched him become a bitter shadow of his former self. Matters did not improve when the Emperor Napoleon arrived in exile in England and settled down with the empress at Chiswick, the country house put at their disposal by the Prince of Wales who in turn had borrowed it from the Duke of Devonshire. Adelina and Henri visited the royal couple several times but with each meeting Henri came away in a worse state of mind. He was seeing it as the end of his world. The splendour and glitter of the Second Empire was gone.

On 28th January 1871 Paris finally surrendered after a four-month siege and a month of cannon fire, the people on the edge of starvation reduced to eating rats, cats and even the elephants in the Jardin des Plantes. Adelina tried desperately to reason with Henri. She too was sorry for the poor Parisiens, for the treasures in the Louvre exposed to bombardment, for the cruel fate of the emperor and empress, and the end of their life at court. Her days in Paris had been among the most carefree of her life. She pointed out that luckily all the family had escaped unhurt, they should be thankful for that and not dwell on the past and what might have been. She wanted no long faces around her. She was young, warm blood flowed in her veins; she needed to be surrounded by gaiety and laughter.

But her arguments had little effect. She did not yet fully realise that little by little she was falling out of love with her husband.

My grandmother was probably born somewhere around this time. If there is any truth in the story that she was the daughter of the diva, one can easily imagine what an unpleasant shock it must have been. Adelina had made it clear to Henri from the beginning of their marriage that she wanted no children, she had neither the time nor the vocation to bring up a family and above all she could not face the risk of damaging her voice.

Since the age of seven, she had instinctively known what was best for her career. Even that small act of singing with her favourite doll clutched tightly in her arms had increased her cachet from five hundred to a thousand dollars an evening. She was a mistress of stagecraft and a confirmed actress, placing her musical career before everything else, allowing nothing to interfere with the perfect organisation of her professional life. If word had got out that under her girlish looks she was in fact calculating, she did not care. Music and the consequent success it brought her was her whole life and everything else must take second place.

Supposing for a moment that there was truth in the well-kept secret that she had a daughter, it could not have been easy to hide her condition from the critical eye of the rest of the world. Physically she would have had few problems. She had always been extremely careful with diet and exercise and it had paid good dividends. She was of such slight build that the voluminous skirts of the day could have hidden eventual changes. Emotionally she could have had some bad moments but she was never a person to panic, keeping a cool head while everyone else was running around in circles, hiding her feelings when necessary.

Although she could have followed the example of many of her contemporaries and reverted to an abortion, it could be that by the time she became aware of her condition it was too late. She would have been adamant, however, that when the child was born she wanted no further part in its life. It was an inconvenience, no more, to be overcome in secrecy and forgotten.

All this is sheer conjecture. If Adelina was ever pregnant, almost certainly Louisa Lauw and Karo would have been aware of it, living side by side with her in her daily life. But in spite of being treated coldly by Adelina towards the end of their relationship, Louisa never gave any real hints of scandal. As for Karo, she remained in Adelina's service until her retirement and her loyalty was absolute. It would be logical to presume that Henri knew too, but there may have been a faint possibility that she managed to hide her condition from her distracted husband, preoccupied as he was at the time with his mind on other matters.

True or not, whether I have believed in nothing more than a fairy story or if my grandmother really was the daughter of Adelina Patti will never be known. Any possible clues or evidence have long since been covered up in the dustsheets of time, and I am not trying to prove anything. I leave it to the reader to draw your own conclusions.

# 7

There is a letter[3] dated "Monday Morning" written in an elegant, sloping hand on a small sheet of paper printed with the Pierrepoint House address, which reads,

> "My Dear Mr Costa,
>
> I have a very bad soore throat and am unable to come to the rehearsal today. I doubt even to be able to sing tomorrow. However maybe, if I remain entirely quiete in my room, it is possible that I shall be better tomorrow. I am, my dear Mr Costa,
>
> Yours very faithfully,
> Adelina Patti"

Whether the "soore" throat really existed or was merely an excuse not to attend rehearsals – which she disliked intensely – we shall never know, but the letter shows the very great care that Adelina always took of her health. She would never dream of singing with the slightest hint of a malaise, least of all a sore throat.

All her life she followed very strict health rules. After the age of forty she ate no red meat and drank only soda water, white wine or

---

3    Letter in Covent Garden theatre archives.

"a glass of champagne to pick me up when I feel weak", as she told a French reporter. Spirits and liqueurs were taboo. She ate lightly, white meat, eggs, vegetables and fresh fruit, and she always slept with the window open, summer and winter. In later years, an impresario[4] wrote that when she was singing she continuously drank an infusion of cherry stalks to keep her voice crystal clear. And apart from the occasional cup of tea, such as that brewed for her by the Tsarina of Russia behind stage in a samovar, she usually steered clear of this drink and coffee too, preferring hot chocolate. Stress had been carefully avoided all her life, if we don't count moments of tension before a performance in front of an unknown audience. Worries and fatigue had been spared her. She kept to a steady routine. Every day she sang her scales and took a siesta and an afternoon walk. Any upsetting incident must be quickly forgotten.

The regularity of her life was largely responsible for her youthful aspect and the preservation of her voice. But exactly what was so special about Adelina's voice that set her apart from her contemporaries? A lot of printers' ink was consumed and many superlatives lavished on detailed descriptions by those lucky enough to have heard her sing. It is difficult to describe a voice in words but they do convey some idea of the special qualities she possessed.

Her biographer Herman Klein, who followed her entire career with meticulous care, recalls hearing her for the first time in 1872 when he was a young man of sixteen. "I recollect more especially the dark, penetrating timbre, the 'voix sombre' of Patti's voice. How unlike it sounded to any other I had heard, so individual in quality, so perfectly in harmony with the personality of the singer, so elusive in its witchery, so satisfying and entrancing to the ear!"

George Bernard Shaw, when he was a music critic writing under the pseudonym Corno di Bassetto, had mixed feelings about Patti. While he admired the perfection of her voice, he disapproved of her unadventurous repertoire and her way of courting applause. Nevertheless, in 1894 he was moved to write, "I never fully appreciated Patti until one night I heard her sing, not 'Una Voce' or anything of that sort, but 'God Save the Queen'. The wonderful even soundness

---

4   Schurmann, *Le Stelle in Viaggio,* p.189.

of the middle of her voice, its beauty and delicacy of surface and her exquisite touch and diction, all qualify her to be great in expressive melody and to occupy a position in the republic of art high above the pretty flummery of newspaper puffs, flowers, recalls, encores and so forth which make it so difficult for people who take art seriously to do justice to the talent and the artistic pains which she condescends to bid for such recognition".[5]

And Lilli Lehmann, a fine singer coming from a family of singers, whose mother was a friend of Wagner and who was therefore well qualified to judge another singer's voice, wrote, "She possessed, unconsciously, as a gift of nature, a union of all those qualities that all other singers must attain and possess consciously. Her vocal organs stood in the most favourable relation to each other. Her talent and her remarkably trained ear maintained control over the beauty of her singing and of her voice. The fortunate circumstances of her life preserved her from all injury. The purity and flawlessness of her tone, the beautiful equalization of her whole voice, constituted the magic by which she held her listeners entranced".[6]

One thing is certain. She must have been quite exceptional if Giuseppe Verdi, when asked to name his three favourite prima donnas, replied, "First Adelina, second Adelina, third Adelina!" And Eduard Hanslick likened her voice to "the dark tones of a Cremonese violin". Much later, when she was sixty-two, a regal lady living in her Welsh castle, she was finally persuaded to record her voice for the Gramophone Company, and although by then her voice had lost its freshness and there are some worn and breathless passages, one still catches a glimpse of the young Patti here and there.

Madame Patti at sixty-two comes across warmly clear, vigorous, exciting, never dull. As well as the exceptional quality of her voice she had a large dose of that other ingredient for success in the theatrical world, charm. When she first appeared as Amina at Covent Garden, Charles Dickens described her as having "… a rare amount of brilliancy and flexibility" and "that talent for success, charm, which is born into few persons and which cannot be bought or taught".

---

5    George Bernard Shaw, *Music in London*, Volume III.

6    Lilli Lehmann, *How to Sing*, London, 1903.

After first meeting her as a young girl, Eduard Hanslick thought in the same vein, "If Patti's singing, acting and personality are regarded as a whole, one must confess to having hardly ever met a more charming individual on the stage. I have heard greater artists as singers and more brilliant voices. I recall more sophisticated actresses and more beautiful women. But Patti's charm consists in making one forget them. What she offers is so completely hers, so harmonious and lovable that one allows oneself to be captivated and accepts capitulation with pleasure. When this slip of a girl steps lightly on the stage, inclines her childish face, radiant with artless pleasure, and regards the audience, intelligently and good-naturedly, with her big, shining, doe-like eyes, she has already conquered… What a youthful, fresh voice, ranging evenly and effortlessly from C to the F above the staff! A silver, clear, genuine soprano, it is wonderfully pure and distinct, particularly in the higher tones… Overall, however, is immeasurable charm".

In the 1870s Adelina's voice was at its best and as usual her engagement diary was full. Her theatre was Europe. With Paris temporarily out of the picture she appeared regularly in London, Homburg, Moscow, St Petersburg and Vienna.

In the summer of 1871, they found themselves neighbours of the tenor Ernesto Nicolini (a Frenchman of Greek origin whose real name was Ernest Nicolas), his wife and five children. Adelina was irritated by the tenor's insistence on imitating her old friend Mario, who had retired that year from public life. They were an eccentric couple. Nicolini's wife kept flying off into scenes of jealousy, accusing her husband of being a Don Juan, and on each reconciliation he arranged for a fireworks display in the garden. The others were amused but the couple's behaviour increased Adelina's dislike. The next season she ran through her usual programme with the usual success and even added the roles of Gelmina and Valentine to her repertoire.

On July 4th 1872 she was summoned to sing for Queen Victoria at Windsor Castle. The queen had already had several occasions to admire her, and was so taken with her duets with the French baritone Faure and the tenor Capoul, followed by her own special version of 'Home Sweet Home' that she presented her with a valuable bracelet. And her collection of jewels was enlarged by five diamond stars received later that year in Russia, as well as two solid gold cups inlaid with precious stones, emerald earrings from the tsar and a diamond tiara from her public in St Petersburg.

It was with mixed feelings that she sang in St Petersburg when she discovered that Ernesto Nicolini was to be Romeo to her Juliet. She was forced to admit to herself that he sang the part with great feeling. He cut a handsome figure in his Romeo costume and together they caused a furore with the audiences, their voices blending perfectly. Yet something about the man irritated her. He was pushy, too full of his own importance and convinced that he only had to snap his fingers for women to fall at his feet, something that she had absolutely no intention of doing. Even Henri was enthusiastic though about their singing together, saying that they made a splendid stage couple.

Later in Vienna she found to her dismay that Nicolini was staying at their same hotel and in spite of her protests and arguments, Henri insisted on inviting the man to join them at their table. She found him quite *antipatico*, always reeling off the names of his latest conquests and even going so far as to show Henri the love letters they wrote him. But since Nicolini was travelling alone there was little she could do to avoid him. She did manage to make a firm stand when her friends the Fischoffs gave a banquet in her honour, refusing to attend if Nicolini was invited. So Nicolini was not invited. The man was most disagreeable and the less she saw of him the better.

Unfortunately, or perhaps fortunately, if she could have looked into a crystal ball and seen the future, at this point the gods must have conspired together because Nicolini was signed on as her partner for all her future starring tours. He continued to irritate her, talking openly about his adventures with the opposite sex, his wife completely set aside, until at one point Adelina was almost tempted to write an anonymous letter to the poor woman telling her of her husband's infidelity. Louisa, wiser and with a broader viewpoint, dissuaded her from meddling. Such goings on were common enough in the theatrical world and very probably his wife knew exactly what her husband got up to on his tours.

By now, Adelina's European engagements were coming so fast on one another that sometimes she scarcely found the time to have her trunks unpacked before they had to be strapped up again for the next journey. The first to suffer from this frenetic activity was Henri who fell ill with a lung inflammation in St Petersburg. He was well looked after and on the way to recovery by the time they had to move on to Vienna, where she was due to sing Rosina in *The Barber of Seville* but he was not judged well enough to accompany them. She was assured there was no cause for concern. The ladies would be escorted by the male members of the company, and Henri stayed behind to convalesce.

At about this time, Adelina's attitude to Nicolini began to undergo a slight change. She no longer despised him, but those traits in his character which had previously annoyed her she now began to find attractive. So she was not altogether sorry to find herself sitting next to him on the train journey through the bleak, unending Russian countryside covered in snow. For once he was silent. She let out an involuntary sigh, hoping they would soon be stopping, and under the furs and rugs that covered her knees, she felt his hand reach for hers. A pleasant, tingling warmth ran through her body and made her heart beat faster. Unseen by the others they sat holding hands like a pair of young lovers until the train reached the next station and they had all climbed down for refreshments and to stretch their legs.

She was rather sorry when, back in their carriage, she found herself sitting next to the French tenor Capoul, although he was excellent company and soon had her laughing at his stories. She laughed and joked but her eyes kept straying across the carriage to where Nicolini sat, apparently asleep in his corner seat. Still he said nothing but she felt his eyes on her all through dinner that evening, and she was surprised, and a little embarrassed, to realise that the hand holding her fork trembled as she raised it to her lips.

From then on their relationship changed. She no longer dreaded having to sing with him but looked forward to playing Juliet to his Romeo, and there was a new naturalness in their stage embraces that seemed to last a few seconds longer than before. She invited him to her table, amused now at his stories, laughing delightedly at his jokes. Now he was no longer a distasteful boor but her "dear Ernesto".

When they had first sung together in 1866 at Covent Garden, the Press had been cool in their comments and his contract with Mr Gye had been severed. He had not returned to London until the spring of

1871 when he had come over with other French refugees to escape the horrors of the siege of Paris. By then his voice had improved, thanks to his wife's coaching, and so had his acting. Above all he had a magnificent stage presence very reminiscent of Mario's, and Mr Gye had signed him on for a season at Drury Lane and then at Covent Garden.

In more ways than one the fall of the Second Empire was to influence Adelina's destiny. Without the Prussian invasion of France Ernesto would probably never have returned to London where he had been so cold-shouldered and they would have gone their separate ways. Without the fall of the Bonapartes Henri would not have become the embittered shadow of his former self and her affection for him might never have reached such a low ebb; indeed, she may even have been persuaded to become Dame d'Honneur to the empress as Henri so desired.

Generally Adelina was not given to introspection or might-have-beens. Her busy public life left her little time for such things. She only knew that suddenly her emotions were getting out of control, and had been ever since that train journey from St Petersburg. There had been nothing more than his warm hand holding hers but they were both aware of the feelings this apparently innocent gesture had aroused.

They had another engagement together in Moscow and one afternoon while Adelina and Louisa were strolling in Petrowski Park, a carriage drew up beside them and Ernesto got out. He seemed very nervous and agitated and after a brief attempt at polite conversation, he suddenly stopped and caught Adelina by the arm. Louisa guessed he wanted to speak to her alone and walked on ahead but glancing over her shoulder she saw that he took at letter out of his pocket and pressed it into Adelina's hand. Then with another brusque movement he jumped back into the waiting carriage and drove off. The whole episode had been so unexpected and everything had happened so quickly that Adelina stood still for a few moments holding the letter in her hand, too surprised to move.

Full of curiosity, Louisa hurried back.

"Go on, open it, let's see what he has to say!" she urged.

Adelina knew that Louisa had no patience with Ernesto, she had never changed her opinion since they had first met, and now she was forced to open the envelope and read the letter aloud, the last thing she wanted being that Louisa suspected her feelings.

To their amazement and Adelina's secret pleasure, it was a passionate love letter. She was moved by his words and found it irritating that Louisa had burst out laughing, saying, "Is it not most amusing?" But to the eternally romantic Adelina the letter was from a man in love, a man daring to risk making a fool of himself. He loved her, of that she was suddenly certain. In spite of his bad reputation, his countless affairs, the trail of broken hearts he had left across half Europe, she knew that this time he was sincere.

Nevertheless she had to allay any suspicion. "However much I wished it, I could never love that man!" she said. But her feet scarcely seemed to touch the ground as they walked back to their hotel.

"Oh, and by the way," she warned Louisa as they entered the foyer, "not a word of this incident to Henri, of course. I would not wish to anger him for nothing".

Up in the privacy of their room she threw herself on the bed and read Ernesto's letter again and again. There was no longer any doubt in her mind. The current that had passed between them had not been just her imagination. Her maid knocked on the door to ask which gown she should lay out for that evening. There was no performance and the night was hers.

"Get out the prettiest gown I possess, the pink silk, and to set it off those new matching diamonds", she told Karo. Tonight she wanted to look her best.

★★★

Shortly afterwards they had become lovers. The story got around, she knew not how, that Ernesto had hidden himself in the wardrobe in her hotel room, waited until Henri went out and then surprised her in bed.

On tour together they had plenty of opportunities for secret liaisons, delightful moments that passed all too quickly. She discovered passion and desire. Ernesto was everything that a woman could wish for in a lover: handsome, virile and capable of moments of great tenderness. He awoke in her feelings she had not known. It was almost as though her life up until this moment had never existed, it had all been a dream and this was reality.

Suddenly she found herself loving everyone around her, but most of all her dear Ernesto. She marvelled at the way he had filled her days He was so male, handsome and arrogant (but never with her), so alive. She lived for the moments they spent together but asked herself how much longer they could conceal their passion from the world.

The main problem was Louisa. This time she would not ally with Adelina against Henri. She openly despised Ernesto and refused to speak to him or to acknowledge his presence. One day when Adelina asked her why, she replied with scorn, "That philanderer! I cannot understand why your attitude to him is so changed or why he is continuously invited to our table! Do you not remember the scandal with that woman, when you wished to inform his wife?"

Adelina did not reply, she remembered only too well. How she understood those other women, their tears and desperate letters, now that she loved Ernesto herself. The thought of his wife and children left behind in Paris scarcely crossed her mind.

Then, "Yes, but he has changed. Do you not find that he is quieter now? Less aggressive? Less disagreeable?" she asked tentatively.

"I find him exactly the same as always, if not worse, and I am only surprised that you let him throw sand into your eyes so easily!" was her friend's retort as she continued to help Karo with the packing of trunks, smoothing skirts and gowns, pleating, folding, tucking everything into perfect place.

Wishing to keep the peace, Adelina said no more. Soon they would all be back in London, she would say nothing until then. She dared not broach the subject again with Louisa but she had the impression that her friend's attitude to her was changing. She must be careful. She wanted none of the inevitable scandal that would certainly arise until she had spoken to Henri herself. It would have to come to that. She loved Ernesto so desperately that she was no longer content with brief meetings and constant partings, she needed him by her side day and night, now and for the rest of her life.

They returned to London and Henri, oblivious to all the signs, continued to admire Ernesto and to invite him to their home, treating him with the utmost cordiality. Nothing was further from his mind than any infidelity on the part of his wife. Adelina, for the time being, let sleeping dogs lie, and treated him with her usual affection.

★★★

In the 1870s Adelina's popularity with Covent Garden audiences was at its peak. Regular favourites, season after season, were *Don Giovanni, The Barber of Seville, Etoile du Nord* and *Il Trovatore,* which after 1872, took the place of *La Sonnambula* in her repertoire. *Dinorah, Romeo and Juliet, Les Huguenots* and *La Traviata* were repeated several times. Innovations were *Les Diamants de la Couronne* in July 1873 in which she sang the part of Catherine and Verdi's *Luisa Miller* which, "in spite of Mme Patti's admirable performance", was not destined to make its mark.

Her most overwhelming success, however, was to be in 1876 in Verdi's *Aida* which was represented for the first time in London and which would remain printed indelibly in the minds of those who saw it as her biggest-ever triumph.

Giuseppe Verdi[7] had composed *Aida* (which, together with *Don Carlos* and *La Forza del Destino* formed what he called his "new operas made with ideas") for the Cairo Opera who had commissioned it as part of the celebrations for the opening of the Suez Canal. It had therefore been presented first in Cairo in 1871 and then at La Scala, Milan in 1872 where the soprano Teresa Stolz, who incidentally was jealous of Verdi's open admiration for Adelina and missed no occasion to show her spite, had sung the title role. It was rumoured that Stolz and Verdi were lovers and for a while his wife, the devoted Giuseppina Strepponi, suffered greatly.

Verdi strongly desired that Adelina should create the part of Aida in London and although at first she had been doubtful of her ability to carry off such a highly dramatic role, these misgivings were soon to be overcome.

The great composer himself had encouraged her. She visited him at his country home in Sant'Agata near Piacenza, Italy, and they went through the part together. The maestro was then sixty-three. Although he was considered the world's greatest composer, rich and famous, he

---

7    1813–1901

lived a simple enough life, dedicating a lot of his time to gardening. With Adelina he worked together at the piano in his studio, the nerve centre of his empire, a crossroads with six doors and a view of the garden beyond the lace curtains.

The studio, with its bare wooden floor, also contained his bed, his desk, books, a shaving stand and a cupboard filled with guns and a collection of duelling pistols. Shooting had been a passion of his when he was young but it had long since been abandoned. Villa Verdi contained more than thirty rooms but the maestro preferred to live and work in this studio on the ground floor, which was cool in summer and warm in winter.

He was pleased and honoured to have the prima donna as his guest, being perhaps the most illustrious of her admirers. So they ran through *Aida* together at the piano and he convinced her that she would have no difficulty with the part. He even allowed her to make several cuts.

Giuseppina Strepponi was a charming hostess and their visit passed pleasantly. The Verdis shared Adelina's liking for dining in style in full evening dress, a habit acquired during their long stay in Paris, and the perfectly cooked maccheroni and risotto served at their table took Adelina's thoughts nostalgically back to her childhood. The couple became her affectionate friends and the *maestro* never made any secret of his admiration for her. He wrote to his friend Giulio Ricordi, the Milanese music publisher, that "…from the first time I heard her in London, when she was hardly more than a child, I considered her a marvellous singer and actress and something exceptional in our art".

Her stay in Sant'Agata over, the last doubts brushed aside, she threw herself wholeheartedly into preparations for *Aida* at Covent Garden. For the first time in years she even attended all the rehearsals. She personally supervised the creation of her costumes by the theatre dressmakers although it had been suggested that they could be ordered from Paris or Cairo. "Fanciful dresses of this sort are always best made for me in the theatre" she said. Her enthusiasm was heightened when she discovered that Ernesto was to be her Radames.

The lovers had done their best to be discreet and up until this time Henri had suspected nothing of her relationship with Ernesto. Their secret meetings continued, wherever they stayed he would take a room in the same hotel and he even wore disguises so as to be near her undetected. Adelina could not bring herself to confess her feelings to Henri so this state of affairs could have continued indefinitely if it had not been for the insinuations, veiled warnings and anonymous letters that began to reach him. To begin with his trust in his wife remained unshaken. But little by little his eyes were opened and he began to suspect that Adelina was greatly taken by her stage partner.

Louisa had already guessed at the truth and tried to remonstrate with Adelina one afternoon as she was about to go out to meet her lover at a secret rendezvous. Adelina, busy buttoning her gloves and straightening the veil on her hat, dark enough to hide her face, was anxious to be off. These precious moments with Ernesto went by all too quickly. But Louisa was being tiresome.

"Adelina, may I speak to you for a few moments?" she asked, standing between her and the door and blocking the way.

"What is it, Louisa, that cannot wait until I return? I do not wish to keep my friends waiting."

Suddenly Louisa, usually so controlled, let go and all the pent-up resentment that had accumulated during recent months came to the surface and boiled over. When her tirade had finished she started sobbing into her handkerchief. So she knew. For a moment Adelina's heart seemed to freeze in her chest. Then impatience took over and this quickly turned to anger. Her friend had no right to criticise her in this way. What did she know of life or love, this German fraulein who had spent so many years as Adelina's shadow, cataloguing her jewels and gowns and pandering to her every whim? Why, she had never even been engaged! Without a word she pushed her brusquely to one side and swept out of the house. The impudence of the woman! Never again would she let her into her confidence. Nothing and nobody would come between her and Ernesto. At that moment she was so furious that she did not give a damn if Louisa went running straight to Henri with her tales. It would be one way of settling the whole affair.

Surprisingly, Louisa kept the secret to herself, hoping against hope that Adelina would eventually return to her senses.

Now that the lovers were so caught up with preparations for the grand opening night of *Aida*, almost always together on stage and off, Adelina's happiness became so transparent that Henri at first began to treat Ernesto more coolly and finally forbade her to invite him to their home. Another crack had appeared in their marriage.

*Aida* opened on the 22nd June 1876 with the Prince and Princess of Wales among the very distinguished audience. It was a triumph. In her Egyptian costume (the way Victorians saw it) with colourful strings of beads and a tall crown, her face stained brown to look the part, she attacked the most dramatic role of her life. Critics, who up until now had doubted the capacity of her lyrical soprano voice (so suited to the music of Rossini and Donizetti) to sustain the part of Aida, were forced to bite back their words. The *Daily Telegraph* critic wrote that never in his experience had he seen at Covent Garden anything more impassioned than her acting, declamation and singing.

Nicolini was a handsome Radames. Singing with Adelina, loving Adelina, his voice seemed to have grown in fullness and was described as "A real tenor of exceeding beauty", whilst the diva's voice had "… taken on a new note of tragic feeling and shades of poignant expression". One can imagine the couple rushing backstage with the applause and frantic shouts for yet another curtain call still ringing in their ears, pushing their way through the mass of outstretched hands, the kisses and congratulations, Ernesto's arm holding her closely all the while until they reached the safety of her dressing room. She had lost Louisa and Henri in the crowd and her maid turned discreetly away. With the brown stain beginning to run with the heat and emotion, she must have kissed her Radames.

Surely this was the happiest moment of her life. His arms were strong around her and their bodies fused together but then there was a knocking on the door and the impatient voice of Henri, demanding that it be opened, shattering the spell.

# 8

A false semblance of normality cloaked the last, weary months of their marriage. She said nothing, anxious as usual to avoid trouble. He said nothing, hoping desperately that in this way the affair would blow over. She could never find the courage to face Henri with the truth; he avoided looking the truth in the eyes.

Adelina and Ernesto were once again booked to sing together in Russia the following winter, but Henri refused to let her go. She was uncertain whether he guessed the whole truth or if he was just suspicious. In the end, pulled in one direction by her passion for her lover and in the other by her fear of rousing Henri to uncontrollable anger, she agreed to give up the idea. As a consequence they had to pay a forfeit of 200,000 francs for breach of contract.

Henri decided they would winter in a romantic Naples, trusting that the warmth of the southern Italian city would bring them together again. Unfortunately he had reckoned without Nicolini. No sooner had Ernesto heard of Henri's plans than he cancelled his Russian tour and decided he needed some sea air and rest too, and he took on an engagement for that winter at the Teatro San Carlo in Naples.

Adelina resembled a pawn in a game of chess, moving to command. Aware of Ernesto's plans, Henri then announced that she would go to Russia after all. The Russians had refused to accept her forfeit, they could not do without Patti and protested that 200,000 francs would never compensate for her loss. Before they left Henri wanted to take his wife away to some quiet place and they went together to

Dieppe for two months' restful holiday by the sea. Adelina was often pensive, her manner absent, but she treated Henri affectionately and the poor man was lulled into a false sense of security. They had taken a suite in a hotel with flower-filled balconies overlooking the sea and, in spite of herself, Adelina felt the relaxation and peace having their effect. She had been through too many emotions during the past few months and her feelings were in a turmoil. Henri was patient with her and kind. Back in his beloved France he became more like the old Henri she had thought she loved, putting himself out to please her in a thousand little ways. So much so that when the two months drew to an end she was almost sorry to leave their quiet hotel. The thought crossed her mind that if they had been just an ordinary couple, out of the public eye and living normal lives, she might even have been willing to stay on here in Dieppe indefinitely with Henri. Perhaps if they had stayed another month... But no, their time was up.

Louisa had not accompanied them to Dieppe but had been away on holiday and they had arranged to meet her in Paris before journeying on to St Petersburg. There were engagements to be carried out, a contract to be fulfilled, her public was waiting. Resigned, she helped Karo pack their belongings and said a sad farewell to Dieppe and to many other things. All this time Ernesto had been writing to her, and at first she had been reluctant to open his letters (addressed to Karo for safety) not wanting to destroy her newfound peace of mind. But then the temptation had been too much and the letters had been memorised, kissed, cried on and destroyed.

They were in Moscow when the bombshell fell. In spite of all her precautions, Henri had come across one of Ernesto's letters. He was still anxious to avoid a showdown but Adelina was aware that "his eyes blazed with revenge". This time it was really all over between them and they became strangers.

After Moscow they moved on to St Petersburg where, to Henri's fury, they were joined by Ernesto. Nicolini, his Neapolitan engagements carried out, had agreed to sing free for twelve appearances to make up for his earlier breach of contract. The first opera on the list was no other than Gounod's *Romeo and Juliet* with the lovers in the title roles. Henri threatened the theatre manager and the impresario that his wife would not sing unless they changed the tenor, but now it was Adelina's turn to fly into a rage. In the end the theatre manager was persuaded to change the programme to *La Traviata* and to substitute Nicolini. But then the management did an about-turn, and when the curtain went up on *La Traviata* it was Ernesto who sang Alfredo to Adelina's Violetta!

Henri had been publicly made a fool of and his anger knew no limits. His courtly manners were forgotten as he raged at his wife, scene following ugly scene and he even struck her across the face, shouting that he cursed the day he had married her, "a strolling player". At last, unable to bear any more of his fury, Adelina broke down, confessed that she loved Ernesto and asked for a divorce. Henri, who had expected this, had kept one of Ernesto's letters (which he had not opened) to produce as evidence in his favour in front of a Court of Law.

At this point Louisa took to her bed with a nervous breakdown. She had been Adelina's friend and confidante for fourteen years but now she could stand no more. The doctor ordered an immediate change of air and she left.

Later she wrote in her memoirs, "Adelina heard with perfect indifference of my approaching departure. Our leave-taking was extremely cold, more as if I were a stranger to her than a friend, an almost sister. For me I had lost the person I most loved in the world. A few weeks later the Marquis de Caux experienced a similar loss".

A few weeks later Adelina and Ernesto eloped to Italy.

★★★

Maurice Strakosch, back on the scene again, chose this moment with timely efficiency to book the couple on a tour in Italy with appearances in Milan, Genoa, Florence, Rome, Naples and then again in Milan.

Alone together at last and in a romantic Italy that was more than ready to welcome them, the lovers delighted in their new happiness. There was no longer any need for subterfuge or pretence, they were free at last.

By now the whole world knew of their affair. They were together day and night, on stage and off, openly living together and sharing a suite at hotels. It was Ernesto she found by her side in the mornings, Ernesto who planned her days and kept any trouble or interference away, Ernesto who adored her more than she had ever imagined.

But there was also work to think of. Maurice had arranged for their tour to begin on Saturday 3rd November at La Scala in Milan with *La Traviata*, the opera Verdi had written in 1853 for La Fenice Theatre in Venice, adapted from the French comedy *La Dame aux Camelias*. Once again Adelina was Violetta to Ernesto's Alfredo. Her appearance had been preceded by a month of American style publicity and the price of tickets was unusually high, so much so that regular opera-going Milanese were disgruntled and in some cases quite hostile as they took their seats.

Italian audiences, and particularly those at La Scala, were the most discerning of all, knowledgeable and experienced in the art of operatic music. So it wasn't so very surprising that when Adelina appeared on stage there was a glacial silence, not one pair of hands clapping. She had to steel herself to cover her fear and find the courage to break down the barrier of antagonism she sensed so acutely.

For this big occasion, in the first act of her first appearance as Violetta, she had chosen to wear a new creation from the House of Worth, a concoction of pink silk and tulle with appliqués of flowers and leaves in darker and lighter shades of pink, a long train covered with ribbons and lace, feathers and frills trailing softly on the floor. It was the *dernier cri* of fashion, with diamonds scintillating as she moved. A figure so slight as to make her appear taller than she really was, her appearance, "jet black hair and sparkling eyes", her stage presence and poise all came to her aid.

She sang the first act to an almost silent house, but slowly the greatness of her voice began to work its magic as it filled the theatre, supple, velvet smooth, crystal clear, perfect. Now it was filled with new depth, new feeling and warmth, at last there was real passion. And at the end of that first act the sophisticated Milanese broke into an applause that shook the house, shouting and gesticulating their enthusiasm. At the final curtain the audience rose to their feet for a standing ovation, the stage was strewn with flowers and, led by Princess Margherita in the royal box, the enthusiasm was never-ending. Evidently the public was anxious to make amends. She had conquered again.

The critics were on her side, condemning the public, one writing that "the Milanese should have realised from the start that to hear Patti sing was worth any price. They should willingly have paid as they had never paid before, not for Pasta, nor for Malibran, nor for Rubini… and before looking and listening they should have accorded the great artiste an applause the moment she appeared on stage".

One of the most famous critics of the day, Filippo Filippi of *Perseveranza* wrote, "Patti is truly that queen and that diva of song whose fame was publicly announced…she is the greatest, the most surprising singer of our times".

Equally impressed was the critic of that authoritative newspaper *Corriere della Sera* who wrote, "Patti the actress is in no way inferior to Patti the singer. She is all intelligence, all soul, all passion and is never exaggerated nor affected nor mannered; she is always real. In that *Traviata* only Patti was a live person, the others seemed like cardboard figures by comparison. And in the last act there were several moments when, incredibly, the actress seemed even greater than the singer". Almost as an afterthought it was added that, "The tenor Nicolini is an excellent Alfredo".

For that first night it was rumoured that the Teatro della Scala had taken the unprecedented sum of 42,000 lire, an all-time record.

After Milan they were due to appear in Florence at that same Teatro Pagliano where Adelina had sung twelve years before. With Ernesto at her side she was to give four performances for a fee of 8,500 lire in gold each evening. The programme was to include *Il Trovatore, La Traviata, La Sonnambula* and *The Barber of Seville.* For a time Ernesto had studied in Florence under the maestro Vannuccini; in 1859 he had appeared at the Pagliano and in 1860 in *I Puritani* at the Teatro Della Pergola.

The weather in Florence was unwelcoming again, it rained heavily, but this time she was not interested in sightseeing which she limited to admiring the view of domes and towers from her hotel window.

Their first performance was on Saturday 29th December 1877 in *La Traviata* and all tickets were sold out several days previously. On the night the local newspaper, *La Nazione,* reported that the police had a hard time keeping the streets around the theatre free from the pushing public in spite of the pouring rain. The carriages of the crème of Florentine society, who had flocked to hear and see the diva, were held up as they approached, one behind the other, inch by inch, along the Via Ghibellina.

Seat prices had been kept at a more reasonable level than in Milan, an entrance ticket costing two and a half lire and a box one hundred lire. Carabinieri in black and scarlet uniforms were posted in the foyer to keep order and to prevent people from smoking (for which distasteful habit the café was open).

It was a gala night and as the carriages drew up in front of the theatre their doors, lined in velvet and silk, were opened by liveried lackeys and the passengers, dressed up for the occasion in their richest gowns and jewels, stepped down on to a carpet laid across the puddles. The local aristocracy crowded the foyer in a vivid profusion of colours and scents. It was the big Florentine occasion of the year and the ladies rivalled one another in elegance.

Adelina peeped through the heavy curtains and was impressed by the distinguished guests in the rows of boxes. The sala blazed with brilliant colour and tiaras and necklaces flashed in the flare of jets, diamonds reflecting the light with each turn of a head. The audience was animated; it was an occasion to see and be seen. In Italy a fairly frequent presence at the opera was, and still is, a guarantee of one's social position, indispensable for professional men, politicians, affluent shopkeepers and aristocrats alike.

The prelude began, the curtains opened, lights were dimmed and the house was hushed to silence. The swish of her skirts as she crossed to the centre of the stage seemed unnaturally loud. As had happened in Milan, Florentines did not applaud her entrance, unwilling to concede any favours, although a thousand arms raised opera glasses to fix her every move. Suddenly she froze with fear, a sensation that still gripped her occasionally before she began to sing when she found herself on an unfamiliar stage and with an audience on the defensive. Then she gained control and her voice came over loud and clear, the first notes filling the theatre and carrying up to the top tiers of boxes. She had overcome the barrier that divided them and the audience began to applaud. From that moment she carried them along with her, every scene was met with enthusiasm, every act closed with cheering and at the end she took nine final curtain calls. Later in her dressing rooms – one for her gowns with their long trains and the other for her makeup and toilette – that had been specially constructed for her on the same level as the stage to save her the bother of steps, she was happy at the way the evening had gone. Now she had conquered two of the most difficult audiences.

The theatre management, too, had been so kind, not only with her new dressing rooms – she remembered that twelve years ago she had had to climb a narrow flight of stairs – but with those charming little touches she appreciated: the set of ivory-backed brushes with her initials, the objects in silver gilt vermeil that she had found on her dressing table, two candelabras and no less than three gas lights– such splendid treatment as she had rarely experienced.

Her first night in Florence had been a resounding success. She was aware that she was singing now, at thirty-four, as she had never sung before. For the first time in her life she was completely happy and fulfilled and it was that happiness and fulfilment that had added an extra dimension to her voice. Smiling, she turned as Karo came to help her out of her gown and she impulsively kissed her on the cheek. Life was just beginning and it seemed that the future stretched ahead as bright as the diamonds that shone in the tiara Karo was carefully removing.

The critic Biaggi, who twelve years earlier had some reason for reserve after hearing her sing was now amongst her most enthusiastic admirers and was at no loss for words in his next front page *Musical Review*. Recalling his criticisms, he was now anxious to stress that these were no longer valid. He wrote, in the flowery language of the times, "The sacred spark of life has animated the clay. Now the Signora Patti is an artist in the most noble, the highest sense of the word. She is a great artiste and worthy in every way of her fame… no longer singing from the throat, but from the mind and from the heart". He goes on, "The Signora Patti, singing in her smoothly modulated voice without affectation and without exaggeration, gives us, in conclusion, that which we have lately been missing in her colleagues. She is a delight and she is a benediction".

She sang four operas in Florence and each time the audience came away convinced that the performance they had just seen and heard was her best ever.

Equally enthusiastic were the critics and the public in Rome and Naples.. In March, they returned to Milan where they had their greatest success in *Aida*, giving ten consecutive performances at La Scala.

Maurice Strakosch in his *Souvenirs* wrote of the tournée, "One cannot imagine the enthusiasm for the diva in Italy, like something out of a fairy story that cannot find any comparison except for that received by Christine Nilsson during her last tour in Sweden. In the cities where Patti passed through, the hotels were packed. People came in from the surrounding countryside to hear the famous singer. They slept in the streets, in the piazzas, and this is the literal truth. In spite of the vast size of the stages where Patti sang, these were covered with flowers every evening, the entrance ticket without any guaranteed seat cost twenty francs. Even if one was not fortunate enough to see Patti, she could be heard from the end of the corridor, and that was enough".

He goes on to say that, unfortunately for him, in view of the enormous takings at the ticket boxes, he had ceded his tournée for a minimal fee, otherwise with these earnings he could have lived tranquilly on the interest alone.

Maurice does not forget Ernesto, saying, "Nicolini, who had a beautiful tenor voice, shared the applause with Patti. He left excellent memories in Italy and the warm welcome he received in this last tour showed that he had not been forgotten".

The lovers' Italian idyll was interrupted by the unexpected arrival of Ernesto's wife, Madame Nicolini. She had brought male assistance with her and there was a terrible scene and a fight which ended up with Ernesto being kicked down the stairs of their hotel!

Henri, who had returned to Paris, took his revenge by announcing his intention of sequestering any sums that his wife might earn in France. As a consequence, several years were to go by before Adelina decided to return to that country. Although they were separated it was to take her eight long years before a divorce was granted by the French courts.

Strakosch had been against her marriage to Henri from the beginning and he writes, "In fairy stories, all the good fairies unite to promise the bride and groom a happy future. It is fair to assume that one of these was not invited to the wedding of Adelina Patti and that the bad fairy used her evil influence to put discord in that marriage".

Obviously her elopement with Ernesto was the talk of the town and the popular Press had a great deal to write about. One interesting, though not impartial, version of the facts is that given by the German soprano Teresa Stolz, who wrote to Giuseppe Verdi and his wife, "What must I say of the diva Patti? After all the scandals born in the theatre and in her own home, I can only conclude one thing, this woman is heartless, she has never loved either her husband or her lover. The stupid Nicolini has served as a useful way of liberating herself from the marquis, she herself said as much to her intimate friends, and so even those who tried to excuse her by calling her blind passion for Nicolini fatality, later blamed her, calling her a woman without heart and without principles. In any case she does not possess any talent as a woman since, without love, she has let herself be compromised so far by an imbecile like Nicolini! To permit him to abandon his wife and five children for a capriccio of her own can only be the work of a woman who is completely selfish. I did not love the marquis but now he fills me with compassion and she has become disagreeable to me as a woman, because as an artist I am one of her most passionate admirers".

The spite of a jealous rival? Teresa Stolz had also sung the part of Aida with a lesser degree of success. Or could there have been a grain of truth in some of her affirmations? Certainly, Adelina was selfishly egocentric like most prima donnas. But as far as a prima donna is capable of love, she loved Ernesto Nicolini. One imagines Giuseppe Verdi and his wife, both friends and great admirers of Adelina, reading the letter with much disbelief.

★★★

After their heady Italian experience, it was time to return to London where Adelina had another season ahead at Covent Garden. Her favourite old theatre was by now beginning to lose a little of its gloss: the sets and costumes looking seedier year by year due to generally incompetent stage management. But still the public flocked to hear Patti as she rang the changes in nine of her favourite roles and sang, for the first time at Covent Garden, the title role in Rossini's *Semiramide*. She had first sung this part of the Babylonian queen as an experiment in Bad Homburg shortly after her marriage. Now, for this new presentation, Rossini specially composed three new cadenzas. He wanted her to try the role although most people considered it too dramatic for her capacities – in England it was still associated with the names of two great drama queens, Grisi and Tietjens – but the composer insisted that it was also a part suited to Adelina. Tietjens had died the previous year and now Adelina felt ready to attempt the role in London. Fortunately for her it proved to be one of her best interpretations, so from now on it was included regularly in her repertoire, her 'Bel raggio' and the duet with Scalchi in the part of Arsace almost bringing the house down. The music critic of the *Pall Mall Gazette* found her, "always natural, always entering into the spirit of the character she undertakes… queenly, not through any deliberate assumption of regal airs, but because in the exercise of her high dramatic faculty she becomes Semiramide herself. She is as queenly as it is possible to be without ceasing to be womanly", which could be a fitting description of the real Adelina at this time and from now on.

During her marriage to Henri he had encouraged her friendships among London society ladies such as Louise, Duchess of Manchester, Lady Londesborough, Lady Hamilton, the Marchioness (later Duchess) of Westminster and Lady Dudley. They had also been frequent visitors to Marlborough House, residence of the Prince and Princess of Wales, who had given a dinner and a ball in their honour on their return from honeymoon. But now, probably due to her new status and without Henri, Marquis de Caux to push her into aristocratic circles, her friendships began to undergo a subtle change and she settled into a happy, quiet domestic routine with Ernesto.

# 9

For several years Adelina had employed a secretary and business manager, an Italian by the name of Franchi. With the help of Ernesto, who had great trust in him, he was now to bring about several changes. The first question that came up was one of her fees. They discovered that Mr Gye of Covent Garden was still paying her only half the amount that the impresario Colonel Mapleson received for Adelina's friend and rival Christine Nilsson, one hundred pounds a performance as opposed to two hundred. Adelina's indignant reaction to this news caused Mr Gye to raise her fee immediately to two hundred guineas a night. This saved her pride and was to remain her cachet at Covent Garden for as long as Mr Gye was manager.

In the same way, her fees requested on Continental tours were steadily raised, not only because the money was welcome but also to protect her image and her name since many lesser singers were now getting fantastic sums. Madame Patti's great drawing power meant that she could ask whatever sum she desired. Her contemporary biographer Herman Klein writes that, "It was not Patti, but Nilsson who led the way in the demand for higher fees. The former did not follow the example of her Swedish contemporary abroad until she found that foreign operatic managers were willing to pay her more. This they really did because they knew her to be under all circumstances what Americans call a money-making proposition".

A new era was about to begin in Adelina's career, that of her American tours. Unfortunately the first of these was, as Klein puts it, "marred by pure mismanagement". She was persuaded by Ernesto and Franchi to revisit the country of her childhood. They had heard that vast profits were to be made there by touring operatic stars. Her first trip to America was to be in the form of a concert tour and to save on expenses it was agreed to do without the services of an American agent and also – even more risky – to cut down drastically on advertising. They were convinced that her name alone would be enough to draw in the crowds. Of course they did not know that in America the pull of advertising was then, as it still is now, indispensable for success in any venture.

Twenty years had gone by since her last appearance in New York and a new generation of opera-goers had grown up knowing little or nothing about Patti. She was enormously disappointed at her first concert to find the theatre barely half full, and they took a meagre $3,000 – meagre that was, to the diva Patti. Her second concert was even more of a delusion, making only a third of that amount. They were consequently forced to let her sing for charity as a belated form of publicity, reducing the price of seats from ten to five dollars each, and at last things began to improve.

Once her initial disappointment was overcome, the practical side of Adelina, to whom a fiasco was almost unknown, took over. She realised that the cause of the debacle was an obvious lack of publicity. The remedy was found in a certain Mr Henry Abbey, the American manager of Sarah Bernhardt and she decided to put herself in his hands for the rest of the tour. Henry Abbey wasted no time and signed her on for a trip to the Eastern States, which made a reasonable profit.

On their return to New York, those theatregoers who were by now aware that Patti was in their city, requested that she sing in opera. To cut down on costs, a supporting company was put together that was not up to her usual standards and she appeared with them in opera at the old Wallack's Theatre on Broadway in February and March 1882. This turned out to be another near-disastrous move.

Disillusioned, Adelina might well have left America for good if fate had not intervened in the form of her old acquaintance Colonel Mapleson, that same impresario who Maurice had badly let down when they first arrived in London. They met up while she was taking part in the Cincinnati Opera Festival during her tour. Back in New York he approached her again. By now he was a successful impresario on both sides of the Atlantic, arranging the season at the Academy of Music in New York amongst other activities, and he talked Adelina and Ernesto into appearing at this theatre the following winter. An agreement was signed and the couple returned to England.

This was the beginning of a period which she might well have privately thought of with amusement as her American Circus Years. Now that he had caught such a big fish in his net, Mapleson spared no effort in organising grand annual tournées in the United States, backed up by a great blaze of publicity, and, to her delight, it was highly profitable for the diva. By now she no longer left all financial matters to others but was becoming very interested indeed in making money.

The first of these tours began in early November 1882. They arrived in the port of New York on the *Servia* and, according to reports, a crowd had been waiting on the wharf all night to greet the diva. She herself had been up since half past four in the morning, unable to sleep for excitement. Mapleson had arranged for a welcoming party and a band, which struck up 'God Save the Queen' as soon as she appeared on deck. In his memoirs Mapleson tells us that "Everyone bared his head, the Englishmen partly from traditional reverence, but most of those present from admiration of the lyric queen who had come for another reign to the delighted people of New York"[8].

Mapleson had done his job well and this time the city of New York was ready and waiting for Adelina. Her room at the Windsor Hotel was filled with bouquets, telegrams and cards and surmounted by a large banner with "Welcome" picked out in roses. At midnight she was serenaded outside the hotel and when she made an appearance at the window an orchestra and chorus played and sang the grand prayer from *Lombardi*. Then, "after three hearty cheers for Adelina Patti people went home and she was left in peace".

Between 6th November and 29th December she made seventeen appearances in New York. She sang Lucia, Violetta, Marguerite, Leonora, Rosina, Dinorah, Amina, Semiramide and Linda de Chamounix and, whether Ernesto sang with her or not, received a fixed sum of £900 a performance, the highest fee she had been paid so far. This time she

---

8    Mapleson, James, *The Mapleson Memoirs*, edited by Harold Rosenthal

was backed up by a strong supporting company, the programme was attractive and the whole enterprise turned out to be a success. After New York, the company went on a long tour for which she received a record $175,000. So much interest was generated by this tour that according to Mapleson, "Amongst the numberless enquiries at the box office several were made as to how long Mme Patti remained on the stage in each of the different operas, and the newspapers busied themselves as to the number of notes she sang in each particular work, larger demands for seats being made on those evenings when she sang more notes… A party of amateurs[9] would buy a ticket between them, each one taking twenty minutes of the ticket and returning with the passout check to the next. Lots were drawn to decide who was to go in first and in the event of anyone overstaying his twenty minutes he had to pay for the whole ticket, correctness of time being the essence of the arrangement".

While people were busy counting her notes, she was surprised to discover that she had another royal admirer, King Kalakaua of the Hawaiian Islands, who sent a delegation to her New York hotel to confer her with the Royal Order of Kapirlani, of which she was made a Knight Companion, in the form of a jewelled star on a red and white striped ribbon. Her tour was not without the usual alarmist reports in the Press. A smallpox epidemic in Baltimore made her decide to give that city a miss and she travelled on to her next engagement in Philadelphia, where a newspaper reported that "Mme Patti had been devoured by mice". This had the effect of people rushing to the box office to demand their money back. Meanwhile a reporter from the Philadelphia Press nipped quickly around to her hotel to find her alive and unharmed and highly amused at all the fuss. This is his account of her interview: "So you were bitten by rats last evening?" "Oh no, it was not so bad as that," replied Patti, laughing as she recalled the adventure. "I hardly, however, like to mention it at for I am really so comfortable in this hotel. When I went to bed last evening, my maid turned the clothes over for me to get in, and out jumped six mice, a complete family in fact, nice fat little fellows. I was not frightened – at least I was only astonished. I took my bonbons box and scattered some sweets

---

9    From the Latin 'Amator', lover of art

on the carpet so that the tiny intruders should have some supper and I went to sleep without any apprehension. In the middle of the night, however, I was awakened by a sharp pain in my ear. I put my hand to my head, when a mouse jumped to the floor and I felt blood trickling on the side of my cheek. I got up and called my maid and examination showed a bite on my left ear. It bled a good deal and today my ear is much swollen. I shall not put any bonbons down tonight, and when I sleep in the daytime I shall place my maid to act as a sentry".

This is one of the longest reported conversations by Adelina that I have come across and shows a different, soft and kind side to her character. Following this account, enterprising manufacturers of mousetraps sent her their latest inventions and she sent them all back, joking that in future she would keep a cat.

The company then went to Washington, Chicago, St Louis, Cincinnati – where the temperature was forty degrees below freezing – and then Detroit where she finally succumbed to a bad cold after walking through piled up snow to get to her carriage and was unable to sing. The public there was so disappointed that they threatened to demolish the theatre until a doctor's certificate was produced convincing them that she was really ill. In fact Adelina stayed behind in Detroit for five days after the rest of the company had left for Canada (where the customs confiscated all their musical instruments, costumes and properties and would not release them until Colonel Mapleson signed an undertaking that the troupe would leave the country within two days). She caught up with the others in Pittsburg where she opened the season in *La Traviata*.

On the way to Washington again she suffered from a sore throat and her appearance in that city had to be postponed for one night. When she appeared the following evening with Scalchi in *Semiramide* they received an enormous ovation. After a private party for the company at the White House, given by President Arthur, Adelina closed the Washington season with Violetta at a matinee to an overcrowded house. Incredibly, people paid just to stand in the corridors with no hope of seeing her and very little hope of hearing more than a few notes. In early March the company returned to New York for a five-week season at the Academy of Music with a programme packed so full that they sang a different opera almost nightly.

It was at this time that the new Metropolitan Opera House was nearing completion and Henry Abbey, who had been granted the lease, began to lure away as many of Mapleson's company as he could, with promises of higher salaries and better conditions. He had also approached Adelina who was quite tempted but then wavered, deciding to stay with Mapleson if her fee was raised to £1,000 a night, at that time equivalent to $5,000. The Metropolitan had been built by the Vanderbilt family in response to the Astors` refusal to rent them a box for the 1880 season at the Academy of Music. The management had been in negotiation with the Royal Italian Opera Company at Covent Garden and Mr Gye's son had supplied them with plans and workings of Covent Garden theatre, assisting them in the phase of construction. They were therefore almost ready to go ahead.

According to Mapleson, after Adelina had received a visit from Henry Abbey offering her $5,000 a night and $50,000 deposited in a bank as payment for the last ten nights of her engagements, as well as a super deluxe train for her tours, specially constructed for her and complete with all luxuries including a conservatory and fernery, Adelina was "so upset that she had not even spoken to the parrot, which was a sad sign".[10] Nicolini, acting as her spokesman, told Mapleson that "Madame Patti held him in the highest esteem, and would on no account throw him over, considering that his engagement with her would be just as good as Mr Vanderbilt's.

Mapleson must have breathed a sigh of relief. He had watched not only some of his best singers but also his chorus, wardrobe mistresses and stage managers filter away to the Metropolitan where they had been offered up to four times as much money. Determined not to lose Patti he agreed to the same terms as she had been offered by Henry Abbey and the following day she sailed to Europe on the *Arizona* leaving Franchi behind to wind up the details of her new contract.

Other artistes had already jumped onto the American bandwagon. "The divine Sarah", Sarah Bernhardt – that slight, pale-faced actress from the Comedie Francaise for whom Adelina had given a charity

---

10 Parrots were fashionable travelling companions of prima donnas of the day and Adelina's, called Ben Butler, had been trained by her and Ernesto to swear in French and to call out "Cash!" every time he saw Mapleson approaching!

concert in Paris – after she had taken London by storm and made inroads into the heart of the Prince of Wales, had starred at Booth's Theatre in New York and had been serenaded at midnight outside her hotel in Madison Square by an enthusiastic crowd.

Lillie Langtry had also recently discovered America, with the assistance of Henry Abbey, and had been regaled with that same 'God Save the Queen' welcome played by a brass band in a tug on her arrival at the port of New York. Feted by some, cold-shouldered by others, she was besieged by journalists from the popular Press, to whose questions she replied amiably enough as long as they did not touch on the subject of Bertie, the Prince of Wales, and she was also scathingly criticised for her early efforts at acting. Yet, nevertheless, she was earning more than $100,000 on a four month tour, always drawing vast, curious crowds wherever she went due to her notoriety and the fact that she was now "living in sin" with the twenty-two-year-old millionaire from Baltimore, Freddie Gebhard. Lillie's first profitable trip to the States had lasted fifteen months.

By 1883 Lillie's love affair with the Prince of Wales had been over for some time. Both had found other consolations and she had given birth to a baby girl, the daughter of Prince Louis of Battenberg.

Lillie Langtry had first met the Prince of Wales in 1877 at a small dinner party set up for the occasion, and, already intrigued by the gossip about this statuesque beauty from Jersey whose enigmatic appearance, dressed in simple black, had made its impact on London society, he did not waste much time on preliminaries. Her husband, Edward Langtry, slipped quietly into the background as she openly became the prince's mistress, accompanying him on weekend trips to country houses, to Ascot and even to Paris. Princess Alexandra, who was by then resigned to her husband's infidelity, accepted Lillie with good grace and she was invited to Marlborough House and on board the royal yacht *Osborne*, officially escorted by the Prince's son Eddy. The prince's early passionate love for Lillie had been replaced by a lasting friendship. When her husband refused to grant her a divorce, her money was running out and she had turned to a theatrical career in 1881, the prince had given her his full approval and support, bringing along his friends for her first appearance on stage in *She Stoops to Conquer* at the Haymarket. So with Prince Louis perpetually away at sea, her affair with Bertie over, and no hope of a divorce, she had badly needed the dollars that her American tour had netted.

Adelina had no such pressing need for cash, but encouraged by Ernesto she was growing to appreciate it more and more, and she left the American shores in a far happier frame of mind than she had the year before.

With her American public reconquered, her fame securely impressed on people's minds, from now on things would be easier. In a single night the Academy of Music took in $14,000 when she appeared in *Semiramide* and on tour her Lucia had reached similar levels. She was satisfied that if things continued in this way, her fortune, already considerable, would grow and consolidate in a way that even Papa, in his wildest dreams, could never have imagined.

*** 

Colonel Mapleson was as good as his word and for her next American tour they travelled in a special train. Adelina had her own sumptuously appointed carriage described as "the most superb and tasteful coach on wheels anywhere in the world", four coaches were for the more important members of the company, four for the chorus and orchestra, four were sleeping cars, three were boudoir cars, and then there was Colonel Mapleson's private car and four coaches for their luggage.

In sensuous luxury, Madame Patti soaked in her solid silver bath while the wheels beneath her sped along the tracks. For privacy she turned the eighteen-carat gold key in the door. It was equally pleasing to sit at the £2,000 Steinway piano in her white and gold drawing room upholstered in silk damask, the walls covered with gilded tapestry and the ceiling hand-painted by artists from Paris. There were Italian paintings on the wall panels; the wood was sandalwood, the lamps in rolled gold. Her coach alone had cost $60,000 but it was worth every cent: the diva was happy and the attention the train attracted was excellent publicity. They covered the enormous distances that separated them from one engagement to the next in rest and relaxation. As well as Ernest, Adelina had an amusing travelling companion in her parrot Ben Butler who had by now added several English phrases to his repertoire and copied Adelina when she whistled him a tune.

Meanwhile, Ernesto cossetted her with a thousand little attentions. One journalist who was privileged to interview her in her coach, looked on in amazement as "Nicolini suddenly began ringing electric bells to summon valets to close a small ventilator and it was not until his adored Madame had been wrapped in shawls that the interview could proceed". Before this, on her arrival in New York for the 1883 season, preparations had been made by Mapleson for a great welcome but unfortunately things went wrong, and he writes, "I arranged to charter sixteen large tug boats covered with bunting to meet the diva, eight of them to steam up the bay on each side of the arriving steamer and to toot off their steam whistles all the way along, accompanied by military bands. All was in readiness and I was only waiting for a telegraphic notification. Some of the pilots at Sandy Hook, moreover, had promised to improvise a salute of twenty-one guns and Arditi[11] had written a Cantata for the occasion, which the chorus were to sing immediately on Patti's arrival. By some unfortunate mistake, either from fog or otherwise, the steamer passed Fire Island and landed *La Diva* unobserved on the dock, where there was not even a carriage to meet her. She got hustled by the crowd and eventually reached her hotel with difficulty in a four-wheeler. The military band had passed the night awaiting the signal which I was to give them to board the tugs. On learning of Madame Patti's arrival I hurried up to the Windsor Hotel where I was at once received.

'Is it not too bad?' she exclaimed, with a comical expression of annoyance. 'It is a wonder that I was not left till now on the steamer. As it was, by the merest chance one of my friends happened to come down to the dock and luckily espied me as I was wandering about trying to keep my feet warm, and assisted me into a four wheeler. However, here I am. It is all over now and I am quite comfortable and as happy as though twenty boats had come down to meet me.'"

She was soon to find out that a battle was in progress between the old Academy of Music and the new Metropolitan Opera House now under the management of Henry Abbey. Mr Abbey had put a strong company together, with Adelina's friend the beautiful and talented

---

11  Luigi Arditi, 1822–1903, an Italian composer and conductor who lived mostly in England and was one of Adelina's admirers.

Christine Nilsson as *prima donna assoluta,* and had spared no expense on new scenery and costumes ordered from the House of Worth in Paris. The artists were paid high fees, obviously too high because the Metropolitan was to lose $600,000 during the 1883/84 season. Later Henry Abbey resigned and the theatre remained closed until the following autumn.

When she arrived in New York, however, the hopes of both theatres were flying high and they opened on the same evening of October 22nd, continuing with packed programmes until Christmas and then reopening from mid-March to mid-April. Adelina arrived on the scene early in November 1883 and made her debut in *La Gazza Ladra,* the opera Rossini had composed in 1817 and that had not been presented in New York for many years. Now, although appreciating Adelina's Ninetta, both the New York public and Press found the opera too antiquated so she continued to appear in her old favourite parts for the rest of the season.

In an attempt to anticipate the moves of Henry Abbey, Mapleson arranged for her appearance in Philadelphia to take place five weeks earlier than originally planned and she had a highly successful night in Verdi's *Ernani,* which took $10,000 in box office receipts. For the American Press, interest in the actual opera seems to have been overshadowed by how much each performance made. However, at her next performance in Boston, things moved more slowly due to insufficient advance publicity since the company had been expected much later. Here she was due to sing in *La Traviata* and, as stipulated in her contract, to receive the $5,000 she was paid for every performance by two o'clock on the same day (this sum was equivalent to about £1,000 in English money of the period). When Adelina's secretary Signor Franchi arrived punctually at two o'clock for her fee, poor Mapleson who was, as he says, "at low water just then" went to collect the takings at the booking office only to discover there was just £800 and that he was therefore £200 short. Franchi at first indignantly declined the money and threatened to sever Madame's contract, but two hours later he was back again.

"I cannot understand," he told Mapleson, "how it is you get on so well with prime donne and especially with Madame Patti. You are a marvellous man and a fortunate one too, I may add. Madame Patti does not wish to break her engagement with you, as she certainly would have done with anyone else under the circumstances. Give me the £800 and she will make every preparation for going on to the stage. She empowers me to tell you that she will be at the theatre in good time and that she will be ready dressed in the costume of Violetta with the exception only of the shoes. You can let her have the balance when the doors open and the money comes in from the outside public, and directly she receives it she will put her shoes on and at the proper moment make her appearance on the stage".[12]

Mapleson, who had almost resigned himself to losing his prima donna but keeping his £800, was therefore obliged to hand the money over to Franchi who congratulated him on his good luck. Later when the theatre doors opened, Franchi presented himself again and was given a further £160, the rest of the takings. To continue in Mapleson's own words, "I begged him to carry it to the obliging prima donna who, having received £960 might, I thought, be induced to complete her toilette pending the arrival of the £40 balance. Nor was I altogether wrong in my hopeful anticipations. With a beaming face Signor Franchi came back and communicated to me the joyful intelligence that Madame Patti had got one shoe on. 'Send her the £40', he added 'and she will put on the other'. Ultimately the other shoe was got on, but not, of course, until the last £40 had been paid. Then Madame Patti, her face radiant with benignant smiles, went on the stage and the opera already begun was continued brilliantly until the end".

The life of an impresario can be difficult and one sympathises with Mapleson who says that on that particular tour, once he had paid Adelina her £1,000 fee and distributed several hundred pounds among all the other members of the company, he found he had just an average of twenty-two dollars a night for himself.

On the other hand it was the name Adelina Patti that drew the vast American public and without the diva he would probably not have gone on tour at all, since so much had been spent on competing with the Metropolitan in New York. They went back to the Academy in January and after a reasonably good opening, secured a full eleven thousand-dollar house for their benefit night.

---

12   *The Mapleson Memoirs*

During her stay in America, Adelina had developed a sincere loathing for the Hungarian coloratura soprano of the company, Etelka Gerster. The feud had started when Gerster discovered Adelina's name was larger than hers on the playbill and that seats cost more when Adelina sang. Her jealously was fanned into flame by an unfortunate incident in Chicago when Adelina's name was on all the bouquets passed on to the stage at the end of the first act of *Les Huguenots* in which Gerster was the queen and Adelina Valentine. In that particular act the queen does a lot of brilliant singing while Valentine scarcely sings a note. But basket after basket, bouquet after bouquet, set piece after set piece, the label on all the flowers had Adelina's name on it, and everything was passed to her. The audience grew restive, indignant at this slight on Gerster, when at last one simple little basket was handed to her and the whole house broke into ironic cheers and applause. It turned out that there had been an embarrassing mistake: the flowers had been intended for Patti at the end of the opera. Furious at this mismanagement, livid at being put into such a ridiculous position, Adelina steeled herself to get through the rest of the opera in her usual faultless style, but once back in her hotel room she threw herself on the floor in a storm of rage bordering on hysteria and "kicked and struggled in such a manner that it was only with the greatest difficulty she could be got to bed". Never one to suffer fools gladly, she raved at the stupidity of the ushers who had made the mistake in the absence of Signor Franchi. Later she even went as far as to accuse Mapleson of having arranged the whole debacle in order to lower her value in the eyes of the public and accordingly pay her less for future performances, immediately afterwards saying she had been joking. But the incident rankled for some time. If there was one thing Adelina could not tolerate it was loss of dignity.

From then on she took it out on Etelka Gerster, accusing her of "having the evil eye". Whatever went wrong, she put the blame on her rival. And in true Italian style she made the sign of the horns with her fingers whenever Gerster's name was mentioned. She even made the sign when passing her hotel room and nearly missed digging her extended fingers into the eyes of Gerster's unwary husband one evening when he opened the door to put his boots out before going to bed!

After the incident with the bouquets things reached such a climax that Adelina refused to sing in the same operas as Gerster ever again, to which slight her rival retaliated by swearing that she, too, would never again sing with Patti. Alarmed at the clash between his two prima donnas, Mapleson decided that Adelina could take a few weeks' rest since she was now already two-thirds of the way through the fifty appearances that bound her to her contract. Possibly he thought a rest would calm her frayed nerves too.

The rest of the company were scheduled to go on a tour of the Far West but Gerster, free from her dangerous rival, capriciously refused to budge. When Adelina heard of this she offered to go on tour in Gerster's place and presented herself to the impresario, her trunks packed and ready to leave. Meanwhile Gerster changed her mind, instructed her maids to pack her belongings and announced that she too was ready. So once again poor Mapleson found himself setting off with the two prima donnas on the same train.

More than anything else, Adelina had decided to "go along for the ride", curious to travel across the entire breadth of America to San Francisco in her comfortable luxury train. It was too unique an experience to miss and she had jumped at the chance. But it was in fact Gerster's tour and Adelina knew this, having her own carriage detached from the rest of the train as they approached the station of Cheyenne. Already, before reaching the station, their train had been met by two carriages full of notables and high-ranking government officials as well as a compartment stacked with Pommery and Mumm champagne packed on ice, and another filled with cigars. A public holiday had been proclaimed for the occasion and there was to be a ceremony of welcome with speeches and a brass band.

After the band of the 9th Regiment, specially called in from their military station, had played for Gerster, she was escorted to her hotel. Two hours later it was Adelina's turn, her carriage was brought into the station and again the band struck up, playing a mixed medley of tunes she found it hard to recognise. "Please ask the bandmaster what they are playing," she said to Mapleson, who obligingly began to edge his way through the tight circle of musicians. But the bandmaster rushed towards him gesticulating wildly and imploring him not to touch the musicians. If one fell, they would all fall like a set of ninepins. They had been on duty for the past thirty-six hours waiting for the arrival of the train, during which time they had "taken considerable refreshment" and he had had a difficult time getting them on their feet!

That evening Gerster starred in *La Sonnambula* as planned and it was a grand occasion. They were astonished at the elegance of the audience; after all they were in a town consisting of little more than two streets and supposedly populated by cowboys. But the public at the theatre could have competed with that at Covent Garden, the ladies in elegant toilettes and dripping diamonds, the gentlemen all in full evening dress.

Salt Lake City was their next interesting stop, and while Gerster was at the Theatre Adelina and Ernesto spent the first day sightseeing, visiting the Mormon Tabernacle with Colonel Mapleson. They noticed that the acoustics were excellent, there was room to seat 12,000 people and it would be the perfect place to hold a concert. At first the Mormons flatly refused but Mapleson was not one to be easily put off. He invited the Prophet Taylor, the successor of Brigham Young, to visit Adelina in her private carriage for lunch the next day with as many of his apostles as he cared to bring. The cooks were given instructions to prepare a splendid meal. Adelina complied, the prospect of singing in the Tabernacle appealing to her as much as it did to the impresario.

During lunch she played the part of hostess perfectly, charming the prophet and his apostles, saying how much she would enjoy singing in their wonderful Tabernacle and even going as far as to enthuse about the Mormon doctrines and to express a strong wish to join their church herself. She wound up by singing them three of her favourite songs. Carried away by enthusiasm, she realised she may have gone a little too far but Prophet Taylor was impressed. His apostles argued that their Tabernacle was no place for a concert, being a place of worship, but the prophet was unable to resist this petite madam of world fame when she turned her dark, shining eyes on him and sang 'The Last Rose of Summer'. Her voice spoke to his heart. He gave his consent to her holding a concert in the Tabernacle the following month on the company's return from San Francisco.

Mapleson happily suggested three dollars a seat as the right price to ask, at which point one of the apostles objected since he had five wives and the total would have been too much for his pocket! The price of seats was therefore fixed at two dollars and one dollar each. That same evening they performed in *Lucia di Lammermoor* in the Salt Lake City Theatre with the prophet present in the audience.

It took their train about thirty hours to cross the state of Nevada. They stopped at Reno to refill the engine with water and here a crowd of reporters scrambled on board, all anxious to interview the diva Patti in her luxury carriage. Instead, to their disappointment, Mapleson handed out sheets of typewritten interviews and they had to make do with these, one of the earliest examples of press releases in history. They eventually reached San Francisco after a twelve-hour hold-up at Truckee, where a recent avalanche had buried a stretch of the railway lines under snow and a squad of 1,500 Chinese workers had been called in to clear a way. To pass the time Adelina played the piano to a crowd of admiring Native Americans who had gathered outside the windows, clamouring to hear her sing.

By the time they reached the west coast she had had enough of snow and ice and was thankful for the Californian sun. The city of San Francisco went wild when they heard she had arrived. They had expected the soprano Gerster and the scheduled appearances were in her name, but to their delight they now discovered they had the extra bonus of Patti.

Due to the mix up before the trip Adelina did not have single concert booked so Mapleson rapidly got to work and put an announcement in the following day's paper to the effect that Madame Patti, travelling with the company on a pleasure trip with her husband, would exceptionally give a performance the following Thursday, the only free night in their schedule. This started off one of the most extraordinary mass events that the city had ever seen. One young man took up a position outside the box office as soon as the newspaper came out and he was shortly followed by another and then another until there was a queue a street long, some bringing folding chairs and refreshments to pass the night more comfortably.

Mapleson writes that, "The Adelina Patti epidemic gradually disseminated itself from the moment of her arrival, and began to rage throughout the city from early the following morning. Many ladies joined the line during the night and had to take equal chances with the men. Towards morning, bargains for good positions in the line reached as high a price as £4, a sum which was actually paid by one person for permission to take another's place. The next morning I rose early and took a stroll to admire the city. I observed a vast crowd down Montgomery Street. In fact, the passage within hundreds of yards was impassable, vehicles, omnibuses etc. all being at a standstill. On enquiring the reason of this commotion I was informed by a policeman that they were trying to buy Patti tickets which Messrs Sherman and Clay had for disposal. On forcing my way gradually down the street, and approaching Sherman and Clay's establishment I saw, to my great astonishment, that there was not a single pane of glass in any of the windows, whilst the tops of the best pianos and harmoniums were occupied by dozens of people standing upon them in their nailed boots, all clamouring for Patti tickets.

Messrs Sherman and Clay solicited me earnestly either to remove Patti from the town, or, at least, not to entrust them with the sale of any more tickets, the crowd having done over £600 of damage to their stock".

At eight o'clock that same evening Adelina was serenaded by an orchestra directed by Professor Wetterman in the courtyard of the Palace Hotel which had been brilliantly lit up for the occasion, and she came out onto her balcony to listen and asked Signor Arditi, the conductor travelling with the company, to thank them on her behalf.

Etelka Gerster was popular in America and she too had her admirers, enjoying her own dose of success first as Lucia and then in *Elisir d'Amore*. But when it was Adelina's turn to appear at the Grand Opera Theatre, there was a near riot. On the day of her performance as Violetta the entire police force was called in to protect the theatre from the frantic crowds pressing for tickets. Although it had been announced that the tickets were finished there was a queue of hopefuls three or four streets long and the line remained, day and night, for the entire length of their four weeks' stay. Patti fever had never run so high as that time in San Francisco.

Enterprising cafes and restaurants sold coffee, sandwiches, dinners and suppers to the people queuing and camp stools were hired out at four shillings each. The police did their best to keep order but when it was announced that a limited number of gallery tickets would be sold there was a general rush to the box office and the crowd surged

107

forward, smashing the front windows and overturning statues and plants in the foyer. Ticket speculators were by now charging up to £10 and many of the tickets sold were forgeries. By the time the doors were opened the fever had reached such a pitch that not only was all the standing room occupied but people were dropping in through a hole they had made in the roof, landing on the heads of those sitting in the gallery!

The ladies of San Francisco had dressed up to the nines, sparkling with diamonds and jewellery. From the beginning to the end of her performance, Adelina was almost buried under bouquets, huge flower arrangements and an outsize globe of violets from the Italian community.

Since many of those who had paid for standing room had smuggled in folding stools under their clothes and had blocked all the aisles, Mapleson was arrested the next day for violating fire regulations and given a heavy fine, but this was later reduced to seventy-five dollars to be taken out in opera tickets.

In view of the overwhelming success of her first appearance, Mapleson announced that Madame Patti would appear again the following Tuesday in the part of Leonora in *Il Trovatore* with Ernesto as Manrico. If there had been a rush for tickets for her first appearance, there was now a raging battle to obtain tickets for the next. The local *Morning Call* of March 15th 1884 wrote, "To one who has stood on Mission Street opposite the Grand Opera House yesterday forenoon and 'viewed the battle from afar', it seemed that a large number of people had run completely mad over the desire to hear Patti sing. Such an excited, turbulent and, in fact, desperate crowd never massed in front of a theatre for the purpose of purchasing tickets. It absolutely fought for tickets and it is questionable whether, if it had been an actual riot by a fierce and determined mob, the scene could have been more exciting or the wreck of the entrance of the theatre more complete. After the throng had melted away the approaches to the box office looked as if they had been visited by a first class Kansas cyclone in one of its worst moods".

On March 18th the great day came round and it took twenty policemen inside the foyer and forty more outside the theatre to keep some kind of order and to let in only those lucky holders of genuine tickets, although most of the forgeries were so cleverly done that it was almost impossible to tell them from originals.

By now the foyer had been restored to its former splendour, the huge glass fountain in the centre splashing water and eau de cologne, the rose trees, violets and rare tree orchids arranged in elegant profusion and one wall hung with English, American, Italian and (for Etelka Gerster) Hungarian flags.

The representation of *Il Trovatore* is described by the impresario as "one unbroken triumph". A few days later Adelina gave a concert at the Pavilion to an audience of nine thousand, and on 27th March a grand ball was held in her honour at the Margherita Club, the whole place transformed into a bower with such a rich profusion of flowers as she had never seen.

Etelka Gerster, in the meantime, continued to make her scheduled appearances "delighting her audiences with the clear, birdlike quality of her voice", but the ill feeling between the two prima donnas grew daily. When the news spread that Adelina had been kissed by General Crittenden, Governor of Missouri, (in her own words "… he suddenly leaned down, put his arms around me, drew me up to him and kissed me, saying, 'Madame Patti, I may never see you again but I cannot help it.'") Gerster could not resist a dig at her rival. She knew well enough that General Crittenden was an old man but when a reporter asked her opinion on the matter she said, "I don't see anything to create so much fuss."

"You don't?" asked the reporter.

"Certainly not! There is nothing wrong in a man kissing a woman old enough to be his mother!" Adelina at the time was a youthful forty-one. When she felt the floor rocking in her hotel one morning, Adelina is reported to have screamed, "Gerster!" maliciously attributing the earthquake to the hated soprano's evil eye. Fortunately the earthquake was not too serious and their last performance in San Francisco took place as planned.

As promised, from San Francisco the company travelled back to Salt Lake City where by now the Mormons were enthusiastically looking forward to her appearance in their Tabernacle. A special railway line had been laid down from the main Salt Lake City line right up to the entrance to the Temple, so when she had dressed in her train she only had to step down and she was there.

Among the most impatient to hear Patti sing was the Prophet. The evening was to make history throughout the state of Utah with over 14,000 people present and the proceeds reaching nearly $25,000.

After this triumph, the train left for Omaha and Chicago and then returned to New York. Adelina and Ernesto opened the season with *Romeo and Juliet* and this was followed by *Elisir d'Amore* and *Semiramide* but although the programme had a discreet success, the reception received from the more jaded New Yorkers did not compete with the enthusiasm they had raised on tour.

The Metropolitan Opera House had been closed for some months now, Henry Abbey near to ruin after his lavish spending, so in view of this and the fact that Colonel Mapleson had always paid her regularly (if sometimes reluctantly) and was backed up by the Academy of Music, a guarantee in itself, Adelina did not hesitate to sign on with him again for the following season. Since 1882 she had received nearly half a million dollars from Mapleson on her American tours and they were obviously too good a proposition to give up.

★★★

They sailed back to England on the *Oregon* and now, the hurly burly done, the American shores behind her, her only desire was to make a definite break with Henri, to come to some agreement for a divorce and to marry Ernesto. On the advice of her lawyers she offered to divide her fortune with Henri, settling on him the sum of £60,000, and both parties sued for divorce in the French courts. The divorce was finally granted the following year.

Then the Covent Garden season came around again and she sang her old favourite opera parts. But Covent Garden was not what it used to be, now that it was no longer under Mr Gye's management.[13] The theatre grew a little more dusty and shabby year by year. Subscriptions had dropped off and although Patti Nights were still a big draw, Londoners no longer seemed to be crying out for Italian opera as they

---

13 Frederick Gye retired from management of Covent Garden in 1877. He died in December 1878 from "a gun accident".

had been in the sixties and seventies. Adelina, aware that fashions and tastes were changing with the times, was willing to bend in the wind. Italian opera was no longer called for? Then she would give concerts. Whatever happened she would survive. Her place was at the top and that was where she intended to remain.

# 10

The day her carriage first turned into the courtyard of Craig-y-Nos she had the strangest feeling of having come home. She had heard that the property was for sale from her host, Sir Hussey Vivian, and he had accompanied them on the long journey through the wild South Wales countryside. The higher they climbed the more their surroundings resembled a dramatic stage setting with craggy mountains on one side and a wooded valley on the other, and Craig-y-Nos was looking its best, suspended on a sunny ledge with grounds sweeping away below.

For some time now Adelina had wished for a country retreat where she could relax between tours, a place to spread out her belongings without the thought of having them all packed up again at the end of the season. Since Pierrepoint House in Clapham Park she had never had a proper home of her own. Now, at forty, she strongly felt the need to end their nomadic existence, moving from one expensive and often gloomy hotel to another with countless stays at other people's country homes. Her friends were kind with their pressing invitations, she was made to feel a welcome and important guest, but it was time to put down roots. She saw herself as Lady of the Manor and Ernesto as a country Squire. Craig-y-Nos was the ideal place.

The name, in Gaelic, meant "Rock of Night". The house held a commanding position on the road from Brecon to Ystradgnlais in the Upper Tawe Valley. It had originally been built for the local Davies Powell family in 1842 by the architect T. H. Wyatt and when Adelina first saw it there was just the central building without the side wings.

But she immediately saw its possibilities. The position was ideal, the River Tawe running through the valley below would be excellent for Ernesto's favourite pastime of trout and salmon fishing, and she was sure the pure, fresh country air would benefit her voice. There is also another little known reason why she chose Wales for their home; the Welsh were mostly Protestants and would not be too shocked by the fact that she and Ernesto were not married, both waiting for divorces, and there would be none of that cold-shouldering they had sometimes come across in more Catholic circles.

The sale went through in Ernesto's name, Adelina providing the cash, with the clause that the house was for Adelina's "sole and separate use to exclusion of any estate or interest of any husband of hers therein." A protection against Henri, officially still her husband.

But before moving in there was work to be done. Adelina, with her usual enthusiasm and efficiency, called in local companies and the first job was to build the side extensions. The builder understood that she would want these in the same grey limestone as the main section, material that was readily available and near to hand. But, "No," insisted Adelina, "I would prefer the Old Red Sandstone." It was pointed out that this was mined some twelve miles away and transportation would involve considerable work and expense. "No matter," replied Adelina, "It is such a pretty pink colour." New plumbing was put in and, for the very first time in a private house in Britain, electricity, worked by a generator on the grounds, the responsibility of the Swansea firm of Mr Legg, Sanitary, Electrical and General Engineer. Furnishings and fittings were supplied by Messrs B. Evans & Co., Silk Mercers, Outfitters and Complete Furnishers of Swansea, who had precise instructions from Madame on every little detail. Adelina wrote from Paris to another Swansea tradesman. Mr Blanchard who was to supply the bedroom carpets, "… these must not cover the whole of the floor, it must be left uncovered all round the room in a width of one metre, or in English measure one yard and a quarter: these carpets are to be of very good quality but not too dear…"

The detail as to the size of the carpets was very probably due to Adelina's practical American good sense (in this way it was easier to sweep around them and eliminate dust) and was not, as many thought, due to a parsimonious saving on the price.

Victorian embellishments of a clock tower and a fountain in the front courtyard were added, this latter topped by a large stone stork and surrounded by flowers.

The grounds too came under Adelina's constant supervision. She employed the services of a Mr William Barron, Garden Architect, to lay out the park the way we see it today, one of the most striking features of his work the terracing of grassy banks leading down from the castle to the river. New trees and flowering shrubs were planted to replace old ones that had to be removed and the pond was stocked with trout and salmon to supply the river lower down for Ernesto's fishing. Bridges and a boathouse were built in rough timber and later Adelina enjoyed boating on the pond among the swans and waterlilies on a summer afternoon. She ordered a summerhouse to be constructed near the rose garden, its outside walls painted her favourite pink with white woodwork and topped with a pink tiled roof, from where she could overlook the tennis courts and the croquet lawns. Inside, the summerhouse was comfortably furnished and it even had the modern innovation of a flushing toilet with a blue and white patterned china base and a polished wooden seat.

Above the grass terraces she had a lofty glass-domed winter garden built, a marvel of Victorian architecture. This was to become a pseudo tropical paradise and a constant source of wonder to her guests, a room everyone preferred to all the others in the house.

The rooms of the "castle", as it was known when the extra wings were added, were illuminated by gas and electricity with a central heating system of hot water pipes pumped by machinery in the cellars. In the years to come other additions would be made but meanwhile Adelina was delighted with her castle and threw herself enthusiastically into her new role of Chatelaine, ready to entertain in lavish style now that she had so many guest rooms at her disposal.

The castle with all its improvements as well as her costly divorce from Henri all, however, cost money, so back they sailed to America for another dollar-raising tour.

They were back in New York in late October 1884, Adelina, Ernesto, the inseparable Karo and the parrot as well as Adelina's new secretary and manager Mr Charles Levilly who had replaced Signor Franchi. It was the twenty-fifth anniversary of her first appearance on the New York operatic stage and Colonel Mapleson had planned great celebrations for the occasion, beginning with a repeat of her first-ever part, *Lucia di Lammermoor* with her original partner the tenor Brignoli. Unfortunately this was not to be; Brignoli died suddenly the day before her arrival. Mapleson says that, "She was very much grieved to hear of poor Brignoli's death and sent a magnificent wreath to be placed on his coffin". She also offered to pay the funeral expenses but these had already been taken care of.

Mapleson had put a good company together for the season, including Madame Scalchi the Italian soprano, the young Californian Emma Nevada who had recently impressed him in Europe where he had spent the summer talent-scouting, Adelina's friend the conductor Arditi and the baritone Galassi. This time he was not worried about possible competition from the Metropolitan Opera House since they had signed on a German company for the season. To use his own words, "They ultimately resolved to try a German opera rather than have no opera at all".

On 10th November Adelina appeared as Rosina in *The Barber of Seville*. By now she was fully recovered from a rough Atlantic crossing. On her arrival she had told reporters "This is the last time I shall come to America as the physical discomfort of crossing the ocean is too great for me to be repeatedly subjecting myself to it". Her next role was Rossini's *Semiramide* and for her twenty fifth anniversary appearance instead of Lucia as planned, she sang the part of Martha. As the opera closed, an immense American eagle appeared at the back of the stage with the word "Patti" and the dates 1859-1884, and to her surprise the band of the 7th Regiment came up to the footlights and played the march that the same bandmaster, Cappa, had written for her twenty five years before. It was difficult for her to conceal the real emotion that overcame her and her voice choked as she thanked him.

This celebration was followed by one of Mapleson's theatrical parades with "a carriage with four milk-white steeds" escorting her like a fairy-tale princess to the Windsor Hotel, torch-bearers and fireworks and bands playing below her window far into the night. But evidently not everyone thought this put-up show an adequate tribute to the diva. One journalist later wrote, "As a demonstration it was the most pitiful affair I have ever witnessed. In fact it seemed to me such a humiliation of the great artist that on the next opera night I suggested to my colleague of *The Times* newspaper that something adequate and appropriate to so interesting an anniversary be arranged. He agreed and within a fortnight or so a banquet was given in Madame. Patti's honour at the Hotel Brunswick".[14]

The New York season closed at the end of the year with *Les Huguenots* and the company moved on to Boston, the first stop on a tour that Mapleson, always with an eye on good publicity, announced as Adelina's "positive farewell" to America and the last chance that people would have to hear her sing.

One or two incidents occurred on tour which would have badly shaken another woman but which Adelina, as usual, took calmly in her stride. In Kansas City railway station her carriage was mistakenly detached from the rest of the train and shunted some four miles down the track with the diva, the servants and Colonel Mapleson, who had just arrived on a friendly call, on board. Ernesto, who had got off the train to stretch his legs, was left standing open-mouthed on the platform. Suddenly a goods truck came running down the rails straight into Adelina's carriage, hitting it with such force that it sent her furniture and ornaments hurtling to the floor and shattered most of the glass in the windows. A mess of broken jam jars and bottles of Chateau Lafitte littered the carpet, mixed up with overturned vases of flowers and Ernesto's best cigars. Seeing Mapleson's horrified expression Adelina burst out laughing, reassuring him that he was not to blame. She then bent down to clear up the mess with the maid's help. Although she was not due to appear that evening she paid a visit to the opera where she found the Mayor waiting to escort her to her box. The house went wild with cheering as though to make amends for the distraction of their railway workers earlier in the day.

Then the company left for San Francisco, with several scheduled stops on the way, but since Adelina was free from commitments her carriage was attached to the San Francisco Express, which meant, to her relief, just three and a half days of fast comfortable travelling, rest and

---

14 Krehbiel, *Chapters on Opera*. This turned out to be an all-male affair, the puritan New York wives refusing to accompany their husbands because Adelina at the time was an adulteress, openly living with her lover.

relaxation. Looking forward to visiting San Francisco again, she was sure she could count on a warm welcome, full houses, and enthusiasm for Italian opera still running high (unlike New York where little by little Italian opera of the old school was gradually losing ground). In New York not even the magic of her name had been enough to draw the enthusiastic crowds of previous years, those crowds Mapleson had been counting on, and they had left near to financial disaster. She was however confident and full of her usual optimism that things would pick up on tour, and she was to be proved right.

In San Francisco she made many more appearances than scheduled because the other prima donna of the company, Emma Nevada, caught a bad cold in Cheyenne which developed almost into pneumonia and forced her to keep to her bed for three weeks. To Mapleson's annoyance he was therefore obliged to pay Patti the agreed sum of £1,000 a night every time she appeared. But the enthusiasm aroused by her duets with the mezzo-soprano Sofia Scalchi whenever they sang together more than made up for the expense. Their *Semiramide,*their *Aida* and their *Linda di Chamounix* were the magical highlights of the tour. Mapleson tells us that in San Francisco, "… the largest and most brilliant audience ever gathered in a theatre were there to hear Patti and Scalchi sing in two of the most difficult roles in the whole range of opera". They "electrified the audience" and "the Press unanimously accorded me the next morning the credit of having presented "the best operatic entertainment in that distant city the world of art could afford"

As in most American cities it was a brilliant audience that filled the theatre in San Francisco, the ladies outdoing one another with the elegance of their toilettes, usually in white, and in the number and size of their diamonds. American theatres, unlike their English counterparts, were kept well dusted and clean and there was no risk of a lady ruining a white gown from an evening at the theatre as might happen, for example, at Covent Garden. Added to this, American theatres were well heated during the winter months and a daring décolleté did not mean risking pneumonia.

Opera lovers in San Francisco who were not lucky enough to find tickets devised other means of getting into the theatre, some even going so far as to wrench off the gratings along an alleyway and to slide down on their stomachs into the cellars of the theatre in the hopes of hearing a few of Patti's magical notes!

From a lodging-house facing one side of the opera house an enterprising person had fixed up a rope from which it was possible to swing up to the roof of the theatre, climb down through a ventilation shaft, walk downstairs to the foyer and obtain a pass-out ticket which was then sold for two dollars. One man repeated the act four times until he was spotted by the police, arrested and the swing confiscated. There was even an assault by ladders with admirers desperately climbing up and entering through the windows of the dress circle until this too was discovered and the iron shutters firmly closed.

Adelina, probably unaware at the time of the antics people were getting up to so as to catch a glimpse of her or hear her sing, was again involved in a dangerous incident that might have killed her. Someone in the audience threw a bomb (aimed at a banker seated in a box near the wings but missing the target through nervousness) and it landed in the centre of the stage just as she was about to approach the spot for a third curtain call. Panic and pandemonium broke out.

"You might have killed Patti!" someone yelled.

"I wish I had!" was the reply, "She has made enough money as it is!"

This was not the first, nor was it to be the last dramatic episode that occurred while she was actually on stage, but even then, a few feet away from death, she did not lose her nerve. She was truly sorry that the episode had taken place in San Francisco, the city that loved her most where people had gone out of their way to show their affection and wild appreciation, and she did not intend to let the gesture of a madman spoil her stay.

★★★

With the passing of the years, Adelina's awareness of her own importance had of course increased. Although there was some truth in the fact that all her life she remained basically unspoilt, and of a friendly, practical nature, it was also inevitable that a lifetime of public adulation would have some side effects on her personality. She was the acclaimed Queen of Opera throughout the world, the *prima donna assoluta*, charming, glamorous, rich and successful, sought-after and admired. Years of red carpet treatment had created a mantle of self-centredness around her. It was of course no longer true as Klein wrote of her as a child that, "…the fact that she had begun to earn large sums of money made no difference whatever to her". Money did make a difference, fame and success did make a difference. And now, with an adoring Ernesto ready to pander to her every whim, she had come to expect the treatment accorded to a queen.

That Adelina knew she was number one is illustrated by an incident of theatre bills in Chicago, their next stop on that particular tour, where her name was not printed in letters one-third larger than that of Emma Nevada as stipulated in her contract. Either she or Ernesto had spotted the fact that the posters were not following the rule that her name must always appear one-third larger than anyone else's. An agreement was an agreement and Madame Patti was put out. Ernesto was seen to fetch a ladder and climb up to measure the exact size of the letters with a ruler and their suspicions were confirmed. Mapleson was compelled to change all the bills, which he cleverly contrived to do by slicing out a portion of the centre of the letters that spelt out Emma Nevada's name and piecing the two halves together again!

When they arrived in Chicago in April 1885, construction had just been completed on the new Auditorium. Designed by Adler and Sullivan it seated 6,000 but held many more and astonished Mapleson with its "surpassing grandeur", its four miles of steam pipes for central heating, its 70-foot stage, Japanese and Chinese-style grand salons, ample dressing rooms and above all, perfect acoustics.

In this splendour, Patti and Scalchi opened the festival with *Semiramide*, with an orchestra of 155 musicians conducted by Arditi and a cast and chorus of 750 people. They appeared together again on the fourth evening in *Linda di Chamounix* to a crowded auditorium that somehow packed in 9,000 people. For Adelina's Aida the following week the hall was filled to double its intended capacity with an audience of 12,000 standing and seated, and as so often happened when Patti sang, traffic blocked the streets all around. No expense had been spared on new scenery and decorations and the two-week Opera Festival was a resounding success, described in the local paper as "… the greatest musical undertaking that has ever been accomplished anywhere" with a total presence of 190,000 for the thirteen different operas on the programme.

The following month, on 2nd May, Adelina and Ernesto sailed for England and home, this time to Craig-y-Nos.

★★★

How good it felt to be home again among the peaceful Welsh hills after the frenzy and glitter of America. They were worlds apart. Here she could sit at the window of her spacious drawing room and look down across the valley bathed in soft June sunshine or walk in the Winter Garden that had been built to the south when the weather was too damp to stroll out of doors. She was loved and pampered by a staff of forty, mostly locals, in each of whom she took a friendly personal interest, and who would never forget her or their days at the castle.[15]

Now she delighted in entertaining. In the summer months she dined with her guests at a long table in the Winter Garden. Here she dazzled everyone with her toilettes, priceless diamonds flashing under the electric lights, the conversation flowing now in English, now in French, her rich contralto speaking voice surprising those who heard her for the first time and were only familiar with her high soprano notes.

Her pride and joy was the expensive new Orchestrion, worked by electricity, which had been specially ordered from Fribourg in Germany. They had it installed in Ernesto's billiard room and after dinner Adelina and the guests would sit there on the long divans (the game of billiards being suspended) and listen to its rich, organ-like tones. She was often tempted to sing along to its accompaniment, the beauty of her voice making her guests feel lucky indeed to be among the chosen few. People all over Europe and America fought and clamoured to get into the theatres or even to see her step out of a carriage and here she was, in her castle, singing just for them. And with the assistance of her Orchestrion she began to discover and appreciate Wagner, whose music was later to mean so much to her.

---

15   Later donated to the city of Swansea and now known as the Patti Pavilion

Later there would be a private theatre where she and Ernesto would act and sing for their assembled guests, but this was still in the future. Already she was said to have spent the vast amount, for the times, of £100,000 on improvements, and an elaborate system of electric burglar alarms protected her jewels and possessions and her expensive wardrobe of over three hundred couturier gowns. Life was enjoyable and Adelina was thoroughly satisfied.

That season, in spite of the gloomy outlook for Italian opera in London, Colonel Mapleson took over the management of Covent Garden, which had been closed since the previous year. After visiting the diva at her castle he proudly produced a contract drawn up in great detail with Madame Patti, indispensable for the success of his new venture. They were to present her in a series of eight operas between 16th June and 16th July and she was to be paid £4,000 with an extra £500 for each additional appearance, the money to be paid in advance by two o'clock on the day. In addition, Mapleson agreed to deposit £2,000 in cash with her bankers, Rothschild, of New Court, St Swithin's Lane. She was to provide and pay for her own costumes but was to be under no obligation to attend rehearsals – this last clause, in Mapleson's opinion, to be "condemned by all lovers of music".[16]

The exciting novelty for Adelina was that for the first time she was to sing the title role in Bizet's *Carmen.* Her feelings about this part are best described by Klein, then music critic of *The Sunday Times*, who happened to visit her the very day before her debut. Klein was nervous at meeting his favourite diva, but his friend reassured him. "You need not hesitate… She is very wonderful… Like the Queen of England she makes you feel perfectly at your ease in her presence without losing an iota of her sense of dignity. Yet such is her charm, her natural simplicity, her magnetic power, above all her sustained vivacity and spirit, that you never for a moment cease to realise that the Patti of the drawing room is the Patti of the stage – and of your dreams".

---

16 He complains in his *Memoirs* that during the years with him in America she never once attended a rehearsal. Rehearsals to her were an unnecessary waste of time and energy and the habit of avoiding them – encouraged by Maurice when she was little more than a child and he would stand in for her –was one she kept for the rest of her life.

So Herman Klein visited the prima donna in her suite in the gloomy Midland Grand Hotel and remembers that she "…came forward and greeted us with much cordiality. I had already met Nicolini and it was he who formally presented me to the famous 'little lady'. Her bright smile and gracious manner instantly put me at my ease. She bade me sit beside her and began to talk – in those deep, rich, contralto tones that always belied so curiously the brighter timbre of her singing voice".

Klein remarks that she looked astonishingly young. Although she was forty three "…she did not appear to be a day more than thirty and her movements seemed still to retain the impulse and freedom of girlhood. The merry laugh, the rapid turn of the head, the mischievous twinkle in the keen dark eyes when she said something humorous, were as natural to her as that rapid, forward élan when she extended her hand to Alfredo in the supper scene of 'Traviata'". He agreed with his friend that "the woman was as unaffected, as fascinating as the artist."

She chatted of her favourite roles, Rosina, Zerlina, Violetta, adding, "But in reality I cannot make a definite choice. I love each of my characters in turn as I sing it", and then, "Maybe I shall like the next one best". Saying this, she indicated the Spanish costume of Carmen hanging over a chair, a dainty Spanish skirt of yellow satin with a crimson shawl flung carelessly across it. Carmen! She enthused, her voice rising in excitement, that it was the part she had been longing to sing for years.

"I adore the opera. Ah, poor Bizet, how I wish he were still alive to hear me! I love the story, I love the music, I love the Spanish scenes and types, *enfin, j'aime tout ce qui est Carmen!* You will see me dance; you will hear how I play the castanets. I have never longed so impatiently for anything in my life". At this point Ernesto interrupted her in French, probably alarmed that she was showing too much excitement, telling her to rest her voice which by then had risen to a pitch. She quietened and getting up gave the signal for her guests to leave, holding out her hand "with a regal gesture that seemed quite natural, nay inborn, and just as naturally, albeit the custom was not English, I took the hand and kissed it" writes the smitten Klein.

Sadly, her dreams of presenting a dazzling, sizzling, triumphant Carmen, in spite of her enthusiasm, were destined to collapse. She could not get away with the part. Her performance fell painfully flat. She never managed to get under the skin of the sensual and passionate Spanish gypsy, the audience got no whiff of sweat or sex and were not convinced.

As Klein remarks, "Her personality could express a vivacious nature with distinction and grace, but was never fitted for the embodiment of a commonplace woman of the people… In a word, her Carmen proved to be clever but colourless. It was a skilful tour de force, nothing more". *Carmen* was repeated once more and then dropped. It must have been a scathing disappointment to Adelina and whether or not as a result of this, she missed a few performances due to "hoarseness" during the rest of the programme and had to be substituted at the last minute by an indifferent debutante. None of which contributed to Mapleson's popularity with the press, which was coldly critical.

1885 was to be the last year in which Adelina appeared at Covent Garden on a regular basis as she had been doing continuously since her arrival in London in 1861. Klein writes that, "This particular night (the last performance of the season, *Il Trovatore*) was practically the last in the history of her unbroken quarter of a century's work – unique, brilliant, amazing in every sense – as the unchallenged and unapproachable star of London's leading opera house. Few could have guessed that it marked the close of a great era in the story of opera in Great Britain".

After her last magnificent rendering of Leonora, she was presented with a very valuable diamond bracelet by a committee of admirers who called themselves the Patti Testimonial Fund, and who made the following address, "Madame Adelina Patti, "You complete this evening your twenty-fifth annual engagement at the theatre which had the honour of introducing you, when you were still a child, to the public of England, and indirectly therefore to that of Europe and the whole civilized world. There has been no example in the history of the lyric drama of such long-continued, never interrupted, always triumphant success on the boards of the same theatre, and a number of your most earnest admirers have decided not to let the occasion pass without offering you their heartfelt congratulations. Many of them have watched with the deepest interest an artistic career which, beginning in the spring of 1861, became year after year more brilliant, until during the season which terminates tonight the last possible point of perfection seems to have been reached. You have been connected with the Royal Italian Opera uninterruptedly throughout your long and brilliant career. During the winter months you have visited, and have been received with enthusiasm in Paris, St Petersburg, Berlin, Vienna, Madrid and all the principal cities of Italy and the United States. But you have allowed nothing to prevent you from returning every summer to the scene of your earliest triumphs; and now that you have completed your twenty-fifth season in London, your friends feel that the interesting occasion must not be suffered to pass without due commemoration. We beg you, therefore, to accept from us, in the spirit in which it is offered, the token of esteem and admiration which we have now the honour of presenting to you".

This moving speech was followed by the National Anthem, cheers and applause, and Adelina was greatly touched. They still loved her, these dear Londoners, and her heart went out to them. For the occasion Colonel Mapleson had organized another of his torchlight processions and when she stepped out of the stage door in Flower Street (then known as Hart Street) her carriage was waiting escorted by torch bearers and followed by a band as well as a milling crowd of admirers kept at bay by the police. There was a row of cabs and carriages waiting behind ready to follow. The band struck up as they moved off just before midnight on the half-hour journey to the Midland Hotel and half London was kept awake by the cheering and singing and the noise, (attracting passers-by and hundreds of roughs). Sadly, although she was to make sporadic appearances at Covent Garden again, this was the end of an era and Londoners were going to miss their Patti Nights.

Images are used with kind permission of SelClene Ltd, owners of Craig Y Nos Castle.

Images are used with kind permission of SelClene Ltd, owners of Craig Y Nos Castle.

# 11

Patterns of sunlight filtering through the lace curtains dappled the rose pink walls and pastel carpet with light and shade and danced on silver and crystal scent bottles and powder bowls. She sat at her dressing table in front of the big window facing the valley. It was all hers, as far as the mountains beyond, the freshly laid out terraces leading down to the river and the wooded park and lawns. It all seemed too good to be true, especially on a day like today.

Karo was bending over her putting up her hair, arranging soft curls on her forehead, fluffing it out at the sides to frame her face, secure in her long-practised movements as Madame's personal maid. The younger maid, Patro, hovered behind them tidying up, ready to help, nervously excited, but today Karo wished to attend personally to every little detail of her mistress's toilette. Adelina studied her reflection in the mirror. She was pleased with what she saw. Forty-three and not a wrinkle, apart from those minute, almost invisible lines at the corner of the eyes; her complexion was fresh, the skin on her brow and neck were as smooth as it had been when she was twenty. Dipping the tip of her little finger into her rouge pot, she reddened her lips again and then rubbed some into her cheeks. A touch of powder with a swansdown puff and she was ready. Her eyes, large and dark, had no need of art to set them off.

At last the day had come. Her gown from the House of Worth, sent over from Paris by special courier, was spread across the bed next to a pair of silk gloves and a concoction of flowers and ribbons and veiling for her head. Everything was ready. Today, 10th June 1886, she was to marry Ernesto. Yesterday they had both signed the official marriage contract and there had been the formality of the ceremony in front of the vice consul for France in Swansea, with Thomas Johnson, her friend from the Paris *Figaro* and Wilhelm Ganz the conductor acting as her witnesses. Today, her real wedding day, she was as excited as any young bride. She picked up the delicate bouquet of lilies-of-the-valley, forget-me-nots, narcissus, violets and white heather to inhale its sweet scent.

The house was full of wedding guests and she had woken early, had her bath and then breakfasted alone. She had made Ernesto understand that today etiquette demanded that he take breakfast below with their guests. The servants would be kept busy running from room to room with jugs of hot water. Although three bathrooms had seemed sufficient, and indeed a luxury when one thought of other country houses, they were hard-pressed when all thirty four bedrooms were occupied. She smiled. Today she would let others worry about the domestic arrangements; she had other things on her mind.

There was a brief knock and Ernesto came into the room. He stood in the doorway, uncertain of his welcome at this moment, afraid of intruding. Adelina's heart jumped as she saw him reflected in her mirror, so handsome in his morning suit, and she could not resist running into his arms. He held her close, her body warm and familiar under the smooth satin of her negligee, and it took all Karo's loud protests for him to let her go.

Laughing, Adelina released herself and plucked a tiny sprig of flowers from her bouquet, pinning them to his lapel.

"*Voilà, mon mari*, now you are quite perfect!" she said and pushed him gently towards the door.

His eyes held hers. "*A bientot, ma mignonne*," and he took both her hands in his and raised them to his lips. Ernesto adored her still, and she adored him. After so many years together, facing criticism and often cold-shouldering from people who could not appreciate the depth of their feelings for one another, today they would be married and that would put a stop to all the malicious gossip that she guessed went on behind their backs.[17]

Karo slipped the gown over her head and shoulders, pale blue silk and ecru lace, soft to the touch, caught up here and there with tiny imitation bunches of forget-me-nots and lily-of-the-valley to match her bouquet. The little headdress was pinned securely on to her coiffure and when her feet stepped into size one Parisian shoes she was ready.

Her only regret was that Papa was no longer there to accompany her to the altar a second time, nor, for that matter, were any of her family to be present. But her old friend Monsieur Maynard made a very good substitute and he was kind and reassuring during their ride together to the church, side by side in the open landau. The carriage and the horses' harnesses were decorated with flowers, and so were the roads and villages on their way, with gay bunting hung across the roads and the local people dressed up in their best clothes to cheer them. Ernesto followed in another landau with his witnesses, and another six or more carriages carrying wedding guests made up the procession. Even the sun came out to shine on them.

A carpet had been laid from the church gate to the porch, and this time there was no lack of music at her wedding, with a choir of Welsh children crowding the churchyard singing a chorus with words and music specially written for the occasion. There was a simple Protestant ceremony and afterwards Adelina signed the register with the French version of her name, Adele Jeanne Marie Patti.

They all went back to Craig-y-Nos for the wedding reception and the felicitations, the kisses, and the inspection of gifts and telegrams that had arrived from all over the world. Champagne corks popped as they sat down to a delectable spread that chefs had spent days preparing. Lord Rothschild had sent a magnificent set of diamonds and there were gifts from "Bertie and Alix" the Prince and Princess of Wales, the Queen of the Belgians and the Queen of Romania. Henry Irving gave the bride an exquisite mother-of-pearl fan. A brass band provided the music and later in the evening bonfires were lit in the grounds, and the

---

17 Over the past years, she had often been attacked by a spiteful Press, particularly in America. Only three months previously, *The Wasp*, a Californian journal, had written that people went to her performances "Not to hear a great artist but to see a great wanton – a beautiful sensualist the fame of whose adulteries had overspread the globe"!

party broke up after a fireworks display. A new era had begun. She was married at last.[18]

Career-wise from now on things would be less frenetic and more profitable. Those breathless trips across two continents were gradually to slow down and she would have more time to devote to leisure, to Ernesto, and to her new home.

★★★

One of the wedding guests was the American impresario Henry Abbey, apparently fully recovered from his colossal flop three years earlier with the New York Metropolitan. Encouraged by Ernesto he now proposed to Adelina another farewell tour of the United States, this time a concert tour with perhaps some opera to wind up with in New York. This project fitted in very well with Adelina's desire to concentrate more on concerts. Italian opera in England had gone from bad to worse and as far as Covent Garden was concerned, the antique glory associated with the theatre had vanished and there seemed to be little hope of its coming back.

Before taking off for America again, she accepted a proposal from Mr Ambrose Austin (manager of St James' Hall and organiser of the annual Scottish and Irish ballad concerts) to give four concerts at the Royal Albert Hall that same month and in July. Backed up by high-ranking artists such as Trebelli and Edward Lloyd and by an orchestra conducted by Mr W. Cusins, these concerts turned out to be a great success and Mr Austin made a large profit. These were the first of the famous Patti concerts which were to continue to draw in packed houses for the next twenty years.

On the afternoon of July 15th 1886 she appeared in a special benefit

---

18  But not without difficulties. She had had problems with the church ceremony being held in Swansea because of her divorce from Henri (finally granted by the French courts after she had agreed to settle his financial claims amounting to a million and a half francs. Henri continued to live in Paris and bothered her no more), and she had to thank the Reverend Glanley, rector of Ystradgynlais and his little parish church for having a religious ceremony. Twice she had appealed to the Vatican for the annulment of her marriage to Henri but this had been refused. In return for Madame Nicolini divorcing Ernesto, Adelina paid her $50,000 as well as paying for the education of the five Nicolini children. Her marriage to Ernesto had cost her dearly but she never regretted a penny of it.

performance in aid of Colonel Mapleson, who now found himself in a very sticky financial position and full of debts, possibly due to her failure to join him in America the previous year on what had then turned out to be a disastrous tour. In a sudden rush of solidarity she and Ernesto sang the roles of Rosina and Almaviva in *The Barber of Seville* at Drury Lane. Tickets sold easily at exorbitant prices, London being full of foreign tourists that summer, and with Arditi conducting the orchestra and the Diva in full voice, Mapleson managed to net in a considerable sum.

The newly-weds enjoyed a sweet late summer at Craig-y-Nos but they were already making plans for the future. She could in fact quite easily have retired at this stage, but as with many prima donnas, no such thought crossed her mind. She was now thinking of building her own theatre at home, a stage where she could entertain her guests, and another dollar-raising tour would enable her to start work on this project without touching her flourishing bank account. So Mr Abbey's proposed farewell concert tour in America to be followed by some opera in New York if all went well, and to be paid at the fantastic rate of $5,000 for each performance (or a total of $250,000 with a guaranteed minimum of fifty performances) was far too appetising a dish to refuse.

As things turned out this was not to be her very last farewell to America. Several such "farewells" were to follow during the next seventeen years, but it was always good publicity and guaranteed to pull in the public. Who could resist the opportunity to hear Patti sing for the very last time? But at the signing of the contract it is possible that she believed in good faith that this was indeed her last American tour. She had no hesitation and the tour was arranged for the coming winter and the spring of 1887, starting off in New York.

New Yorkers, associating the diva with opera rather than with concerts, did not unfortunately give her tour that brilliant send-off that she had been counting on. Her four November concerts at the Academy of Music met with cool indifference. But once out of the city and on the road, the tour got off the ground and box office takings were said to have touched "unparalleled figures". In fact it was such a financial success that it enabled Mr Abbey to book the Metropolitan Opera House in New York for the following April. Here Adelina was to be featured in six "farewell" operas with the support of excellent singers such as Scalchi and with Signor Arditi conducting. It was a gamble that paid off. This time the New York public rose to the occasion, response was overwhelming and tickets were sold for a total of $70,000.

In *Chapters of the Opera* H. E. Krehbel writes, "Prices of admission were abnormal, and so was the audience. Fashion heard Patti at the Metropolitan, and so did suburban folk, who came to $10 opera in business coats, bonnets and shawls. Such audiences were never seen in the theatre before or since".

For some reason, among the six operas she chose to sing at the Metropolitan, she included her ill-fated version of *Carmen*. It is possible that she thought her American public would reverse the negative reception it had received at Covent Garden and was desperate to try again. But she was to be bitterly disappointed. The audience was cold and the critics hard, one writing that "This was not *Carmen*", and she never sang the part again. Apart from this faux pas, the rest of her programme in her favourite old parts brought her the usual triumphant success.

After their return to England in May 1887, that summer she sang in two concerts at the Royal Albert Hall arranged by Ambrose Austin.

Meanwhile, Colonel Mapleson had again been trying desperately to entice Adelina into his net for a series of operas at Her Majesty's Theatre, in spite of a general lack of interest in such an enterprise. He was not a man to give up easily and in his memoirs he writes that he "secured the services of Madame Adelina Patti at the small salary of £650 per night". That year Queen Victoria had been on the throne for fifty years and various Jubilee celebrations had been planned, so Mapleson was counting on the crowds of visitors who would be attracted to London from the provinces and from overseas. There is, however, some mystery shrouding this affair because at the time Henry Abbey had the exclusive rights to Patti's London appearances. In fact she appeared on the stage of Her Majesty's Theatre just once in the role of Violetta in *La Traviata*, and did not honour the rest of the agreement. Excuse followed excuse. She had "accepted an invitation from a wealthy banker for a trip up the river to be followed by a dinner" and "took a violent cold from having been placed in a draught with a light muslin dress on". Difficult to believe, with her excellent health and with Ernesto always ready to place a shawl around her shoulders at the slightest ruffling of the air.

So Lilli Lehmann stood in for her but the house was almost empty, public attention directed to the next time she was due to appear on 5th July in *The Barber of Seville,* Theatregoers and performers were to be disappointed again. Nicolini arrived at five o'clock on the day of the performance to say that Madame was still too ill to appear and although many people had already arrived and had sent away their carriages, they were all turned away.

Nicolini promised that she would appear in *Faust* the following week, but on Mapleson's request for some cash to help him face the losses he had incurred and to pay the orchestra and artists, offered the poor impresario only fifty pounds. To continue the story in Mapleson's words, "I replied that that would be scarcely enough for the orchestra and that the entire representation would be jeopardised. He thereupon went home, stating that Madame Patti would not sing that evening unless the orchestra was duly secured. I immediately made arrangements with my orchestra, "and notified the fact to Madame Patti by half past three through her agent at her hotel who, after seeing her, informed me that it was all right. She was then lying down in view of the evening performance, for which her dresses had already been prepared by herself and her maid".

As Mapleson was leaving the hotel, Henry Abbey arrived and accompanied him to the box office, only to discover that four or five hundred of the best seats were still unsold. Understandably, the public were holding back until the last minute to avoid any further disappointments and to be sure the Great Lady herself would appear. Although the sum of £650 for that evening's performance had already been deposited at Adelina's bank, Mr Abbey decided there and then that she would not perform; Madame could not risk facing a half empty theatre. And that was that. Mapleson waited until eight o'clock but no Patti appeared and no word was sent. In order to placate the public he was forced to put on a free performance of *Carmen* with Trebelli in the leading role, and tells us that "The audience was numerous and enthusiastic" and that it all "went off admirably". But by now he was very much in the red. He continues, "I wrote to Madame Patti the following day, entreating her not further to disappoint the public and to stand by the announcement Signor Nicolini had given me of her appearance the following Tuesday in *Il*

*Barbiere*. To this I had no reply, and I afterwards learned that Madame Patti had gone off by a special morning train to Wales to avoid meeting the chorus and employees who, hearing of her probable flight, had assembled in large bodies at Paddington to give her a manifestation of their disappointment".

Such self-centredness and apparent indifference to the difficulties of others were all part of the prima donna's make up. Her careful avoidance of any unpleasantness or stress, the cosseting she received as her due from Ernesto and her entourage, the strict regime and self discipline of her everyday life, were all part of the protective wall she had erected around herself for the perfect preservation of her voice. At forty-four her voice was still perfect. Her cancellations at the slightest sign of a chill, the refusal to attend rehearsals with their frustrations and frayed nerves, her desire to be always comfortable on stage and off, all these things and more had made her what she was, the unrivalled international star, the Queen of Song. Without the egoism there would have been no diva, no legend, no story to tell.

No doubt she had been swayed by Henry Abbey's insistence that she was under contract to him and not Mapleson, perhaps there was even some truth in the story that she had caught a cold, but was it possible that she was entirely unconcerned about the plight of the impresario who had gone to great expense, as well as the entire theatrical company she had let down? The heart of a diva can be hard.

Poor Colonel Mapleson had difficulties paying off the rent of Her Majesty's Theatre (which he had also gone to considerable expense refurbishing, repainting and having new carpets put down) and paying the artists, the orchestra, the clerks and bill posters, not to mention the sixty Italian choristers who had come specially from Italy and whose expenses and salaries and tickets for the return journey had to be found. One wonders if his mind went back to that April day twenty-six years before when he first set eyes on Adelina, a young girl quite unknown in Europe, sitting demurely in the foyer of the Arundel Hotel where she had sung 'Home, Sweet Home' for him and told him she was certain she would draw in the money. He had taken one gamble too many on his find.

Mapleson's future enterprises were mostly destined to failure and after another unsuccessful season at Her Majesty's Theatre in 1889 and a final fling at the New York Academy of Music seven years later, he spent his last years in poor health and financial difficulties. After his death in 1901 his eldest son sent a letter to *The Times* (referring to an article they had published) stating "...that he died a poor man, leaving his widow destitute and that the many artists and musicians whose fortunes he made have entirely forgotten their indebtedness to him, is sufficiently sad, without having ridicule cast on his memory by *The Times*".

But this was in the future. In the summer of 1887 Adelina strolled around the grounds of her Welsh estate under a parasol, boating on the pond or watching Ernesto fish for trout in the stream, supervising the extensions and improvements, blithely indifferent to the plight of her old impresario.

★★★

Adelina does not appear to have made many enemies. Few bore her any rancour if we exclude Ernesto's first wife, justifiably jealous, one or two rival sopranos and the colleagues involved in her desertion of Mapleson's programme. Some journalists, particularly in America, had attacked her for her morals. But now she was to meet a new Dutch manager, a certain Schurmann. Two years earlier she had been contacted by Signor Pollini, Director of the Stadt-Theater in Hamburg, and had signed a contract with him for eighty representations, one every three days, on a European tour. Through a series of mishaps this contract arrived in the hands of the thirty-year-old Schurmann and in 1885 Adelina discovered she was under contract to this person for a tour covering Austria, Hungary, France, Spain and Portugal. They disliked one another on sight. In his malignant chapters on Patti in his book *Les Etoiles En Voyage* he writes, "Escorted by Signor Nicolini, her so-called husband, and followed at a respectable distance by her French secretary Monsieur Levilly, by the maid Patro and by a manservant, Madame Patti studies me from her mediocre height and turns her back on me saying, 'I do not know this man, I only know Signor Pollini. What a ridiculous way of doing things, to be passed from hand to hand like a suitcase'". [19]

---

[19] *Les Etoiles En Voyage*, published in 1893

Schurmann goes on to relate a series of incredible anecdotes and one can only hope that Adelina, no great reader at the best of times, never bothered to look at his publication, or that she even heard of it.

The best-known and funny-sad story goes as follows (and he himself admits that if she ever found out about it she would have had the right to be scandalised). It was time for her appearance in Bucharest where Ullmann, acting as Schurmann's secretary, had preceded the company. At a certain point Adelina put her foot down and refused to go on to that city with an emphatic, "I will not go, it is too cold, there is snow everywhere, I don't want to catch my death. No, a hundred times no, you will never make me change my mind!"

Schurmann was desperate. In spite of the high prices charged, every ticket for her appearance in Bucharest had been sold and as he says, every impresario's idea of hell is the torture of having to refund a superb cash intake.

At the Post Office, Schurmann twisted the pen around in his fingers trying to find the words to send the fatal telegram to Ullmann in Bucharest, when suddenly he had a brilliant idea. Well aware of Adelina's love of pomp and ceremony, for brass bands, ovations and flowers, he sent the following message, "At any cost we must have an ovation at the Bucharest railway station on the part of the Italian aristocracy (at the time well represented in the city). Send the following telegram by return… The Italian and Romanian nobility are preparing a magnificent welcome for the arrival of the Signora Patti. The Ministry will be represented. Sleighs, torchlight and music. Telegraph hour of arrival".

According to Schurmann when Adelina read this telegram sent back by return, it had the desired effect. She went pink and then white with excitement and he fancied he saw "a tear or two of noble pride" on her long black lashes. "What really nice people. When do we leave?" she asked. "Tomorrow morning," replied the crafty Schurmann.

The following evening as they stepped down from the train, they saw the platform crowded with sixty gentlemen in full evening dress, impeccably turned out in spite of the cold. Torches were flaming, the band played the national anthem, flags flew and flowers were offered in profusion. An old gentleman welcomed Adelina in Italian in the name of all the nobility of Bucharest and she thanked them with a voice that shook with emotion. Then, nodding and smiling her thanks, she climbed into a waiting sleigh. There was an explosion of applause, cheering and shouting and escorted by the sixty aristocrats she made a triumphant entrance into the city.

At the hotel doors, while the cheering doubled in volume, Schurmann asked his secretary to follow them inside. "Impossible," Ullmann replied. "I have to watch my costumes otherwise they'd probably run off with them".

"Who?" asked the curious impresario.

"Those gentlemen. You asked me to organise a big welcome and I enlisted all the chimney-sweeps and labourers in the area at two francs each. The hire of the costumes was five francs each, the purchase of white ties and gloves make a total of three hundred and twenty francs".

Schurmann was delighted, particularly since the trick had been played on Madame Adelina Patti.

Later there was to be a tragedy in the over-packed theatre while she was singing the mad scene in *Lucia di Lammermoor*. The gallery was swaying with the weight of 600 people and, not finding any other place, a few idiots decided to climb up onto the scenic arch above the stage. A certain Rubenstein lost his balance and precipitated down into the wings, injuring a child and a chorister. There was panic and the orchestra and the other singers took flight, alarming the public who imagined a general disaster. The only person to remain calm was Adelina.

Schurmann says, "Patti did not move. After having reassured the audience with a gesture of her hand, she finished the aria without any accompaniment and only left the stage after the entire house, enthused by her *sang froid* and her virtuosity, had called her back for four curtain calls".

After this further demonstration of calm in the face of a crisis, she went on to give thirty more performances under Schurmann's management (and not the original eighty agreed with Pollini). This tour brought large profits to the waspish impresario, a total of nearly £44,000, from which Adelina made a net profit after deducting all expenses, of £11,500. This sum, added to fantastic profits on her forthcoming American tours, meant that in less than two years she earned approximately £100,000. No other singer had ever earned such an amount in such a short time.

But a sad event clouded the autumn of 1887 for Adelina. In October her old friend and mentor Maurice Strakosch died in Paris where he had been living for some years. The previous year he had published his *Memoires d'Un Impresario* written in the third person, describing the early years with his little sister-in-law as well as his association with other singers. Adelina was understandably sad to hear of his death. She had Maurice to thank for much of her success, and another link with the past was gone.

★★★

During Adelina's last American tour, Henry Abbey had discussed the possibility of her visiting South America where huge sums were paid to artistes of her calibre. Ernesto had been enthusiastic at the idea. He was all for promoting his wife's career and making as much money as possible, unlike Henri who had been more wrapped up with their acquaintances in high circles and the courts of Europe. Another American manager, Mr Marcus Mayer, was contacted and agreed to sound out the South American opera houses for them. The result was impressive. If the diva came, they said, she would be paid more than any other artiste had ever been offered, £1,000 for each performance plus a percentage on the box office takings that would probably reap in half as much again.

She accepted immediately. The tour was to be a long one lasting nine months, from December of that year until September 1888, with stops in Paris and Madrid en route to Lisbon where they would board the *Congo* sailing for Buenos Aires. In Europe they always travelled by train with an enormous amount of luggage including a folding billiard table which they set up in their hotel rooms for an after-dinner game. Their party included Ernesto; Carlina Patti, Adelina's niece; Adelina's English friend and adviser, Augustus Spalding; the inseparable Karo; and the American managers, Henry Abbey and Marcus Meyer.

By a coincidence Adelina celebrated her forty-fifth birthday in Madrid, the city of her birth, and was therefore much feted by the Spanish public as "a true daughter of Spain". Like a new species of chameleon, she could choose her nationality to suit the occasion.

The party finally reached Buenos Aires where she appeared in twenty-four representations and since the Politeama Argentina seated 5,000 and was packed out every time, there was a record cash intake at the box office, of which she received £38,400 (£1,600 a night). This was the highest fee ever paid to any opera singer up to that time.

Then they moved on to Montevideo where she gave eight performances at the Teatro Solis. They had to cut out a planned stop in Rio de Janeiro due to an outbreak of yellow fever, and the party returned to Buenos Aires. Now it was time for four "farewell" evenings and a "benefit" where it is reported that "scenes of the wildest enthusiasm were enacted" and that "bouquets and floral tributes were thrown upon the stage in such profusion that the prima donna, when coming forward to take her calls, was actually compelled to tread among flowers. The President of the Argentine Republic and other notables made her handsome presents and attentions of every kind were showered upon the distinguished visitor".[20]

In all, the tour was a great success and certainly her biggest success financially. She earned a total of £50,000, most of which was pure profit. Her coffers full to bursting, in excellent health and spirits, she sailed back to Europe with her entourage from Rio de Janeiro on the *Ionic*.

20  Herman Klein, *The Reign of Patti*

# 12

Adelina's own private theatre was officially opened in August 1891. She had been in enough theatres all her life to know exactly what she wanted; here there would be absolutely no damp, dust or draughts but everything would be in perfect working order, warm, comfortable and efficient. There was a delicately blended décor, the main colour scheme in pale blue and ivory touched with gold (the work this time being carried out by J. Lacasas of London), with seating for 180 or even 200 at a pinch. The chairs were upholstered in pale blue velvet and the cream walls panelled and columned and decorated with the names of Adelina's favourite composers, Rossini, Verdi, Mozart, Gounod, Auber, Donizetti, Handel, Beethoven and Wagner. Stage curtains were in sapphire blue velvet richly draped and tasselled and the act drop showed the diva herself as Semiramide in her chariot drawn by galloping horses.

With a local architect she had created a miniature jewel. There was a clever mechanism by which the floor, normally sloping down towards the stage, could be raised to the same level and so create a ballroom 62 feet long. In the same way the orchestra pit, large enough for twenty musicians, could be raised to the height of the floor. For the times it was as perfect as engineering could make it.

Craig-y-Nos Castle was packed with important guests for the opening ceremony. Musicians, impresarios, journalists and critics rubbed shoulders with a sprinkling of the aristocracy that so impressed her. Important people from nearby Swansea and the local St David's

Amateur Operatic Society directed by Mr W. F. Hulley, were taken up by special trains to the little station of Penwyllt where Adelina had her own private and comfortably furnished waiting room, and were met by carriages sent from the Castle for the drive along narrow country roads to Craig-y-Nos.

Madame Patti Nicolini, as she was now called, and Signor Nicolini greeted all the guests and the artists and offered them refreshment in the winter garden. On the programme that evening were the first act of *La Traviata* with Adelina's Violetta being supported by local singers, an Entr'Acte by the orchestra and then act III of *Faust* with Ernesto singing the title role and of course Adelina as Margherita. To the diva it was all a game, light entertainment, but her audience took the whole affair as seriously as though they were at Covent Garden. The orchestra was mostly made up of Swansea amateurs and was conducted by her old friend Luigi Arditi who was a house guest with his Irish wife. Local enthusiasm for this event ran high. To have the chance of appearing on the same stage as Madame Patti was an undreamed-of privilege.

Before the music started it was planned for the famous actor Henry Irving to make an inaugural speech. As things turned out he was detained at the last minute and sent his protégé, the young actor William Terriss, who managed to learn the long, elaborately worded address in just two hours. A hush fell in the little theatre as he stood in front of the curtains.

"Ladies and Gentlemen", he began, "I stand here as the humble and inadequate "representative of the first of living English actors. It had been the intention of Mr Henry Irving to signalise his appreciation of Madame Adelina Patti's transcendent talent as singer and actress, and to mark his strong sense of the close alliance connecting the musical and dramatic arts, by speaking a few inaugural words on this occasion – one that is unique in operatic and theatrical annals alike. For we are met here to be present at an initial performance held in a theatre which, at the generous behest of the Queen of Song, has been erected and provided with every mechanical appliance perfected by modern science in the very heart of a wild Welsh valley, teeming with the beauties of nature, but remote from the busy haunts of men. "As far as Mr Irving is concerned, circumstances have intervened rendering his personal participation in tonight's celebration impracticable. He has, however, empowered me as his envoy, and I have been accepted in that character for the performance of this agreeable and sympathetic duty by our gracious and gifted hostess, the chatelaine of Craig-y-Nos – the good fairy who haunts the 'Rock of Night' –the true friend of the poor whose benefactions have for a dozen years past ripened unnumbered throughout the length and breadth of this picturesque region. In this beautiful theatre, dedicated to the allied arts and adorned with the counterfeit presentments of great musicians and dramatists, you will this evening be privileged to listen to that incomparable voice which ever binds its hearers in a spell of wonder and delight. I will not retard your supreme enjoyment by further dilating on the attractions of that which you have your eyes to see and ears to hear, but will conclude my grateful task by declaring the Patti Theatre open for the late summer season of 1891".

After the applause had died down, Arditi raised his baton and the Swansea Orchestra began to play the nostalgic prelude to Verdi's *Traviata*. Electric lighting, a great innovation, illuminated the scene as a slim and youthful Adelina appeared on stage dressed in pink satin embroidered in white and trimmed with roses, afire with an array of diamonds such as most of those present had never seen or even dreamed of. She was a sensation and according to the local newspaper the next day, "Her superb voice fairly electrified her hearers, accustomed as they are to hearing artistes of the highest rank". They were carried away and Patti's "unrivalled genius" asserted itself again.

Later, in a magical afterglow, everyone sat down to supper entertained by their host and hostess and a vote of thanks was proposed by the local Member of Parliament (that same Sir Hussey Vivian who had first shown them Craig-y-Nos). Her little theatre had functioned perfectly. One of its most spectacular features was the lighting system operated by a switchboard, "a wonderfully clever contrivance" as it was described in *The Cambrian*. This switchboard controlled a total of 281 lights including footlights, limelights, wing and ground lights and a thirty-bulb chandelier, as well as the illuminations in the main part of the theatre.

No expense had been spared. Scenery, mostly painted by Mr Halley and Mr Rigo from London, was sufficient to stage thirty different operas and was stored in a scene dock by the side of the stage, high enough so that it did not have to be rolled. Below the stage was a room with machinery and props, and more props were stored in a loft above. There were elaborately furnished dressing rooms with divan beds so that they could be turned into extra guest rooms on the first and second floors.

In a day when electricity was only installed in public buildings and even gas lighting was frowned on as being "vulgar" by owners of large houses, who preferred to pay at least three lamp-and-candle men to take care of their old-fashioned illuminations, almost every room in Craig-y-Nos was lit by electricity. An underground boiler and engine near the winter garden drove electricity to a dynamo which then sent it by cable to a switchboard and then on to fourteen accumulators in an adjoining building. From here it was carried by heavy cable to the castle, the winter garden and the theatre as well as to several electric motors. One of these motors fan-dried the larders and another drove the large Orchestrion in the billiard room. There were auxiliary dynamos driven by gas for emergencies so that there was never any fear of a blackout. I am going into all these details to show you the perfect efficiency of a Patti-run house, a trait also reflected in her general life.

Before lunch Adelina enjoyed a stroll in the lofty glass winter garden, calculating twenty times around it to the mile. Here she also dined with her guests on fine summer evenings. At the south end of the top gardens, past the conservatory to which it was connected by a covered passageway, and in front of the rows of greenhouses and vineries, the winter garden was furnished with a scattering of bentwood rockers and cane and wood tables and chairs. One wall was lined with large potted palms and exotic plants. The east side was left clear to give an unbroken view down across the valley to the River Tawe. Here and there it was enlivened by parrots and cockatoos in their hanging and standing cages. Unlike the rest of the house that was furnished in the overpowering Victorian style, heavy with furniture and drapes, the winter garden was not too cluttered and with its central fountain illuminated at night the effect was of light, airy elegance.

Adelina had a passion for her exotic birds and always stopped to talk to them. Usually they were housed in the aviary at the far end but when she was in residence and there were guests they were brought out to occupy their cages. Pinky and Jacky were particularly friendly parrots and said, "Come in", when she tapped on the doors of their cages and then bowed to her and said, "Madame Patti, good morning!" as they had been taught. In these blissfully carefree days she was so carried away that she even made enquiries into the possibility of housing a family of monkeys in the garden. Luckily for the garden, and probably because of the damp Welsh winters, she was dissuaded.

She also had several much-loved little dogs who had their own small house near the laundry on the north side. There was a servant whose only duty was to look after them and exercise them. Each one had his own basket and chest-of-drawers personalised with his or her name – Fifi, Mabs, Kaiser, Beauty and Ricci. And every morning they had a fresh ribbon tied on and were taken to see "Mummy", jumping all over her and barking delightedly until it was time for their morning walk.

Meanwhile, Adelina's career was not neglected and her vocal engagements began to settle into a pattern that was to continue until her retirement. There were the Albert Hall concerts and the provincial concerts organised by Percy Harrison (who had been arranging annual concerts for her in Birmingham since as far back as 1874). He now took over from Ambrose Austin as her official concert manager. She was paid a fixed sum of £600 for each appearance in the provinces and 800 guineas in London.

One exception to this routine had been her singing Juliet in French for the first time. She could not refuse when Monsieur Gailhard, Director of the Paris Opera, rushed over to Craig-y-Nos unannounced and unexpected, begging her to take on the part as a special favour to both himself and to Gounod, always her fervent admirer. She protested that she would only have two weeks in which to study the role in French and he left Wales without a definite answer but was overjoyed to receive her telegram forty-eight hours later, "My Dear Colleague – I was deeply touched by your visit to me at Craig-y-Nos. You invite me to assist in the performance of an artistic masterpiece conducted by the maître himself. My answer is yes. Patti"[21].

She studied the part hard and was word perfect. This was her first appearance in Paris since her separation from Henri and public and

---

21   Gounod, who was overcome by this unexpected stroke of luck.

critics alike were enchanted. She was described as "looking positively more youthful than when she had last sung the part at Covent Garden a dozen years before". It was also reported that "from a dramatic point of view, the famous artist that night took the sternest of French critics by surprise and not a word was uttered or written save in unstinted admiration".

There was another record-breaking tour in North and South America in the Winter and Spring of 1889–90 under the excellent business management of Henry Abbey and Maurice Grau. In Buenos Aires her fee was £1,250 a night plus £2,400 – half the box office takings…and this was well over a century ago.

Again she travelled in her own luxury railway carriages emblazoned with her name, a spectacle which people came running from miles away to see. Her monogram entwined with flowers decorated every room. Her salon suite was upholstered in pale blue velvet, her bedroom inlaid with satinwood and complete with brass bedstead and embroidered and monogrammed coverlet, and, naturally, there was also a piano, a bath and all comforts including electricity. She took her own Italian chef from Craig-y-Nos and her favourite dog. Her most important and enthusiastic audiences were in Chicago, where she appeared in December 1889 in the recently completed eight- million-dollar auditorium and in Mexico City where the rich section of society showered her with costly gifts including a solid gold crown. President Diaz and his wife, to show their admiration, gave her a pair of ruby and diamond earrings, and she was said to have earned £32,000 altogether for a total of forty-three appearances.

On the sea voyage back to Liverpool from New York Adelina caught a severe cold, the result of not being well enough wrapped up against the Atlantic wind during her walks on deck. This was bad news, especially since she had an important engagement at the Albert Hall on May 14th. This time she did not want to let her public down. Against her better judgement and Ernesto's remonstrations, she insisted on going ahead and singing although she was hoarse and had a sore throat. The audience did not understand what was going on when she substituted easier pieces for those on the programme and gave them just one encore of 'Home Sweet Home', although they shouted loudly for more. For perhaps the very first time she strained her voice so badly that she was forced to cancel the next concert scheduled for June and to take a complete rest.

A warning bell had sounded. She was just three years off fifty. Her adult career had proceeded uninterrupted for thirty years. Her lovely voice had reached its apex but from now on, year by year, little by little, she was to reduce its range, lower the register and concentrate on the medium tones which were now reported to be "more rich, more resonant than before". A journalist wrote, "The tones that had so long enraptured the musical public were found as bright and rich as ever. What if the extreme notes be not so elastic or ready at command as they once were, what if the daring flights of vocalisation be less spontaneous, there is surely compensation afforded in the increase of volume, in the ripe mellowness of the middle and lower registers".

The public clamoured for her but from now on she rationed her appearances out wisely. As she was to tell an interviewer some ten years later, "The whole harm to a voice comes in pushing it up and down, in trying to add notes to its compass", and, "High gymnastics are very beautiful but lose the middle notes and you lose it all. The very high and the very low notes are the ornaments, but what good are Gobelins and pictures if you have no house to hang them in?"

★★★

After the official opening of her theatre, Adelina's house party went on for several days. In her guest rooms she offered hospitality to the Spanish Ambassador, Baron Julius de Reuter (founder of the international news agency), Edward Lawson, owner of the *Daily Telegraph* and Graham Vivian, Lord Swansea's younger brother, as well as many other distinguished guests. The theatre floor was raised to the level of the stage and the following night it was transformed into a ballroom and the diva waltzed with her guests until the small hours. The Rock of Night rang out with such music, festivity and laughter as it had never heard before.

In those happy days at Craig-y-Nos there was never a dull moment. Life went with the same swing as Adelina's Viennese waltz. A week after the inauguration they put on a matinée performance, the third act of *Martha* and the balcony scene from *Romeo and Juliet*. Being a matinée it enabled people to come up to the castle for the day so they had sent out many invitations and the theatre was packed full with enthusiastic Welsh friends. The set programme was followed by one of Adelina's favourite encores, 'The Last Rose of Summer' which she sang first in English and then in Italian, and 'Il Bacio' (The Kiss) the lilting waltz which Luigi Arditi had written specially for her.[22] Ernesto seemed to be back in good voice again – his once fine tenor had hardened and recently he had cut his singing down drastically – and Adelina was in her usual sparkling form, "…rendering the music of Juliet as no other living artist can render it" and "With more passion and grandeur than when I heard her last in this character at the Paris Opera nearly three years ago".[23]

Luigi Arditi first met Adelina when she was a child during a visit to the Patti home in New York. Caterina Barili, Adelina's mother, was anxious for him to hear her child sing and he says, "Her determined little airs and manners then already showed plainly that she was destined to become a ruler of men… she demurely placed her music on the piano and asked me to accompany her in the rondo of *Sonnambula*". The effect "that child's miraculous notes" had on the Italian conductor was devastating and he "wept genuine tears of emotion", her voice "stirred his innermost feelings with its extraordinary power and beauty". He was "simply amazed, nay, electrified, at the well-nigh perfect manner in which she delivered some of the most difficult and varied arias without the slightest effort or self-consciousness".

Everyone agreed that Adelina was a charming hostess but sometimes she was too energetic. She admitted that she could not bear sitting still and doing nothing, and she "could not tolerate indolence of thought or manner in those around her". She kept her guests on their toes, organising their days and evenings and keeping them very much awake with her lively conversation.

Her biographer and fervent admirer, Herman Klein, was a frequent visitor at the castle during this period and, while enjoying their conversations together ,he found her strangely reticent to talk about herself or her past. She would willingly discuss her colleagues or

---

22  Luigi Arditi, *My Reminiscences*, 1896

23  Herman Klein, *The Reign of Patti*

various celebrities, some of whom she admired, others she criticised, and talked about them freely saying, "I have confidence in your discretion". Klein finds this reluctance to discuss her past "singularly modest" for someone with such a glorious career behind her. She did speak of her childhood and of her early days in New York when they stood her on a table and she astonished them with her *Casta Diva* but her reminiscences went no further.

Perhaps he never guessed that while walking with him in the gardens or around the winter garden, chatting and relaxed as they admired the parrots and cockatoos or the peacocks strutting on the terraces, she was afraid of letting slip some secret from her past. She preferred to keep the conversation on safe and neutral ground, discussing her plans for the day and the evening's entertainment.

Together with Klein and Augustus Spalding, an old friend whose experience as an amateur actor proved invaluable, she got up a pantomime, which in those days was a comic mime show with lively music that was about to become all the rage. Mr Hulley and some of his Swansea musicians were called in, and after raiding the hampers of wigs and costumes with which the theatre was well stocked, they put on such a hilarious show that the audience was doubled up with laughing.

Adelina's day at the castle did not begin early. She liked to lie in an hour or two longer and have a leisurely breakfast in bed before sitting down at her desk and attending to her correspondence. After this she had made a regular habit of practicing her scales for at least half an hour, sometimes accompanying herself on her new toy, a zither. If anyone was strolling in the gardens below they could enjoy the trilling scales and cadenzas that floated out of her window and across the valley.

Her guests spent the day pleasantly enough, the men shooting duck or pheasant with Ernesto or fishing in the river, with perhaps a game of tennis in the afternoon. The ladies took carriage rides, enjoyed a game of croquet in front of the summer house or boated on the pond.

The highlight of the day was dinner in the winter garden, the hostess at the head of the long table always elegant in one of her latest Paris gowns and matching jewellery, the guests sitting down either side and Ernesto at the foot. Adelina was adept at carrying the conversation along in several languages, laughing and joking in her clipped, precise

English with frequent interruptions in French to Ernesto, asking his opinion with an *"Entends-tu, mon ami?"* to which he invariably replied, intent on his dinner and his champagne, *"Oui, ma mignonne"*.

These were times when champagne flowed liberally. Silver and crystal glinted under the bright electric lights, fruit bowls were piled with peaches grown in the peach house under the kitchen garden wall and grapes from the Vinery on the south side. The table was decorated with roses or orchids and gardenias from the hothouse, and the Italian chef prepared cordon-bleu dishes which were served by footmen under the watchful eye of Longo the butler. Dinner usually went on for a couple of hours.

Afterwards they broke the custom of men remaining at the table smoking and passing the port while the ladies adjourned, a stuffily British habit not to Adelina's taste. Instead, the gentlemen rose with the ladies and escorted them through the morning room and the hall to the new north wing, on through the dining room to the billiard room. Here the ladies leant back on cushioned divans, coffee was served and it would be Ernesto (he allowed no one else to touch it) who put rolls of music into the Orchestrion. He had given up smoking by now but he kept a special stock of cigars for the men. Conversation mingled with the click of billiard balls, fragrant cigar smoke mixed with coffee and the heady scent of flowers, and over them all flowed the rich organ music of the Orchestrion.

In this relaxed after-dinner atmosphere the temptation to sing was usually too great for Adelina to resist and, at first softly and then gathering volume, her voice wove a spell of nostalgic beauty that her listeners would never forget. When Adelina sang to them it was an emotion that went straight to the heart.

# 13

"She came, she sang, she conquered!" a journalist enthuses in *The Cambrian* on August 15th 1884. "Madame Patti came down from her pedestal to befriend the poor and destitute".

Shortly after Adelina's arrival in the Swansea Valley it had been suggested to her that in view of her great standing it might be advisable to give the occasional charity concert, hiring a local hall and paying the musicians and singers, especially since Swansea General Hospital was in debt and many other local charities were crying out for funds. After some hesitation she agreed and the first concert in Swansea raised the considerable sum of £830. It was a wise move. "In descending from the standpoint of fame to mix with the people amongst whom she dwelt, she ascended another throne – the throne of the affections of a grateful people" a local journalist writes.

Up until that time she had avoided giving "something for nothing" (apart from the traditional benefit nights expected of an opera star). From an early age she had been taught that if people wanted to hear her sing they had to pay, and pay in advance by 2pm the same day. She had a name for being egoistic and parsimonious and appeared to be as oblivious to the needs of the poor as a chrysalis in its silk cocoon.

Her whirlwind career had left little space for charity. If she had given in to one request she would have had to give in to another and yet another. The demands for her free services were countless and she had made a rule of refusing them all. But now, with London opera seasons a thing of the past and European tours reduced to a minimum, time was no longer such a problem. Always her own best public relations officer she realised the importance of winning over her new Welsh neighbours. Life had taken on a slower pace, she let herself relax in congenial surroundings, she was happy in her relationship with Ernesto and gradually the sharp corners of her character were smoothed and softened. Madame Patti's charity concerts were to become an annual event, alternating between three of the towns nearest to Craig-y-Nos, Swansea, Brecon and Neath. It was an occasion for public holidays when Wales' most famous citizen stepped down from her railway carriage at the station. She was met by local dignitaries and the mayor and escorted by a military band, her carriage cheered by crowds all the way to the town hall, the streets hung with bunting and flags. Speeches of welcome and of thanks and a gala luncheon – although she never ate much before a concert – preceded the performance. It was almost like being back in the Mapleson parades, but this was far more genuine and sincere. Naturally, Adelina revelled in the attention.

The ice broken, her popularity grew. In recognition of her services in 1897 she was made a Burgess of Brecon with a solemn ceremony, and many years later, in 1912, she was made a Freewoman of Swansea, becoming the only woman in Britain with the freedom of two boroughs.

It is not surprising that they began to call her the "second Queen of England". Her life was certainly far more brilliant and varied than that of Queen Victoria, by now weighed down with widowhood and mourning and the troubles of State and permanently dressed in black. Even the Queen's faithful retainer and friend John Brown had died and her days passed dimly behind the walls of Balmoral, Osborne and Windsor.

In the winters of 1892, 93 and 94 Adelina made three more American tours still under the management of Henry Abbey and Maurice Grau, now joint directors of the Metropolitan Opera House in New York. On the first of these tours she gave concerts which also included excerpts from opera in costume, and these were very popular, playing to packed houses with people pushing for standing room. She wound up in New York at the Metropolitan in what was to be her last appearance in America in complete operas, her well-loved *Lucia di Lammermoor* and *The Barber of Seville*.

The second tour was equally successful but the third appears to have been *"nato sotto una cattiva stella"*[24] Everything went wrong. She caught a bad cold on the outward voyage and had to cancel her first appearance in New York. There was also a financial crisis in America at the time. After a whole series of mishaps they sailed for England the day before she should have given her last concert so the tour wound up without its star. This caused a lot of criticism in the American press and a journalist who up until then had been one of her most fervent supporters wrote, "… That she was not well advised in taking this step there is no question. It left behind a very disagreeable impression".

Things went better in Europe. After a very successful season in Nice in January 1893 in her familiar roles of Rosina, Violetta and Juliet, she went on to Milan, probably with a little trepidation, to sing in *La Traviata* at Teatro alla Scala. Her old admirer the composer Giuseppe Verdi was there, busy with rehearsals for his new *Falstaff* and he was delighted to meet up with Adelina again. She need not have worried because this time at La Scala, a real testing ground, they gave her a royal reception with endless applause and standing ovations, her greatest triumph in that famous opera house. Verdi, who shared a box with Giulio Ricordi, the Milan music publisher, had tears running down his cheeks as Adelina sang, admitting that he found her divine.

Afterwards they travelled south to Florence, one of the cities touched on her romantic flight with Ernesto six years previously, and then back up to Nice where they enjoyed the Riviera sunshine until the middle of March. She carried on as usual with her provincial tours in England, her charity concerts in Wales and her summer appearances at the Albert Hall, her fees maintained at a high level. When the organisers of the Norwich Musical Festival wrote to her, perplexed by the sum she had requested, "Why such a fee at a musical festival?" back came her crisp reply, "I am a musical festival!"

In the early 1890s Adelina began a musical flirtation with Wagner. She was counted as being "the greatest living exponent of the old Italian school" (a form of opera that was by now beginning to tire some of her more critical fans), but after having heard his music in London she fell under its spell. Wagner was difficult to sing and she knew her

---

24  Born under an unlucky star

limitations; she never sang a Wagnerian role but she did sing *Traume* and Elisabeth's Prayer from *Tannhauser* in concert and in German.[25]

Beginning by trying out what she called some "singable" pieces in the privacy of her own home, sometimes accompanied on the Steinway grand piano in the billiard room, at other times by the Orchestrion, in 1894 she studied the song *Traume* in German. Her spoken German was fairly good but up to now she had never sung in that language. Pleased with the result she decided to include it in the programme at the Albert Hall on May 19th, confiding to a friend, "It is a beautiful song and I shall love to sing it, but there is not a single resting-place where I can stop to swallow. From first to last the voice goes on without interruption. It is that which fatigues, and it is one of the things that make Wagner hard to sing. Still, I shall do my best".

Her best was good enough. George Bernard Shaw was in the Press seats at the Albert Hall writing as a music critic under the pseudonym "Corno di Bassetto" and was most favourably impressed, reporting, "We live in an age of progress. Patti has been singing a song by Wagner… What is more, she sang it extremely well, and when the inevitable encore came, repeated it instead of singing 'Home, Sweet Home' or 'Within a Mile'".[26]

After the July concert when she sang Wagner again, George Bernard Shaw wrote, "Patti continued her new departure into Wagnerland by singing Elisabeth's prayer from *Tannhauser*. Now, if I express some scepticism as to whether Patti cares a snap of her fingers for Elisabeth or Wagner, I may after all these years of 'Una Voce' and 'Bel Raggio', be very well pardoned. But it is beyond all doubt that Patti cares most intensely for the beauty of her own voice and the perfection of her singing. What is the result? She attacks the prayer with the single aim of making it sound as beautiful as possible, and this being precisely what Wagner's own musical aim was, she goes straight to the right phrasing, the right vocal touch and the right turn of every musical figure, thus making her German rivals not only appear in comparison clumsy as singers, but actually obtuse as to Wagner's meaning".

He concludes in his usual dry way, "If the song were beautifully

---

25  A study on *Tristan and Isolde*, number five of Five Poems

26  George Bernard Shaw, "Music in London" Volume 111

sung, it simply could not take the wrong expression, and if Patti were to return to the stage and play Isolde, though she might very possibly stop the drama half a dozen times in each act to acknowledge applause and work in an encore – though she might introduce 'Home, Sweet Home' in the ship scene and 'The Last Rose of Summer' in the garden scene – though nobody would be in the least surprised to see her jump up out of her trance in the last act to run to the footlights for a basket of flowers, yet the public might learn a good deal about Isolde from her which they will never learn from any of the illustrious band of German Wagner heroines who are queens at Bayreuth but who cannot sing a *gruppetto* for all that."

Shaw deplores the fact that she had wasted so much of her career on her hackneyed old Rossini pieces before attempting to sing Wagner. Whilst loving her voice he had criticised her in the past for courting applause, for being capable of jumping up from a deathbed scene to collect a bouquet and for the haphazard mix of music presented at her concerts. In spite of these observations he was one of her admirers and writes that she was by now "the most accomplished of mezzo-sopranos". Time had "transposed Patti a minor third down, but the middle of her voice is still even and beautiful and this, with her unsurpassed phrasing and that delicate touch and expressive nuance which make her cantabile singing so captivating, enables her to maintain what was, to my mind, always the best of her old supremacy".

These two Wagnerian pieces were now included on the programme during her concert tours in the provinces. Her public was happy because Wagner's music was becoming extremely popular in Britain.

In early December 1894 Adelina received a command to sing privately before Queen Victoria at Windsor Castle. She had always had a great affection for the Queen and accepted with joy. Wilhelm Ganz, by now her regular accompanist, went with her and she recounted, "Her Majesty received me with the utmost amiability and expressed great pleasure at hearing me again after many years. She conversed with me in the sweetest manner between each of my pieces. Naturally at the end I sang 'Home, Sweet Home' and I could see that it brought tears to the dear Queen's eyes. She was really deeply moved".

Adelina was invited to spend the night at the castle to avoid a tiring late journey back to town and the next day she was delighted to receive a signed photo and a royal brooch with crown and monogram which she was to prize for the rest of her life. At a fun-packed Christmas party fortnight at Craig-y-Nos, Herman Klein broached the subject of another operatic season at Covent Garden, an idea he had been cultivating with Sir Augustus Harris who had restored the theatre to some of its former splendour. He had received permission from Adelina's concert manager, Percy Harrison, and now the only real difficulty was to persuade the diva herself. She was reluctant to return to Covent Garden after an absence of ten years and nervous at the prospect of confronting a London public again.

"Everyone is pining to hear you in opera just once again," Klein told her.

"Everybody? The old subscribers, the *vieille garde,* perhaps. But there is a new generation at Covent Garden now. Are they equally interested?" she asked.

Ernesto's emphatic "No!" to the proposal did not help matters, but Adelina promised Klein that she would talk it over with her husband and her manager, and a week later she met Sir Augustus Harris on Paddington Station on her way to the Continent, tucked her arm into his, and the matter was settled.

Her appearance as Violetta in *La Traviata* on June 11<sup>th</sup> was a sensation. The Covent Garden season had already been underway for a month with Madame Melba and the tenor Jean de Reszke (who had been a revelation as Romeo to Adelina's Juliet in Paris) but now the London public was galvanised at the prospect of hearing the diva Patti in a full-length opera. They wanted Patti, only Patti. The magic of her name still had great drawing power and there was a rush for tickets at any price, just like in the good old days. Every seat was sold out days before the performance and the 'old guard' began to form a queue at the gallery entrance before midday. That night the house was packed with a glittering crowd including the Prince and Princess of Wales, Bertie and Alix, their three daughters and the Duke and Duchess of York, (later King George V and Queen Mary) in the royal box.

When she was young she had hardly ever suffered from nerves. Famous for her *sang froid*, stage fright was something almost unknown, apart from those times she had to stand a real test such as at La Scala, Milan. Singing had always been her greatest joy and facing a friendly audience a delight, but now her stomach churned at the prospect of standing on the stage of Covent Garden again. She was very much aware of the fact that she was now fifty-two years old, an age at which most prima donnas are long past their prime. She asked herself over and over again whatever had made her agree to it. What if it should be a terrible fiasco? She simply could not bear the thought of criticism, after all she had already accomplished everything and she had nothing more to prove either to herself or to the public. But by now it was too late to turn back. In her own words, she said, "When I made my entry, when I looked across the footlights at the familiar picture, as I went on bowing again and again, while the storm of applause seemed as if it would never cease, I felt more like breaking down and crying than singing. But after we had sat down to the supper-table and De Lucia had begun the 'Libiamo' I suddenly regained my confidence and courage. I never lost them again. I think I never sang my 'Libiamo' better!" The old Patti magic wove its spell again. Still incredibly youthful, slim and graceful, she now sang Violetta with such dramatic power, her voice still pure and fresh, that she amazed those in the audience who had heard her a quarter of a century before in that very same theatre.

To celebrate this return, and perhaps to give herself a little courage, the idea had come to her to wear a diamond-studded bodice on her white dress in the ball scene in Act III. With almost careless courage she had the largest diamonds from her collection, 3,500 stones, removed from their settings by a leading Paris jeweller and sewn on to the front and back of a cuirass so as to completely cover her corsage. The effect was of such sparkling light that its brilliance was on a level only with its value. It was reported that no thought of vulgar ostentation crossed her mind but that she looked on the gesture as a gift to the audience. She had a special escort to and from the theatre, a guard outside her dressing room and two Bow Street police officers in costume mingled with the extras on stage to watch the treasure as it danced and shone under the lights. She wore this marvel for two performances, after which the same jeweller put all the stones back into their original settings.

After Violetta she starred in *The Barber of Seville* and *Don Giovanni*, with good supporting artists. The season ended as a success for the impresario Augustus Harris and carried away by her good fortune she promised him she would repeat the exploit the following year, but before this could take place he died prematurely and the plan was left abandoned in mid-air.

The rounds of concerts continued as usual and later that year included a trip to Ireland where she appeared in Dublin and Belfast.

At Craig-y-Nos there was a constant buzz of activity in Adelina's theatre. She cajoled her guests into taking part in a series of mime-plays, her latest craze. After a comic *Bluebeard* and a serious *Tosca* (based on a play by Sardou, not Puccini's opera which was not performed until 1900), it was the turn of *Mirka L'Enchantresse* which had been specially created for her by Georges Boyer, a journalist from *Le Figaro* and Secretary of the Paris Opera. She was exceptionally good at this new art form, now comic, now tragic, communicating emotions, actions and plot without a word being spoken, to appropriate accompanying music. So much so that after two performances of Mirka at Craig-y-Nos she took it to Paris for a charity benefit at the "Gaiete" and then on to Nice and Montecarlo. It was a piece of light-hearted nonsense but in Paris it brought in 30,000 francs.

With 'Mirka' behind her she enthusiastically started rehearsing another mime-play at Craig-y-Nos, based on East Lynn. All this time Ernesto, her best supporting actor, had joined in the fun and games with his little 'Bohemienne', encouraging her as one encourages a mischievous child. But now when he saw her on stage as the widow and dressed in black, he turned pale with anger. It was an "ill omen" and would bring them "very bad luck". But Adelina just laughed at his superstitions and took no notice. In 1896 she gave a Charity concert in Cardiff for the first time. In a letter to her American niece Marie Brooks, after having described her triumphs on the Riviera and how the Czarevitch[27] was so happy to have heard her sing again that he gave her a signed photo, she goes on to write, "I am going to give my Charity concert at Cardiff, which I think will be an "exceptionally grand affair, as it will be the first time I have sung there for charity – my concert was to have been given in Swansea but owing to the impertinent interference of some of the Swansea Committee, who upset all the arrangements, I declined to sing there and am giving the concert in Cardiff instead, but I have arranged that part of the proceeds of the concert shall go to

---

27   Future ill-fated Tsar Nicolas II

the Swansea hospital and the poor of the district as I do not want them to suffer for the stupidity of the Swansea Committee". The reason for this change-about was that someone had inadvisedly decided to lower the price of tickets for the Swansea matinee. Ernesto, when informed, brought it to his wife's notice and she took it as a personal slight. She was indignant. Luckily Ernesto thought of remedying the situation by contacting the Cardiff authorities who were only too pleased to organise a concert in their city.

Herman Klein was as usual a summer guest at Craig-y-Nos and Adelina begged him to accompany them and make a speech in reply to the vote of thanks. He asked, "Why not Monsieur Nicolini?"

"You are joking. You know what his English is like and he cannot make a speech even in French. Besides his health is not good enough for him to make the effort. No, I shall depend on you" she insisted.

With a very good cast of supporting singers the first Cardiff Charity Concert went magnificently and they netted in £800. Adelina brought the house down when she promised the audience that she intended, with the help of two Welsh singers, to learn 'Land of My Fathers' in Welsh. She could not have paid them a greater compliment. A few days later Adelina organised a matinée at her theatre, to which she had invited a large party of friends, and after a new mime and an Ave Maria she persuaded Ernesto to sing with her the duet from Act 1V of *Romeo and Juliet*. Klein writes, "Her singing that day was exceptionally magnificent, but her husband betrayed his growing physical weakness and barely managed to pull through the long duet. It was the last time I ever heard him upon the stage. He had been my first Faust, my first Romeo, my first Radames, my first Lohengrin, and this was the end!"

★★★

When she was young, Adelina had perfected the art of closing her eyes to any unpleasantness and shutting it away in a secret compartment of her mind where it would lie forgotten, like an old garment put away in a trunk in the attic. It stayed there but she never thought about it.

The outward signs of Ernesto's increasingly poor health were plain enough: the flesh had fallen from his fine figure and his once dashing, debonair good looks were almost gone. His face had taken on a thin, gaunt look and even his voice was weaker. Everything cost him an effort. Refusing to think it was anything serious she put his growing weakness down to his age. He would be sixty-three in February and had led an active and intense life so it was hardly surprising that he was not as strong as he had once been. She was confident that a stay on the French Riviera would help him get his strength back. Adelina's hopes were short-lived. Instead of recovering, his condition grew worse and when they returned to London she decided at last that it was time to call in a specialist. The diagnosis was devastating. Ernesto was suffering from such a complication of kidney, liver and lung disorders that there was little hope of his getting better. This time the truth hit her hard and could not be ignored and she suffered with him, never leaving his side, until he managed to gather enough strength to leave the Hotel Cecil for the journey down to South Wales. At Craig-y-Nos they moved him into a separate bedroom.

Recently the physical side of their marriage had slowed down almost to a standstill, but nevertheless she missed him at nights. Waking up suddenly from a bad dream, her heart pounding, when she reached out and found he was not there she would throw a shawl around her shoulders and creep quietly into his room and sit by his bedside until dawn. He needed her constantly in his room and sat propped up against the cushions for hours devouring her every movement with his eyes while she kept up a flow of chatter to distract him from his thoughts. Gradually his health seemed to improve. He missed his outdoor life and longed to get out into the grounds again with his gun slung over his shoulder. Sometimes he spent hours poring over catalogues of guns and fishing tackle.

"Just think of all those fish and I can't go fishing! And all those ducks and I can't go shooting!" he exclaimed one day.

"Never mind, they will wait for you," she said. William Armstrong who was their guest at the time reported this episode, adding, "The enchanting flirt that she gave to her white parasol made even the dying man grin".[28] Occasionally he asked her to bring him one of his precious violins from the collection he had picked up on his travels, mostly in

---

28  A journalist to whom Adelina had confided some of her secrets on singing which he later published as *Madame Patti's Advice to Singers* in 1903.

America, and attempted a few notes on his favourite Stradivarius. But even this was impossible. He had never been more than a mediocre player and the only time that Adelina could remember the Strad being played divinely was a few years ago when the great violinist August Wilhelmj had been their guest. Although by then he had retired, he had still been able to make the Stradivarius and the Guarnerius sing for them with Clara Eissler accompanying him on the harp. Now Ernesto caressed the polished wood of his violins and regretfully replaced them in their cases.

Adelina's thoughts wandered while she sat by Ernesto's bedside. They had been so happy together, he had looked after her so well and was still utterly devoted to her. The only time they had quarrelled, or rather one of the few times she had lost patience with him, was when he first had the idea of raising pheasants on the estate. The young birds were raised near the kitchen garden and she soon grew fond of them, calling them by name and feeding them corn. One afternoon she was sitting reading in the winter garden, completely absorbed in her book until she gradually realised that Ernesto's shots were coming closer and closer to the house. She had given him instructions that if he really must shoot (a sport which she abhorred) it had to be on the far side of the estate and well away from her eyes and ears, but now she had suddenly been startled by a shower of gunshot dropping on the glass roof above her head. She still remembered how livid she had been, running out into the garden and shouting at him to stop. It turned out that he had been shooting at his newly-raised pheasants on the far side of the river but the poor birds, terrified, had fled back to the safety of their kitchen garden with Ernesto at their heels. When the one bird he had bagged was served up for dinner some days later Adelina could not bring herself to touch it.

But what were a few pheasants compared with all the years of love and devotion he had given her? Their early years together had been wonderfully happy and it was difficult to resist a smile when she remembered her initial distaste for this blustering, over-talkative man and how her feelings had changed first to a liking and finally into an overriding passion. She owed him so much, he had taught her so much, and with Ernesto by her side her career had flourished. They had been the perfect duet.

Sometime later, seeing a change for the better, his doctors suggested that he might benefit from some sea air and he left for a holiday at Langland Bay near Swansea. Adelina preferred to sleep in her own bed at Craig-y-Nos and with the excuse that sea air upset her (never mentioned until now), travelled down to Swansea by train to be with him every day, returning home in the evening. After seven weeks he insisted on coming home, but after another relapse the doctors again advised a holiday by the sea, this time in the more bracing air of Brighton. Adelina stayed in London and visited him daily.

It was the year of Queen Victoria's Diamond Jubilee and she had several engagements in the city. At this point she was ready to give up her Autumn concert tour to be with her husband but after some weeks in Brighton his health again showed signs of improvement and they decided the tour could take place as usual. In September he left for Paris in the care of his son Richard, and Adelina saw him off on the boat train from Newhaven in fairly good spirits. When her tour was over she joined him for a brief stay in the south of France, but had to return to London for her concert at the Albert Hall on December 4th. It was almost a relief to be separated. She could not bear it any longer, watching him die, suffering without hope. It was becoming increasingly difficult for both of them to keep up the pretence that he would soon be better. Sadly, she spent Christmas and the New Year alone at Craig-y-Nos. With Ernesto's condition growing steadily worse, as a last resort he went to Pau in the French Pyrenees to take the waters. They telegraphed her to come and she reached his bedside just in time to say goodbye to her dear love for ever.

Ernesto died on January 18th 1898, a month before his sixty-fourth birthday. He was buried two days later and Adelina supervised the funeral arrangements. She spent the rest of the winter months and the spring in deep mourning, first at Sanremo on the Italian Riviera and then in London, seeing no one apart from one or two very close friends. When she next appeared in public on May 26th at the Albert Hall she was dressed entirely in black. Summoning all her courage she finally returned to Craig-y-Nos in mid-April.

The castle was empty and silent without Ernesto. A river of daffodils rippled around the lower lawns, wallflowers and forget-me-nots, her favourite flowers, bordered the terraces and formed little islands in the grass. Rose bushes were sprouting pinky-green leaves in readiness for their summer show but even the scents and colours of her gardens could not warm the coldness in her heart. Ernesto had filled all the corners of her life so completely for the last twenty years that now, alone, she hardly knew which way to turn. He had amused her, encouraged and admired her in everything she did, his unfailing love had buoyed her up and only now she realised just how much. He had been everything to her; above all together they had had *fun*. Now, wandering from room to room, in spite of all the luxury and the forty servants ready to spring at her slightest gesture, the castle was an empty and gloomy place. To make matters worse she had recently begun to suffer from rheumatism. It had started in a knee and when that passed off it moved to her shoulders and the pain was fastidious. She would have to look for a cure.

# 14

Baron Olaf Rudolf Cederstrom was the Swedish born owner of a military gymnasium in London. He was a tall, slim and rather austere figure with a classic profile, blue eyes and a sweeping blond moustache.

Friends had suggested to Adelina that with his massaging techniques he would be able to smooth away the rheumatic pain in her shoulders and, willing to try anything, she arranged to meet him on her return to London where she had an engagement to sing with the Handel Orchestra at Crystal Palace. She was anxious to be in good form for this big occasion. It was estimated that there would be an audience of nearly 23,000.

Cederstrom agreed to treat her rheumatism and when he massaged away her pain with his strong but gentle hands, it was as though, slowly, some of the pain in her soul began to slip away too. She decided that she had spent enough time in mourning and on her next public appearance at the Albert Hall in July it was noticed that she was no longer dressed in black.

That summer the baron was a guest at Craig-y-Nos. She found his company pleasantly soothing. They spent many hours together rowing on the little lake, feeding the swans or taking leisurely walks in the woods while she told him the story of her life. In spite of his youth – he was only twenty-eight – he had an air of quiet authority, a reliability and strength that she found attractive. She began to lean on him and to seek his opinion and approval on the various matters that they discussed. Almost before she realised it, she had fallen in love again.

She presented him to her startled friends backstage at a concert at the Albert Hall on November 14th. It was a raw, chill, foggy evening and the only bright thing in sight was her smile. Brimming over with happiness like a young girl, she introduced him. "This is Baron Cederstrom, my fiancé!" The young man stood quietly at her side, a proud smile on his face as he shook hands with her friends and admirers who were too polite to show their astonishment.

The *Manchester Guardian* came out with the news the following day: "The most interesting fact in connection with the Patti concert at the Albert Hall tonight was that during the interval the prima donna seized the opportunity to privately inform her friends of her intention to get married again. The engagement will not be formally announced for some time, for scarcely a full year has elapsed since the death of M. Nicolini, but I am in a position to state that the happy man is Baron Cederstrom, a Swede of high family, who was a visitor at Craig-y-Nos Castle during the recent summer holidays. The wedding will, according to present arrangements, take place in February".

As things turned out they did not wait until February but were married on 25th January 1899 in the Roman Catholic church at Brecon. This time there were no wedding festivities. They celebrated with a private wedding breakfast on the train to London and three days later left for the Riviera and Italy where they spent the rest of the winter.

★★★

After her marriage Adelina's lifestyle took on more muted tones. Her naturally bubbly personality was subdued under a cloak of ladylike calm. The baron did not approve of her friends – musicians, journalists and a miscellany of European nobility – calling them "hangers-on".

The era of lavish entertaining at her castle was over, the doors closed firmly on the outside world. Perhaps she did not really mind. Ernesto had been stimulating, encouraging her into constant activity and cheering her on from the sidelines. Now she could take life more slowly. Rolf was kind and gentle, handsome, young and titled. Adelina could never resist a title. He would take care of her for the rest of her days. Delightedly the new Baroness Cederstrom ordered a new trousseau from the nuns of a French convent – sheets, pillow cases, tablecloths and napkins in the finest linen all hand sewn and embroidered with her new monogram surmounted by a coronet. Her underwear too was handmade, lace-edged and monogrammed with a crown, right down to the last pair of pantalettes!

Her career, too, ended with her third marriage The concerts continued but she no longer felt the need to strive for success. On May 19th 1899 she reappeared in public at the Albert Hall. She still sang well enough, she still looked youthful and agile as she repeated her old favourites from Italian opera and her ballads, the public still went away happy and convinced that they had had their money's worth, but from now on her voice was on a gentle downhill slope. Not many seemed to be aware of this yet because after a charity performance at Covent Garden in 1900 in front of the Prince and Princess of Wales, the *Sunday Times* reported: "She sang encores after each of her operatic airs, and lavished the full measure of her genius upon a delighted and astonished crowd. I say 'astonished' because the word fitly expressed the feelings with which the old opera habitués gazed upon the still young-looking face of the diva and listened to the ever-fresh tones of her incomparable voice".

The new century saw Adelina Patti still firmly seated on the throne of the Queen of Song, with few possible rivals. She now measured out her concerts more sparingly, limiting her Albert Hall appearances to two a year instead of four and cutting down her travels on tour in the provinces. As for her voice, Klein writes, "The watchful and expert observer could alone perceive the significance of the modifications that were now taking place. So slow, so gradual were they as to be almost imperceptible And so long as the velvety tones remained, so long as the delicious 'legato' and the indescribable Patti manner continued in evidence, what did Londoners care? An extra breath here and there, a transposition of a semitone down or maybe two, "fewer excursions – and those very 'carefully' managed – above the top line of the treble stave, some diminution of resonant power or of sustained vigour in the higher medium notes – what were these, after all, but trifles when one could still derive so much pleasure from the superlative qualities that Patti, and Patti alone, possessed?"

★★★

165

She was beginning to have problems with her health. The rheumatism had come back in spite of Rolf's loving massage and now she began to suffer from neuralgia. The doctors put these troubles down to the damp climate of South Wales and in particular the Swansea Valley where she had her home.

Against her better judgement, Rolf persuaded her to put Craig-y-Nos up for sale so that they could move to a warmer climate. The castle was well heated by hot water pipes but not even Rolf could dissuade her from walking out of doors whenever she felt like it, summer and winter, or from sleeping with her window open.

Widely advertised by the chosen estate agents, Craig-y-Nos was described as "a picturesque country seat most substantially built of stone in more than one style" and "in the first rank of British mansions". Externally it was by now a hotch-potch of mock Gothic with squat side wings, but inside it was luxurious. It was put up for sale with its rich fittings and furniture and even her well-loved Orchestrion, which was estimated at £3,000, "about 18 ft. high and perhaps the finest ever built and of remarkably beautiful and effective tone". They asked a very high price for the entire property and, to Adelina's secret relief, received no adequate offers. So she kept her castle and never thought of selling it again.

★★★

In 1903 when Adelina was sixty, she made what was probably the greatest professional mistake of her life. Carried away by the girlish enthusiasm that had never been very far below the surface, when her old friend Marcus Mayer suggested the possibility of yet another (this time very last) farewell tour in America, she recklessly agreed. She was optimistic, riding gaily on the waves of past popularity on the other side of the Atlantic, and signed the contract that had been drawn up with Robert Grau, Maurice Grau's younger brother. He was to be her manager for the tour with the assistance of Marcus Mayer. This tour was scheduled to last six months with a total of sixty concerts, the terms they offered her were excellent and her stage appearances were to be brief with just two pieces in every concert and a limited number of encores. It seemed well within her reach.

She arrived in New York in high spirits and called a press conference at her hotel in the afternoon so as to receive all the journalists in a bunch and face the fire of their questioning in one go. So as well as inventing press releases some years previously, it may well be that she also invented press conferences.

It took all her tact and *savoir faire* to parry their sometimes too-personal questions. She stressed how happy she was to be back in New York and how this was to be her real and definite farewell tour and their articles the following day were enthusiastic and excellent publicity. The first concert was to be held at the Carnegie Hall on November 4th. With the passing of the years she had become increasingly nervous before facing the public and now she was sick with nerves. Suddenly all her optimism was washed away in a flood of hideous doubts. She remembered the slights, the criticisms and her bitter flight from New York nine years before. They had been so unfair, particularly to Ernesto. She had shut away the unpleasantness all these years but now unhappy memories came back and she was afraid.

New Yorkers' tastes had changed since the days of her early triumphs. Although they still appreciated her Italian *coloratura* style of singing, according to Klein "They raved far more loudly over opulence of vocal tone and strenuous Wagnerian declamation". It was a critical audience that she faced that first night. They had applauded as she stepped out from the wings but she was not the figure that they had imagined. Two-thirds of them had probably never heard of Patti and others expected to see a glamorous young woman and hear the nightingale their fathers had raved about.

It was unfortunate that her voice chose this moment to desert her. She was almost strangled by nerves, her breath coming in gasps, and people in the back rows could hardly hear her. In desperation she managed to close with a passable encore of her old battlehorse 'Home, Sweet Home'.

One reporter wrote that, "The curious shortness of breath is explained by the photographs of Patti at that period; that wasp waist was ruinous to her vocal support, for surely no diva was ever more tightly corseted". The next day critics did not save her. Richard Aldrich said, "She had to reach desperately for high notes, even though her arias were transposed as much as a minor third; these notes were frequently taken with faulty intonation – and that by a singer whose ear in her prime had never let her lose the pitch by a hair's breadth; her runs and arpeggios were dull and uncertain; her trills were subdued and promptly cut off; her phrasing was short and disjointed, showing failure of breath".[29]

Even Klein, her greatest fan, remarks, "Her voice did not carry so well as usual in the big hall, although its lovely quality was unchanged."

Richard Aldrich sums the whole fiasco up adequately: "It was a matter of regret to her sincerest admirers ten years ago that she saw fit to return then, and it must be a matter of much deeper regret that she has come again now to exploit upon the concert stage – very parsimoniously and very cautiously, it is true – the remains of what was once the most perfect, the most beautiful of voices, the most exquisite and consummate art in singing. It is unfortunate that the great artist has not been willing to leave us with memories of achievements which were, in their own particular way, worthy to be put with the supreme traditions of art; that she should be brought, by any temptation, however alluring, to play upon unthinking curiosity by her distinguished name and to a 'last chance' see and hear what have already gone into the history of art".

We do not know if Adelina read these reviews or gave them a quick glance, but if she did read them it had the effect of spurring her on to do better. By the time the next concert came round on the Wednesday she had recovered enough to regain her voice, most of her breath, and her habitual aplomb. Unfortunately the negative newspaper reports had been read and her public was not too warm. In Philadelphia they had to postpone the performance because not enough tickets had been sold and it was not until they reached Chicago that things began to go better. At the end her 'Home, Sweet Home' had the audience spellbound. Armstrong wrote, "People… would bend forward in breathless silence as if fearful of losing a single note, and when she ended, a long sigh preceded the frantic outburst of applause".

Apart from this, she was criticised for having accepted to sing such a limited repertoire and above all because every performance had to include (in agreement with a Broadway songwriter) a song which was described as "deplorably tasteless". But to Adelina, supported by Rolf

---

29   Richard Aldrich, Music Critic on the *New York Times*

(whose love of money seems to have surpassed even hers) it was all a profitable business arrangement.

Four months and forty performances later, the tour came to an end. As usual, she wound up in New York. For her last appearance the box office takings were just $3,180 and in true old Patti fashion she refused to sing until the agreed sum of $5,000 had been paid to her in advance. She waited at her hotel, the audience growing restive, until Robert Grau borrowed the difference from friends.

Outwardly calm and serene, helped by her acting talent, she tried not to show that she was lacerated inside. That she should receive such a humiliation, and in New York of all places! Where were the cheering crowds, the stamping and clapping and endless applause, the masses of bouquets and the adoring public that she had counted on for this final send-off? The agonising truth came to her that she was *old* and New Yorkers were just not interested any more.

She managed to put on a brave show during the last few days in America. With a smile stamped on her face like a carnival mask she told everyone, "Oh, I am so happy! I shall soon be going home!" But no one was fooled. She left New York for the last time amidst great general embarrassment, her only consolation being that she had made a net profit of $50,000.

★★★

Hurt feelings and hurt pride slowly diminished once she was back in the serenity of her beautiful valley. It was difficult to maintain negative feelings in the lush green of the Brecon Beacons, in the luxury of her castle, in the joyous welcome she received from her dogs Mabs, Fifi, Kaiser, Recci and Beauty. Even the parrots and cockatoos seemed happy to see her again. She found flags and bunting hung out to greet her and the fountain in the winter garden lit up in a blaze of colour. One of her maids, Cecilia Page, recalled that she was in bed with influenza at the time and Madame Patti went up to her room to see her and took her grapes from the hothouse, later having chicken soup and her cure-all champagne sent up.

Recently Adelina had turned to religion for comfort. So many of her family and friends were dead by now and she fervently wanted to believe in an after-life. A few years before she had supervised the construction of her own small chapel inside the castle, a place to meditate and pray and be alone. Its quiet colours of blue, white and gold, the light oak wood, the fresh flowers that were always on the altar, all helped to soothe her spirit and give her courage. When Queen Victoria died in 1901 she held a memorial service on the day of her funeral with Father Vaughan saying mass and just a few close friends present. Now she prayed for herself, for Rolf and for Ernesto's soul.

There is no doubt though that the recent stress she had been subjected to (Ernesto no longer with her to cushion her against the rest of the world), had told on her health. When she sang at her next Albert Hall concert on June 11<sup>th</sup> 1904 she was suffering from acute neuralgia. Battling against the blinding pain she insisted on getting through the 'Jewel Song', 'Batti Batti', 'Pur Dicesti', 'Angels Ever Bright and Fair' and 'Voi che Sapete' followed by several encores. Proudly, she refused to announce to the public that she was in the middle of a bad attack of neuralgia. The resulting performance can be imagined, and for once the London critics made no attempt to treat her kindly. She did not sing in London again until the following year.

All things considered, Madame Patti began to realise that it would not be long before she must take a dignified last bow. A heart-wrenching moment for any diva, sad but inevitable.

# 15

At precisely nine o'clock Odile tapped on the bedroom door and held it open for the pantry maid who was carrying Madame's breakfast tray. Swishing back the heavy velvet curtains she turned to her mistress with her usual bright, "Bonjour, Madame!"

Adelina stirred lazily under the covers. What a noise Odile made every morning. Between sleeping and waking, she had a feeling that today was somehow special. She blinked her eyes against the brightness that streamed in through the windows, the glass still pearled with raindrops, happy that at least the weather had improved. It had been pouring for days and all night too, the roads would be so muddy that travelling would be hazardous and – ah yes! Now she remembered! Today she would hear her first finished recording. Excitedly she pushed back the bedcovers and slid her arms into the peignoir that Odile was holding out.

The mingled aromas of hot chocolate and freshly baked brioches hovered enticingly and she was hungry. "Merci, Odile. You may run my bath while I have breakfast and then find me a nice ensemble to put on. Those gramophone men are coming back."

"Aah, tres bien, Madame!" Her maid was pleased. It was high time there was a little excitement in their lives; they had been so dull all the autumn. This record-making was just the diversion Madame needed. Monsieur le Baron was a good, kind man she had no doubt, but she found him too *ennuyeux* (tedious) for Madame's vivacious temperament, often dampening her bursts of gaiety and childish enthusiasm with a cold look or a cutting word. The servants were always talking about the old days when Monsieur Nicolini was alive, champagne flowed like water and there was music and entertaining for weeks on end. Even royalty had come to stay and had a suite reserved for them on the second floor. How she wished she had been here in those days!

She turned to leave, smiling at her mistress as she sipped her chocolate. "Just pop downstairs, dear, and find out if they have arrived. Make sure they are comfortable and ask them when they will be ready."

Adelina attended to her toilette with care. It was quite an occasion for her to have an appreciative public nowadays. The last time had been when she had strolled down to the village shop one afternoon to post a card, only to find that she had forgotten her purse. The woman behind the counter was new and spoke only Welsh. In vain she had gesticulated and told her that she would send a servant down with a penny later on. The woman could not, or would not understand, and by then a small curious crowd had begun to gather outside the shop. The penny stamp had already been stuck on the card and she wished to post it.

"I am Madame Adelina Patti," she said. But the woman was suspicious. Seeing that she was getting nowhere, in desperation Adelina had broken into her *piece de resistance* 'Home Sweet Home', the crowd smiled and applauded and someone explained the situation to the shopkeeper in Welsh.

Odile hurried back upstairs, breathless. The gramophone men had only just arrived and were sitting down to breakfast, she said. They had had a terrible journey in the rain and their hired car had got stuck in a muddy ditch on the way from Pontardawe and had to be pulled out by a carter's horse and then they had to change a tyre in the pouring rain, but they said to tell Madame la Baronne that they would be ready in half an hour at the most.

Half an hour! It would take her far longer than that to prepare herself. Her heart started to beat faster as it did lately when she was under pressure. And she was still not entirely convinced that making these recordings had been a good idea. After the receptions she had been receiving lately she secretly wondered if anyone would bother to buy them. It had been a moving experience to hear the very first wax as soon as it had been made, but that was only natural, it was such a surprising novelty to hear her own voice coming out of a horn.

While she chattered, Odile searched through the rails of gowns in blacks, whites and pastel shades and after much choosing, discarding and choosing again, decided on an apple-green watered silk taffeta with a tight-fitting, long-sleeved jacket and a long flared skirt, not quite suitable perhaps for a December morning in Wales, but she wished Madame to look her best. Adelina nodded her approval. Next she sorted out a pair of pale green silk stockings and high-heeled black satin slippers.

It was almost eleven o'clock before they had finished. Odile was so fussy with her coiffure, piling curls in an outward-springing mass on top of her head, standing like a crown around the plaited bun at the back. Her few grey hairs had been carefully tinted black. When she was ready, Odile stood back to look at her admiringly. Madame looked not a day over forty, she thought. *Quelle grande dame!*

Adelina made her entrance at the top of the main staircase as though she were stepping on to the boards of La Scala. The first thing she noticed was the gramophone standing in solitary splendour in the centre of the hall, its long polished brass horn shining in a sudden ray of sunlight. And then, startled, she heard her own voice floating up to greet her, so true to life, so amazingly real that she fancied it was like looking at her own soul in a mirror. It was magic! She paled and gripped the banister, transfixed. The beautiful notes of Lotti's 'Pur Dicesti' filled the big hall, seemed to fill the entire castle, and she was overcome by happiness. Yes, she had done the right thing, yes! Almost running down the stairs she went across to the gramophone, threw her arms around the horn and kissed it.

★★★

It had not been easy to persuade the diva to trust her voice to the "new-fangled toy" as she called it, invented by Edison in 1878 and since perfected by Emile Berliner. The Gramophone Company in London had already recorded such voices as those of Caruso, Melba, Sembrich and Tamagno, but Patti was unwilling to give in to their advances.

By 1905 they had been putting pressure on her: Sydney Dixon, The Gramophone Company's English manager, refused to take 'no' for an answer and enlisted the services of a Welsh tenor, Hirwen Jones, as a go-between. Jones had often sung at Adelina's concerts as a supporting artist, he was on good terms with the diva and he had already made records with Dixon. So, between them they gave her no peace until she agreed to listen to some gramophone recordings at the Carlton Hotel in London. She admitted that they were interesting and said that if Dixon could make records of her voice which would satisfy her she would consider signing a contract.

At last, her resistance lowered by persuasion from the "talking machine men" she told them, "Well, if you will go to my solicitor Sig George Lewis and arrange everything with him, I will do whatever he agrees to."

Sir George agreed on condition that the Gramophone Company took all their recording apparatus to Craig-y-Nos, set it up ready for immediate use and waited there until the day the baroness said she was willing to sing for them. The royalties were later paid through his office. We probably have to thank Sir George Lewis for this mediation, without which we would never have been able to hear at least a part of the great voice that had once been Patti's.

Fred Gaisberg and his brother Will arrived at Craig-y-Nos with all the machinery necessary for record making early in December 1905 after a complicated journey by train from Paddington to Swansea where they changed for Penwyllt and then took the bus that Patti had sent down for them. When Adelina made the journey to London she was better organised, she had her own saloon carriage ready and waiting to be hitched on at Penwyllt station and it took her straight through to Paddington where it waited until her return. Her own private road had been cut into the hillside from Penwyllt to Craig-y-Nos Castle, which was just a short ride. But she fully appreciated the difficulties others encountered when they came down by train and she had got into the habit of "expecting them when she saw them".

The Gaisberg brothers were put in the care of the agents Mr and Mrs Alcock, who when questioned by Adelina as to what they looked like, replied that they seemed harmless enough young men. "Well, look after them well," Adelina told them.

Two bedrooms had been cleared and here they set up their apparatus, the long recording horn protruding through a curtain, which intrigued Adelina who could not resist peeping underneath to see what was hidden behind it. There was a piano on a dais of wooden boxes and everything was ready. Adelina did not rush straight into the recording sessions but kept them waiting for some days while she prepared herself mentally for this new experience. She had invited the pianist Landon Ronald to accompany her. Everyone waited. Then, one evening after dinner with champagne she asked Ronald to play some 'Tristan and Isolde' and after a little persuasion she agreed to sing. "She sang divinely", he said later, "For her husband, her brother-in-law and myself. We were all quite overcome by her great artistry and agreed that the records must be made the next morning. She assented, and accordingly at twelve o'clock everything was made in readiness for the event".

Ronald continues, "Her first selection was Mozart's famous 'Voi che sapete'. She was nervous but made no fuss, and was gracious and charming to everyone. When she had finished her first record she begged to be allowed to hear it at once. This meant that the record would be unable to be used afterwards but as she promised to sing it again, her wish was immediately granted.

"I shall never forget the scene. She had never heard her own voice and when the little trumpet gave forth the beautiful tones, she went into ecstasies! She threw kisses into the trumpet and kept on saying, *'Ah, Mon Dieu! Maintenant je comprends pourquoi je suis Patti! Oh, oui! Quelle voix! Quelle artiste! Je comprends tout!'*[30] Her enthusiasm was so naïve and genuine that the fact that she was praising her own voice seemed to us all to be right and proper. She soon settled down and got to work in real earnest, and the records, now known all the world over, were duly made".

Once her first enthusiasm was over, however, she realised that there were a few shortcomings. She had difficulty reaching her top notes and she had difficulty with her breath control. She asked her friend Jean de Reszke if he would come over and teach her his method, which she had heard brought excellent results. He did not come but sent one of his pupils, Minnie Saltzmann-Stevens, who wrote to her mother, "Patti is a darling, She looks and acts like a girl… Her voice,

---

30 Oh my God! Now I understand why I am Patti! Oh yes! What a voice! What an artiste! I understand everything!

of course, is wonderful, but some of the muscles are weak and it is for that, I suppose, that de Reszke sent me here. He is sure his method will help her and I think it will… She is so impatient about her work. It is so funny, yet she does try so hard. She doesn't believe in getting up in the morning and says I should stay in bed until nine and then dress very quietly. She doesn't approve of any violent exercise – nothing but a good walk every day which lasts an hour. Then to bed at ten, eat lots of oysters, but don't let anything ruffle or disturb you. Keep everything unpleasant far from you".

Adelina benefited from the de Reszke training. "Those exercises are positively excellent for avoiding the fatigue of too many scales", she later wrote gratefully to Miss Stevens. This tuition occurred between two batches of recordings that December and the second series shows very much improved breath control.

She continued to record most of her favourite pieces and even 'Casta Diva' which she had never dared sing in public. At first she found it difficult to stand still and sing into the horn. She had the habit of throwing back her head for the top notes and making dramatic movements while singing as she had always done on stage, yet they managed to finish by the end of December. She did not tire herself but recorded for just one hour every day, from eleven to twelve o'clock in the morning, and for these sessions she was always elegantly turned out.

Fred Gaisberg later wrote, "I have always instinctively felt that Patti was the only real diva I have ever met – the only singer who had no flaws for which to apologise. No doubt she had so mastered the art of living and protecting herself from the public gaze that she could plan her appearances for just those moments when she was at her freshest and brightest… I noticed that she never over-taxed herself… She was very devout and I was told she offered prayers in her beautiful private chapel to her patron saint for the success of the records".

But as we know the diva could also be temperamental. On occasion she was impatient with herself and the others. "She would be calling everyone 'darling' one minute and 'devil' the next", Gaisberg recalled. But her charm won them all over.

Altogether she recorded about twenty pieces, some, like the 'Jewel Song' from *Faust* and 'Home Sweet Home' were recorded twice. She ended up with a spoken message to Rolf, "God bless you, my dear husband, for the new year 1906. This is a message which I want you to keep for all time, so that you may have my voice ever with you. Your loving Adelina, otherwise Patti".

★★★

Time was precious, other recording companies were after the great Patti, and the wax blanks of the records were rushed back to London to the offices of the Gramophone Company. The first hand-made samples were produced overnight and by the following afternoon they were already on the train to Swansea in the care of their London manager Sydney Dixon. After the adventurous journey from Swansea to Craig-y-Nos already described, they finally arrived at the castle in time for breakfast.

This was the magical moment when Adelina first listened to her own finished records. It was the 18th December 1905. On the 30th of that same month she signed the contract and wrote her testimonial of approval which was to be used for advertising: "Gentlemen, the gramophone of today I find is such an improved instrument for recording the human voice to the older machines with which so many of us are familiar, thus my hitherto objection to allow the thousands who cannot hear me sing personally to listen to the reproduction of my voice through the instrumentality of your gramophone is now quite removed and the records which you have lately made for me I think are natural reproductions of my voice –Adelina Patti Cederstrom".

The records, made in Hanover and shipped back to England, were already on sale in shops all over Britain by 8th February, supported by a colossal advertising campaign in 200 newspapers, including the entire front page of the *Daily Mail*. Shop windows were decorated with boards written in enormous capitals, "PATTI IS SINGING HERE TODAY", and newspaper headlines read, "MADAME ADELINA PATTI HAS MADE GRAMOPHONE RECORDS". The whole business was a national event. Sales of the Patti records went very well in spite of the fact that at £1 each they cost an average week's wages.

Listening to the records today, a century later, at a first hearing one is disappointed. Was this the voice that people slept in the streets, caused

177

near-riots, pawned their jewels to hear? But listen again, and again and some of the great Patti flashes out. Although she was sixty-two and her voice was beginning to fray at the edges, J.B. Steane in *The Grand Tradition – Seventy Years of Singing on Record* finds her "an imaginative interpreter, an accomplished technician with a warm middle voice and a remarkable, sometimes disconcerting fund of energy". Although there were shortcomings like rushing headlong through 'Batti Batti', "in a flurry of snatched breaths and scrambled or missing notes", and in 'Casta Diva', "Nearly all the phrases were broken, light aspiration used and some of the written floriture simplified as for a novice", nevertheless, at other times, her voice is warm and magical. Vigorous and breezy in 'Comin' through the Rye', vividly Spanish in 'La Calasera', according to Steane, "she colours with more emphasis than Callas… The elderly lady singing into the old horn gives one some uneasy moments: a sudden forte in one phrase, a loose bit of timing in another… On the whole I prefer Patti, who in addition to an intimate feeling for the music has retained some accomplishments – the swift turns, the trill with its fantastically fine texture and lightness – that few of the others have ever really acquired. The decorations I find quite lovely, unobtrusive and graceful".

★★★

Later in the spring, Fred Gaisberg returned to Craig-y-Nos with an assistant to record some more versions. This time Alfredo Barili, Adelina's nephew, accompanied her on the piano. Although they were very well treated, "… she was always sending us grapes from the big greenhouses and when we left she loaded us with a basket of choice fruit for our return journey to London", Gaisberg noticed that the whole atmosphere at the castle was quieter. "One must come to the conclusion that Patti was beyond her prime at this time as most of the arias were carefully chosen to lie in the limited compass of the best notes of her voice", he wrote later. "To see her, one was amazed that such a slight wisp of a woman could have exerted such tremendous influence over a vast audience, simply by her singing. She was always *belle soignee* and so carefully groomed that one could see no trace of grey in her hair".

Adelina was happy with this new diversion. Life had recently taken on such a slow pace that sometimes she had a secret longing to run wild, scream, smash the crockery, anything to reassert her brilliant personality and kill the monotony. Naturally she did none of these things. She was the Baroness Cederstrom and had her dignity to maintain. The most she could allow herself to do to let off steam was to walk around the garden, singing.

She began to devise little ways of amusing herself and the others. When Rolf was away she organised musical evenings for the staff. They would all be summoned to the Billiard Room where a table held drinks and a buffet supper and everyone, from Longo the butler down to the newest little laundry-maid would listen, spellbound, as she sang to them accompanied by the Orchestrion and dressed up in one of her stage costumes. Sometimes she wore her Spanish Carmen dress and danced for them and played the castanets. 'Comin' through the Rye' was a favourite, accompanied by a beautiful wink when she reached "But all the lads they smile at me", but it was her favourite 'Home Sweet Home' that always moved them. They all loved her. After a few songs she would turn to the butler and say, "Pop the corks, Longo!" and everyone, including her, drank a glass of port wine or champagne.[31] Pathetic? Not a bit. Just sheer good fun.

At other times, strictly when austere Rolf was away, she would call some of her Swansea friends and put on a mime-play in the theatre. For a few brief hours they recaptured some of the old gaiety that had once reigned in the castle.

Now that she was spending so much more time at home, Adelina took a great personal interest in the domestic staff. She treated them with small kindnesses and Ethel Rosate-Lunn in *My Recollections of Madame Patti* tells us that one day she met the laundry maid coming out of the hot, steamy atmosphere into the chill November air, stopped and told her, "You must wear something around your shoulders when you leave the hot laundry and come outside into the cold air. You will get rheumatism". The young girl laughed, saying, "Oh no, milady, I do not notice it", to which Adelina replied, "No, you do not notice it now but you will one day. I did not have rheumatism when I was

---

31   Ethel Rosate-Lunn, *My Recollections of Madame Patti*

young but I have it now in my shoulder blades". That same evening she sent the girl a shawl, which she had to wear, to the amusement of her colleagues.

Christmas was now the happiest time of the year at Craig-y-Nos. The tradition that had begun with Ernesto was carried on. A large tree stood in the theatre, turned into a ballroom for the occasion, laden with gifts for everyone. Rolf took the presents down and passed them to Adelina who handed them out one by one. There were cheques and jewellery for the house steward and the personal maids, lengths of uniform cloth for the head maids and the same (but of a slightly less expensive quality) for the under-maids. There was a staff dance on Christmas Eve, Adelina taking it in turns to dance with the butler, the chef and the footman while Rolf danced with the head girls. The same Ethel Rosate-Lunn many years later recalled, "She was a most friendly and understanding woman, and how she loved to joke with us. She never lost an opportunity of doing so. Those magnificent eyes of hers would seem to be laughing too and she would clap those beautifully gloved hands together. Yes, she really did enjoy a joke".

Once the festivities were over, Adelina, who had always hated the anti-climax, the silence after the curtain had rung down and the ovations had died away, always travelled abroad with Rolf. They stayed on the Riviera and sometimes travelled down through Italy by train. They also got into the habit of going abroad for a few months in the summer, in June or in August, never missing a Bayreuth Festival in honour of her much-loved Wagner. She found these Bayreuth performances "perfect" and "wonderful".

In 1906, after having made her records, the diva was back in good voice at her Albert Hall concert, and wrote to Miss Stevens, "I had great ovations everywhere. I certainly do open my mouth now…" and, "I sing my scales every day and of course think of you all the time. Open your mouth! My mouth has become so large that I can hardly shut it up properly after I have done singing".

But she was vexed that the newspapers had got hold of the story of her tuition. Was there nothing she could do that they did not write about?

★★★

December of that year saw her official retirement from the stage after a farewell concert at the Albert Hall although there was a farewell tour of the provinces the following autumn and a year later she agreed to reappear at the Albert Hall for Mr Percy Harrison's benefit concert. Newspapers published the story of her life and her successes, and hazarded guesses as to how much money she had amassed during her career.[32] They were probably a long way off the mark but concurred that, in any case, she was "the richest prima donna the world had known".

In a way, it was a relief to have retired. Lately the travelling had tired her as it never used to. And she had found to her dismay that in recent years she suffered increasingly from stage fright. In Paris she had had to steel herself before stepping into the limelight, she had been seen trembling in the wings, wrapped in a shawl and muttering to herself, "I am afraid, I am afraid!" before her entrance. Her reign had been supreme but it was time to step down from her throne and hand the sceptre over to someone else. And in the autumn of 1907 during a quiet season at Covent Garden, she first had occasion to hear the thirty-six-year-old Florentine born soprano Luisa Tetrazzini, who immediately made such an impression on her that she was moved to write, "My dear Madame Tetrazzini, bravo! Bravo! And again bravo! I cannot tell you how much pleasure it gave me to hear you last night and what a joy it was to me to hear your beautiful Italian phrasing... I shall take the first opportunity of going to hear you again. I heartily rejoice in your well-deserved triumph. Yours sincerely, Adelina Patti Cederstrom".

At once Adelina looked on Luisa Tetrazzini as her natural successor, and the two struck up a correspondence in English and French. Patti had long been Tetrazzini's idol and she was flattered at the diva's interest. What Tetrazzini's voice lacked in schooling, it made up for in brilliance, but after their initial enthusiasm the London critics cooled down in their appraisals. Her career proceeded well in America but after the First World War she turned to concert singing, over the years made

---

32 This must have amounted to a huge fortune because for years she and Rolf had been living on her capital interest. And she also had an enormous collection of jewellery and possessions, and her castle.

three disastrous marriages ending up in the law courts, and, ruined in health and also financially, she died in poverty in Italy in 1940.

Adelina had not seen clearly when she regarded Tetrazzini as her successor. The public would have to wait much longer before Maria Callas arrived on the scene.

★★★

After Adelina's last concert at the Albert Hall, the *Daily Telegraph* music critic wrote, "Will any deny her right to be described as historic? Certainly none who have heard her, year in, year out, for nearly two generations, during which the art that she has so long adorned has undergone something like a complete change, and with it public opinion of it. Yet, in spite of this, the diva has gone on her way, looking neither to the right hand nor to the left, untouched by the transitions of music or musical life, singing largely the music of a bygone day, yet singing it as she only could sing it. And none, surely, would have it otherwise".

It was a highly emotional leave-taking. Among the applause, the shouting out for more and more, the flowers that cascaded on the stage until there was hardly room left for her to stand, the atmosphere in the great hall was heavy with nostalgia. None of those present could really believe that this was to be her very last 'Home, Sweet Home'. Not many in that audience of nine thousand went away with dry eyes.

But there were to be more "last times". She sang a full-length Rosina in Jean de Reszke's private theatre at his home in Paris (she had been the one to persuade him to build his own theatre) when it was said that she was in "miraculous voice" at sixty-five.

Occasionally, she came out of retirement to sing at charity concerts, and her very last appearance was again at the Albert Hall on October 20th 1914 in aid of the Red Cross War Fund. She was in Germany when war was declared and had some difficulty getting home to England. Profoundly saddened by these events she closed herself in her castle but "did her bit" by turning one wing into a convalescent home for wounded soldiers.

In the early months of 1919, her health began to give Rolf serious cause for concern and she was visited by several doctors. They diagnosed a weak heart and prescribed a stay in Brighton, and it was here, on the windswept south coast, that she spent her last birthday in February, her seventy-sixth.

★★★

She had spent the afternoon downstairs in her salon, among her souvenirs. They clustered on every table top, ranged along the mantelpiece, filled every shelf in the cabinets; mementos of her past – and what a past – gathered over the years. Looking back, it seemed almost unbelievable that she had done so much, had achieved such acclaim, so much satisfaction. Recently she had contented herself with the little things in life: a chat with Dai Price the gamekeeper or Con Hibbert the head gardener, stopping to talk to a tramp on the road and sending him back to the Craig-y-Nos kitchens for a meal.

She liked to chat *a tu per tu* with the people who worked for her and to help them with their small problems.

She looked around her at the richly-patterned wallpaper and carpets, at the portraits of herself and Ernesto, her piano with its padded stool, photographs of the family, Papa, Mamma, Amelia, Carlotta and her nieces, signed portraits of kings and queens, princes and princesses, dukes and duchesses, all surveying her benignly from their silver frames. Boxes in gold and silver, porcelain and china souvenirs, the Gainsborough, the framed copy of Arditi's 'Bacio', the Beethoven death mask and her little china dog. Lace cloths covered the tables, antimacassars and fringed shawls the chairs. Everything was as she wished, in its exact place.

She was tired, overcome by an immense weariness that had recently made every step an effort. Rolf had carried her downstairs in his strong arms and had placed her on a comfortable divan near the window, well wrapped in shawls although it was mid-August. From here, if she craned her neck she could look out across the sunny courtyard and see the fountain splashing around its stone stork and beyond that the gates and the steep rise topped by the craggy points of Craig-y-Nos.

These past months alone with Rolf had been so peaceful, such a sharp contrast to the life she had loved when she was young, filled with the excitement of travel, fame and success. Now she was cherished and protected, happy in her husband's quiet and reassuring company. She smiled. Lately Rolf could hardly bring himself to leave her side and she had had to insist that he take advantage of such a fine day to walk across the hills; he was young and the exercise would do him good. Really in her heart she had felt the need to be alone for a while, to spend a few hours with her reflections and her memories.

She knew of course that the time was approaching when she must take her last curtain call. This tiredness, this steadily increasing weakness were signs that pointed gently towards the wings. She could not complain. No one could have loved life more than she had or lived life more fully. Heaven only knew that she had had more than her share of good fortune, a superlative career spanning seventy years that they said had made her a living legend.

She must have dozed off because she had been talking to Papa. He was here, sitting near her in the high-backed chair, so natural and so real, not at all like a dream. She must be patient, he said, just the way he used to speak to her when she was a child, the time was not far off when they would be together again. Now fully awake, she realised the absurdity of this. Idly her fingers traced the lace cushion cover, so finely worked by the French nuns. The thought occurred to her that our lives resemble lace. We begin with a single thread but this soon meets and intertwines with other threads, looping the complex pattern of our lives. And then, the last knot completed, at the end we are again left with a single thread that must be cut off. The threads of her life had all fallen neatly into place. Three very different husbands, each one caring for her in his way. Few others of little or no importance. Any flaws in the pattern were unnoticed but just for a moment she was overcome with a sense of loss.

Tea was served discreetly at a table by her side. Not wishing to disturb her, they probably thought she was asleep. There were wafer-thin slices of her favourite chocolate cake and two tiny éclairs beside a glass of peach juice, but she hardly touched it. With the lengthening of shadows across the courtyard a maid came to carry away the tray and to switch on an electric lamp shaded in champagne silk, and to put new logs on the fire against the evening chill. The wood spluttered and sparked, flames coloured the brass fender and fire screen, turning them to reddish gold. Soon the sun would set behind the mountains but in this brief space of time between day and night she would sit here in warmth and comfort and watch, and wait for Rolf to come home and carry her upstairs, lifting her as easily as if she were a child.

It would not be long now.

# EPILOGUE

Adelina Patti died peacefully on 27th September 1919. Her heart, which had given so generously all her life, was tired. Rolf was by her side, her hand clasped in his.

Her body was embalmed and lay in state in her private chapel at Craig-y-Nos until 24th October when it was removed to the Roman Catholic chapel of St Mary's Cemetery, Kensal Green, London. Here a short memorial service was held the following morning. Later, following her wish, she was buried with the famous in Père Lachaise cemetery in Paris, near the graves of her father and her sister Amalia. One can imagine that she envisaged a grave embellished with statues, perhaps a Madonna or an angel. But Rolf had a very sombre and out-of-character slab of black marble erected in their place.

In 1920 all the contents of Craig-y-Nos were sold by auction and Adelina's much-loved and lived-in winter garden was dismantled and removed to Swansea where it remains as the Patti Pavilion. The castle was bought in 1921 for £19,000 by the Welsh National Memorial Association and put to use as a tuberculosis sanatorium for children (in 1947 the children were among the first in Britain to be treated with a new cure: the antibiotic streptomycin). In 1959, it became a hospital for old people, closing in March 1986.

Craig-y-Nos Castle then stood empty for many years and began to fall into decay. There was talk of turning it into a school of music, which would surely have met with the diva's approval, but various offers were turned down. In 1988, it was sold to a consortium of businessmen who formed the Craig-y-Nos Castle Company Ltd. and after a long period of repairs and restoration it opened to the public as a venue for various functions. It was then sold again to Dr John Trevor Jones and his wife, Penelope, who completed essential repair work including a new central heating system and re-roofing the theatre, financing the work by using it to house national antiques fairs, musical events and wedding receptions. On reaching retirement age they then sold it to SelClene Ltd. who continued the restoration and opened part of the castle as the present hotel and wedding venue.

The castle is said to be haunted by the ghosts of Patti and Nicolini and strange phenomena have been experienced. Caretakers who have lived in the castle swear that they have felt her presence, a sensation of being watched all the time. Adelina's ghost is said to "shut the door on people she does not like" giving them a feeling of being pushed away, nudged in the back. The still beautiful grounds are open to the public and today form part of the Brecon Beacons National Park. The theatre was restored in 1960 to the original delicate colours and is often used to stage local musical and operatic productions.

What is left of Patti today at Craig-y-Nos? Very little. When I visited it many years ago I found only a fan, a feather boa and some reproductions of old photographs on display in a little room that was once the laundry.

When his wife died, Rolf gave her beloved parrots and cockatoos to the London Zoo, together with the aviary. He inherited her entire enormous fortune and in 1923 married again, dying on 26th February 1947.

Madame Patti left a vivid, lasting imprint on the memories of local people and as a speaker said when she was granted the Freedom of the Borough of Swansea in 1912, "We have only had one constant, resplendent, radiant light for nearly half a century and that is the incomparable singer who has come to live among us". This seems a very fitting epitaph.

# BIBLIOGRAPHY

Herman Klein, The Reign of Patti The Century Co., New York 1920

Louisa Lauw Fourteen Years with Adelina Patti Remington & Co.,London 1884

Strakosch & Schurmann, L'Impresario in Angustie 1886-1893, Bompiani, Milan, Italy 1940

Harold Rosenthal, The Mapleson Memoirs, Putnam, London, The Career of an Operatic Impresario 1858-1888

Eduard Hanslick, Music Criticisms, Penguin Books

Charles N. Gattey, Queens of Song, Barrie & Jenkins

George Bernard Shaw, Music in London, Volume 111 1893-1894

Eugenio Gara, Cantarono alla Scala Electra Editrice, Milan 1975

Charles Osborne, Letters of Giuseppe Verdi, Victor Gollancz Ltd. 1971

Philip Gossett, William Ashbrook, Julian Budden, Friedrich Lippmann, Andrew Porter, Mosco Carner, The New Grove Masters of Italian Opera, MacMillan, London Papermac, 1983

Rupert Christiansen, Prima Donna, A History, The Bodley Head Ltd. 1984

Anita Leslie, The Marlborough House Set, Dell Publishing Co. Inc. New York, 1972

Michael Aspinall, Jerrold Northrop Moore, Adelina Patti for EMI Records Ltd. London, Issued with Limited Edition of recordings

Ethel Rosate-Lunn, My Recollections of Madame Patti, West Glamorgan County, Library, Swansea

Froom Tyler, Patti, The Lady of Craig-y-Nos, West Glamorgan County, Library, Swansea

Leonora Davies, The Day Patti was Wed a Second Time, South Wales Evening Post, West Glamorgan County, Library, Swansea

Royal Opera, Covent Garden, Archives Office

National Archives, London, The Times, The Telegraph, The Sketch etc.

Archives Office, The Illustrated Sporting and Dramatic News, The Illustrated London News

Biblioteca Marucelliana Florence, Italy, La Nazione (daily newspaper) Florence

The National Museum of Wales

And my grateful thanks to The British Institute Library in Florence